THE SAFE PLACE

A DCI BOYD THRILLER

ALEX SCARROW

GrrBooks

THE SAFE PLACE

Published by GrrBooks

This book is dedicated to Team Boyd.
I can't believe it's been nearly a year since we began this journey.
Your support and advice has been much appreciated.

PROLOGUE

His penknife made short work of the gull. He'd found it among the grass-tufted dunes, dead and surrounded by a drifting cloud of dislodged feathers.

The penknife was one of those Swiss Army ones. A gift from his grandad. *Careful with it, boy. That blade's a sharp one.*

It really was. After he'd gouged the gull's eyes out and severed one of the wings, he'd finally decapitated the dead bird. The penknife had performed very well. Taken its first blood.

The boy wiped the blood off his hands with a fistful of grass, folded his penknife and tucked it away in the back pocket of his jeans. He stood up to survey the beach and pushed the irritating curls of ginger hair out of his eyes.

The beach was deserted.

The school break had been a wet and miserable one this year, the broad sandy beach attracting only hardy dog walkers wrapped up in thick coats. Normally, at this time of year, he found holiday kids to make friends with. But the weather so far had kept them away.

He had just his own company. And his penknife to play with.

1

'So, how long did you say this is going to take?'

Gavin had made a thumb-in-the-air guess when he'd quoted Mr Knight a figure for the job. The old man had said the basement was thirty feet or so in diameter and thirty, maybe forty feet deep – effectively a very wide, very deep well, made of old bricks and crumbling mortar.

'About a week, maybe ten days,' Gavin replied. 'But that depends on how deep the water is, and how fast it's coming in.'

'You gave me a firm figure,' Knight reminded him.

'I gave you an *estimate*,' Gavin replied. He'd met more than his fair share of knobhead building developers who seemed to pride themselves on how much they could screw down a contractor once they'd started on a job. 'If it takes longer, it'll cost more.'

Knight's already pink face pinked up a little more. 'I want it pumped dry as quickly as possible. I need to get the concrete foundation in sharpish,' he insisted.

'I'll do what I can, Mr Knight,' Gavin muttered.

'What you "can do" and what you prom–' The rest of whatever Mr Knight was saying was drowned out by the noise of the pump starting up. The man's mouth was flapping away, jowls quivering, ruddy face animated, while he demanded that he wasn't paying a penny more for this job than had been agreed over the phone. Or at least that's what Gavin presumed he was shouting over the deafening growl of the pump on the back of his flatbed truck.

He could see the eighteen-inch-wide hose inflating like sausage skin pumped full of blended gristle as the first of the basement water came up from below. The leading hump of liquid raced through the hose past his feet, across the raised berm of grass-tufted earth beside his truck and off into the marshland beyond – water going back to where it damn well belonged.

Gavin turned away from Mr Knight, who had given up protesting, and he wandered over to the hump of grass to check that the extracted water was being discharged far enough away from the base of the tower that it wasn't going to seep back into the basement.

He could see dark, sludgy mud shitting its way out of the hose into the marshland a dozen yards away. Not unusual that – most jobs started with the thick sludge at the bottom, which was now giving the Generac Diesel Prime Trash Pump sitting on his truck's flatbed a hearty workout.

He walked down the far side of the grassy berm into the soggy marshland to inspect the gunk coming out of the pipe. Too thick and he was going to have to pull the inlet pipe up a bit from the bottom of the basement or risk the whole thing clogging up. He definitely did *not* want to have to waste time clearing it. Knight had paid him to remove the marsh water from his flooded basement. If he was going to be a dick about their verbal agreement, then so be it. Gavin would pump the *water* out. The crap at the bottom could be Knight's fucking job.

He squatted down beside the discharging hose, not particularly put off by the stench of rancid marsh water. He was used to it in the way a fishmonger was accustomed to smelling of fish. Every trade had its stink: you either became nose-blind or found another job.

The wire basket over the end of the outlet pipe was there to trap large items of debris: shopping bags, nappies, tin cans, plastic bottles and the like – and prevent that crap from contaminating the discharge. It made sense, really... Without a catch-basket, he was essentially fly-tipping using water.

So far the basket contained a few bits and pieces. Some fragments of red brick, the inevitable indestructible plastic bottles of pop displaying labels from another century – Tab, Cresta – and a green glass Coke bottle.

Then he heard something hard rattle down the pipe towards the catch basket and clatter into the mesh. The muddy liquid that pushed past washed it almost clean.

It took Gavin a few seconds to realise what he was looking at, nestled among the detritus trapped in the basket.

'Fuck me,' he gasped.

2

_____

'Come on now, boss. I want you to give me a hundred and fifty per cent this time!'

Boyd glanced up at Minter, who was leaning over the bench press and looking down at him with an expression that lingered halfway between amusement and pity.

'You can do it!'

Boyd really couldn't. The muscles in his arms felt as useless and gelatinous as pork belly. He let the crossbar rattle noisily back into its rack just before his arms collapsed uselessly over the side of the bench.

'Bloody hell,' he wheezed. 'I'm done.'

Minter clearly begged to differ. 'You need to give me one more rep to complete the set,' he insisted. 'You can make that.'

'No, really. I'm absolutely buggered,' Boyd said, puffing.

Minter pulled his best encouraging face. 'Oh, come on now – don't you want to look all hench for that lady friend of yours?'

He was talking about Charlotte. 'She's not my "lady friend",' Boyd garbled between gasps for air. 'Not in _that_ sense, anyway.'

Minter smirked. 'Ah, righto. If you say so, boss.'

'I do. I do say so.' Boyd struggled to raise himself into a

sitting position on the weights bench. 'And this isn't about being *hench*... It's about raising my general level of fitness.'

'Right.' Minter nodded, clearly less than convinced. He cast his gaze across the gym. 'Ah, I see the rowing machine's come available now. Up you get...' Minter offered Boyd a hand. 'Now we've got your heart rate up into fat-burning territory, the real work can start, see? So, we'll keep it in the zone with some cardiovascular work. Let's go.'

Minter pulled him up to his feet and Boyd let his arms hang like unfilled shirt sleeves.

'It's mostly leg and torso work, so –' Minter grinned and patted him on the back – 'you'll be just fine, boss.'

It was his sergeant's endless bloody goading and guilt-nudging that had convinced Boyd to come to the White Rock Gym this morning before work. He was definitely regretting it now.

'I can just about walk still...' he complained. 'I'm not sure I can pull on a pair of oar-handle things.'

'Shoulders, chest, thighs, heart and lungs,' Minter said over his shoulder as they approached the recently vacated rowing machine. 'It's a good all-in-one exercise. Ten minutes as hard as you can go and then we'll call it a day. How about that?'

Boyd looked at the machine. The seat, at least, looked inviting. He slumped down into it and placed his feet on the bracing pedals.

'Grab them handles, boss... I'll just tap in the time.' Minter put ten minutes on the machine's screen clock. 'Now this...' He pointed at a display of zeroes. 'That's your distance. See if you can get that up to three kilometres in the time, okay?'

Boyd had never, ever used a rowing machine before. 'Is that reasonable?' he asked. 'I mean for a beginner? I just –'

'Oh, yes. Easy peas.'

'Easy peas, eh?'

BOYD WAS ABOUT five minutes into the timer and a quarter of the distance he needed to be – according to Minter, anyway – when his iPhone buzzed in the pocket of his shorts. He managed to ignore it the first time around, but when it started buzzing again, he abandoned the rowing, a little too eagerly, and pulled it out, expecting to see either Emma's face or Charlotte's name on the screen.

Instead, he had: UNKNOWN ID.

'Yup?' he answered.

'DCI Boyd?'

'Yup. Who's this?' he asked, trying to mask his gasps for breath.

'It's DI Abbott, sir.'

'DI Abbott? Hang on, what's wrong with using my work phone?'

'I tried that already, sir. There was no answer,' Abbott replied.

'That's because it's not even eight yet, for God's sake.' Boyd shook his head. 'What's the matter?'

'We've got a body,' Abbott informed him.

'Right, well... you're still on shift, DI Abbott, so go and deal with it and we'll hand over when I come in, all right?'

'It's out beyond Camber Sands, sir. That's at least a forty-five-minute drive.'

Abbott, he was beginning to learn, was the laziest bastard he'd ever met. 'So?'

'The D-Sup's overtime ban, sir? If I head out there and wait for you... there'll be several hours' worth to log.'

That man would take literally any bloody excuse to sidestep doing some actual police work, Boyd thought. 'Abbott, if it's a murder, Sutherland will let it go – trust me.'

8

'It's a bone,' Abbott said. 'Been there a while by the sound of it.'

'I thought you said a body.' Boyd glanced at Minter and rolled his eyes.

'Well, not a whole body,' Abbott replied. 'Just an arm or a leg bone. It was dredged up by some bloke pumping out a flooded basement. So... I don't think there's an immediate or obvious crime scene to *secure*.'

That seemed to be Abbott-speak for *It can wait for someone else, sir, can't it?* The idle fucker had gone to the effort of looking up Boyd's personal contact number so that he could say he'd handed the case over, rather than risk being pulled up for tapping into Sutherland's precious overtime budget.

'Right, I'll deal with it, shall I?' Boyd said. 'Get out of my bed, get dressed and –'

'You're not in bed, though, are you, sir?' Abbott cut in. 'Sounds more like a gym?'

Boyd was about to say he bloody well *was* in bed when some knucklehead in the background let out an explosive *ooofff* as a barbell clanked down noisily onto its storage rack.

'Fine. Why don't you go and get yourself a nice cuppa, then?' Boyd sighed. 'I'll come in extra early to take this case.'

'Thank you very much. I'll do that, sir,' Abbott said, the sarcasm entirely wasted on him. He hung up before Boyd could say anything else.

'Aaand fuck you very much,' Boyd replied under his breath.

3

Boyd looked out of the passenger-side window at the sandy hillocks topped with tussocks of hardy grass. At this time of year, without a cheerful blue sky to mitigate the drab browns and olives, the wetlands out here made for a truly bleak landscape. It was the perfect location for Peter Jackson to film some mournful marsh inhabited only by Ring-wraiths and Gollum.

'Cheerless-looking place, isn't it, boss?'

Boyd turned to DS Minter. 'I was just thinking that.' He looked back out of the window. 'Just give me a speck of bloody colour to look at, please.'

'There you go,' said Minter with a laugh. He was pointing at a grubby orange traffic cone half-submerged in a mound of tidal mud.

'Yeah, nice,' Boyd said. 'Classy.'

'It's what you'd expect of wetlands, guv,' said Minter. 'The birds love it out here.'

'Really? Are you sure?' Boyd had noticed the absence of any life at all, even those vicious little bastard seagulls. His personal nemeses.

The drive so far had *already* taken forty-five minutes and, by the look of the ETA on Minter's phone, there was still another twenty minutes or so to go. DI Abbott hadn't been exaggerating. In fact, given how dispiriting it all appeared, Boyd was beginning to understand the man's reluctance to climb out from behind his desk and drive over.

'How're the muscles?' asked Minter.

Boyd flexed one of his arms and immediately regretted it. 'Bloody sore,' he said.

'Ah, that's good news, then,' Minter told him, slowing down to steer them round a hair-pin bend in the meandering marshland road. 'That's tissue damage you're feeling there.'

'Tissue damage? And that's good, is it?' Boyd asked, incredulous.

'That's right and, yes, it absolutely is. It means you've done some useful work. Your body will be reinforcing the tissue, making those muscles a little bit bigger, a little bit stronger for next time. Isn't it a great feeling? Makes you feel like the Incredible Hulk.'

'What?' Boyd muttered. 'Really pissed off?'

'No, I mean, bursting out of your clothes...' Minter sighed. 'I bloody love it, I do, and soon you will too.'

Boyd felt that he'd already, unfortunately, grown rather used to that feeling over the last few years, only in all the wrong places. 'I don't know about that,' he said to Minter doubtfully.

'Oh, you will. Gets me buzzing, it does. If I don't get this feeling every morning and every evening, I feel like I've really let myself down.'

'You do that more than *once* a day?' Boyd said.

'I do. Three times some days. I've got the Ironman Challenge coming up soon, haven't I?'

Boyd vaguely recalled his detective sergeant announcing that a while back. 'When is that?' he asked.

'It's this weekend, boss. Two-and-a-half-mile swim,

followed by a hundred and twelve miles of cycling, then a twenty-six-mile marathon. All back-to-back.'

'Christ.'

'I've booked a day's leave on Monday for muscle recovery,' Minter said.

'A day?' muttered Boyd. He suspected he'd need to be put into an induced coma for months to recover from a traumatic experience like that.

They passed the rest of the journey in a comfortable silence, Boyd ruminating on how anyone could possibly live out here in this godforsaken place without ending up topping themselves, and Minter eagerly looking forward – no doubt – to the physical agony he'd organised for himself this weekend.

Boyd finally spotted the building they were heading for on the horizon, with half a mile yet to go on the satnav. It was a stout and stubby rounded tower, like a scaled-down power-station steam vent. It sat on a spur of marshland that looked like it would all but disappear come high tide. The road, now little more than a rutted dirt track, was meandering back and forth, following the contours of the marshland that was high enough to actually call itself land, bringing them slowly closer to the old building.

As Minter made the final approach towards an apron of weed-tufted gravel, Boyd saw several dumped mounds of aggregate and sand, and pallets of bricks sitting at the old ruin's base, waiting to be used.

Boyd spotted one of their CSI vans parked up beside a flatbed truck and a mud-spattered Land Rover. 'How the hell did Sully beat us out here?' he asked.

'He's always ready to go, isn't he? Tool bags packed. Regular little eager beaver,' said Minter, pulling up beside the van.

They got out of the warm fug of the car into a stiff and bitterly cold gusting wind that was peppering them lightly with spots of salty water. Boyd pulled up the collar of his donkey jacket and fumbled in its pockets for a scarf or gloves, or anything else he might have left there from last winter. He found a beanie but his ears weren't quite cold enough yet to risk looking like some ageing hipster in front of Minter and Sully.

'Somewhat bracing, isn't it, Boyd?' Sully emerged from the driver's side of his van, already kitted out in his white bunny suit, blue gloves and wellington boots. The wind was making the vinyl of his forensics suit snap and rustle.

'Bloody freezing's more like it,' Boyd replied. 'You the first here?'

'Indeed I am.' Sully shook his head disparagingly. 'You desk jockeys are all a bit sluggish in the mornings, aren't you?'

Boyd was about to tell the overly chirpy SOCO that he'd actually been up at six in order to go to the gym this morning, but he thought better of it. Sully had enough material without that comedy gift.

'Some of us have lives outside work,' said Boyd. 'Who else is here?'

'One owner and one contractor,' Sully replied. 'They're both inside.'

Boyd looked at the building. 'So what is this, then?' he asked.

'It's a Martello tower,' said Sully, head to one side, waiting for Boyd to ask.

Boyd shrugged. 'Aaand?'

'Well, since you ask so nicely...' said Sully primly, 'it's a coastal fortification tower built during the Napoleonic Wars. There are dozens along the south coast. Some were repurposed during the Second World War. Others –' he indicated the building in front of them – 'were left to slowly crumble.'

Boyd glanced up at the stubby brick tower. It definitely looked as though it had seen better days; the brickwork at the top had begun to cave in, leaving ragged gaps beneath the circular roof. There appeared to be a sapling growing on the top floor, with a limb sticking out through one of the upper gaps in a desperate attempt to reach daylight.

It was remarkable, really. The only tree in sight from horizon to horizon.

'Right, shall we get out of this bloody cold wind?' said Sully, clapping his hands together and heading for the base of the tower.

4

Sully led the way inside through an arched doorway.

Boyd's eyes took a moment to adjust to the gloomy interior. He found himself standing on a creaking oak-plank floor that was about thirty or forty feet in diameter. Above him was an imposingly low wooden ceiling supported by thick oak beams that ran from one side of the tower to the other. There were eight small arched windows – six of them looking out to sea, the other two landward. It felt vaguely like being on the cannon deck of a tall, rigged navy ship.

He spotted the two civilians having a cigarette and pouring coffee from a Thermos flask. Boyd rubbed his hands together. It wasn't much warmer inside and he watched them enviously.

'So over here we have...' Sully gestured at the younger of the two men. 'Gary Merchant?'

'Gavin, mate,' the younger man corrected him.

'Right. And this is the owner and developer... Stephen Knight,' Sully said, pointing at a ruddy-faced older man.

Boyd stuck out a hand. 'DCI Boyd, Sussex CID. And this is DS Minter,' he said, waving a hand in Minter's direction.

Mr Knight shook it quickly and glared at him. 'How damn

long are we going to have to pause things here? I'm pissing money away every minute we spend standing around doing nothing!'

Boyd ignored him. 'So which one of you called this in?' he asked.

'I did,' replied Mr Knight.

'Where did you find the bone?' Boyd turned to Sully. 'We've double-checked it's human, right?'

Sully shot him a withering look.

'It was pumped up out from the basement,' said Knight, pointing at the snaking hose that ran across the wooden floor and down through an open trapdoor in the middle of it. 'The tower has a large underground storage area that's been flooded with marsh water. I've got to get it all out and fill it with concrete bloody *quickly*.'

'Why have you got to do it "bloody quickly"?' Minter asked.

'That flood water is what's keeping the basement walls standing,' Knight replied. 'You remove the equalising pressure of the water, and the walls will begin to buckle.'

'How much water's been pumped out so far?' Boyd asked.

'Hardly any at all,' said Gavin. 'I'd literally just started.' He also sounded slightly pissed off, Boyd thought.

'So this place is stable at the moment?' said Boyd.

'Yeah, it's not going anywhere for now,' said Knight. 'But I'm paying out good money for Gavin here to stand around doing nothing, which neither of us are too chuffed about.'

'Can we get a look at the basement?' Boyd asked, ignoring the old man again.

Knight shrugged. 'Help yourself.' He pointed towards the trapdoor.

Boyd wandered over and peered down through the open hatch into the darkness below. He pulled out his phone and turned on the torch function.

'Here you go, mate – try a proper one.'

Boyd turned round to see Gavin holding out a long-handled torch to him.

'Thanks,' he replied, snapping it on and aiming it down into the darkness. He could see an old weathered wooden ladder descending into a flickering pool of ink-black water below. 'How deep is this water?' he asked.

'At least thirty feet, I reckon,' Gavin said, turning to Knight for confirmation.

'Yes, thirty, maybe forty feet. It's very deep,' Knight replied.

'Straight down? No intervening floors?' Boyd asked.

'There's an unstable floor somewhere halfway down, I think,' said Knight. 'You'd be daft to put any weight on it, though. It'll be rotted through by now.'

Sully and Minter came over to squat beside Boyd and peer down into the darkness, the three of them blowing clouds of condensed breath into the space between them. The torchlight glinted back at them, bouncing off the black water.

'Looks like Cthulhu could emerge from the depths at any moment,' said Sully, shuddering.

'Who's Ker-thoo-loo?' asked Minter, staring down into the void.

'You read any H. P. Lovecraft?' asked Sully.

Minter shook his head.

'Shocker,' Sully replied. 'Cthulhu is an evil and ancient supernatural being.'

Boyd lay on his front, pulled himself a little further forward, then ducked his head and shoulders down through the hatchway and panned the torch left and right. The beam of light picked out the damp brick wall all the way around. He could see what appeared to be the top of a wooden post emerging from the water, but little else.

'Watch out for those tentacles,' cautioned Sully softly. 'The Great Old One does not like to be disturbed.'

'Tentacles?' queried Minter.

'Oh, yes,' replied Sully with hushed reverence. 'Aye... those poor souls who have glimpsed him... and remained sane, they say he resembles an octopus crossed with a dragon.'

Boyd couldn't help chuckling at Sully's hokey accent – located somewhere between the witches of Macbeth and a wind-weathered Cornish trawlerman.

He pulled himself back up to a kneeling position with a groan. 'We'll need to get a diver down there.' Then he heaved himself onto his feet, groaning again.

'Are you all right, Boyd?' asked Sully.

'I think I might have broken him,' admitted Minter. 'I took him to the gym with me this morning, put him through his paces.'

Sully whistled and winced. 'The gym, eh, Boyd? This on behalf of your new lady friend?'

Boyd ignored him and turned to Knight. 'We're going to have to get a diving team to investigate before you can do any more work on this tower,' he said.

Knight didn't look too pleased about that. 'Well, how long's that going to bloody well take?'

'A few days maybe? I don't know. I'm also going to need you to come to the police station in Hastings to make a statement.'

'*What?*' Knight spluttered. 'Oh, for fuck's sake! That's an hour's drive away, at least.'

'I know,' said Boyd. 'Today, if that's possible?'

Knight shook his head and slapped his hands down against his thighs. 'For fu– It's money I'm losing here, do you understand?'

'Is that me too?' asked Gavin. 'I could be taking my pump to do another job.'

'Yup, both of you, I'm afraid,' Boyd said. 'Sorry, gents.' He turned to Sully. 'How old do you think the bone is?'

'Do you mean the person's age or how long has it been down there?' Sully asked.

'The latter.'

Sully shrugged. 'It's totally clear of any soft material. Decades probably. But, Boyd... FYI...'

'Yup?'

'It's a young bone. A teenager, I'd say.'

5

It was gone half eleven by the time Boyd and Minter returned to the station. Boyd's hankering for a warm frothy coffee had reached epic proportions before they'd even parked the pool car and entered the building, but his thigh muscles were screaming blue murder by the time he'd made it to the first floor.

'Do you want me to go up and get you one?' offered Minter.

'Christ, would you? I can barely bloody hobble,' Boyd said, rubbing his thighs.

He shuffled into the CID's main floor, over to his desk and collapsed into his chair with a groan of relief.

Okeke looked up from what she was doing. 'You all right, guv?' she asked.

Boyd peeled off his jacket and hung it over the back of his seat. 'I made the huge mistake of letting Minter lure me into a gym,' he confessed.

'Ouch,' she replied.

'Exactly. Every bloody part of me hurts. If he wasn't getting me a coffee, I'd hate him right now.'

Okeke laughed. 'Have you just come back from Jury's Gap?'

Boyd nodded.

'I notice from the logs that it came in during Abbott's shift...'

'It certainly did. But you know what Abbott's like,' he said with a sigh.

'Useless?'

Boyd shrugged. 'To be honest, Okeke, I wouldn't know if he's useless. I don't think I've seen him actually do anything yet.'

'He's great at sliding bits of paper around his desk,' offered Okeke. 'So, guv, what's the gist?'

'We've got an arm bone that's been sucked up out of the basement of an old, ruined tower-fort-lighthouse thing,' Boyd said.

'How old's the bone?' Okeke asked.

'Sully says decades. He reckons, from the length of the bone, we're looking at a young adult.'

'Male? Female? Do we know?'

Boyd shook his head. 'Not yet.'

'Want me to make a start trawling through mispers?' she asked him.

'I'm just going to give Sutherland a quick update first, then I'll call a team meeting,' Boyd said. 'Go grab a fag break and a coffee if you want. You've got time.'

'Ah, good morning, Boyd!' said Sutherland. He appeared to be annoyingly pleased with himself.

'You sound happy, sir,' Boyd said.

'I am. I had my Weight Watchers weigh-in this morning!' He tapped his round pot belly. 'Lost nearly two pounds this week!'

'To make space for Christmas, eh?' asked Boyd.

'I fully intend to have a disciplined Christmas and keep this weight off,' Sutherland replied firmly, 'despite Mrs Sutherland's mince pies.'

Boyd hobbled over to the spare chair and let himself gently down into it.

'What's up with you, Boyd?'

'Gym. Minter,' Boyd replied.

'Well, that wasn't particularly clever, was it?' Sutherland snorted. 'Minter's an absolute fanatic.'

Boyd conceded that with a nod. 'Let's just say his idea of an entry-level workout and mine vary greatly.'

Sutherland had the night shift's logs printed out and spread across his desk. 'I see DI Abbott handed over a job this morning?'

'He raised your concern about tapping into overtime pay, sir,' Boyd said. *And he's a useless, lazy arse.*

'Quite right,' said Sutherland. 'So then, a human bone all the way over at Jury's Gap, eh? Crikey... Another few miles and this would have been Kent's shout.' He pursed his lips. 'Pity, that.'

'Dead folks can be so bloody thoughtless, can't they?' Boyd said.

Sutherland, oblivious, nodded his head. 'Yes, they can, Boyd; yes, they can. Have you just come back from the scene?'

'Yeah. A humerus bone was pumped out of the basement of some old fort, tower-like thing.'

'Ah, yes... They call them Martello towers, don't they? There's quite a few of those in Sussex, I believe.'

'So Sully was educating me,' Boyd said. 'Are you okay if I crack on and pick a small team?'

'A very *small* team, please.' Sutherland's lips clamped shut, as though he was frightened Boyd might reach down his throat and help himself to some of the dwindling budget for the year. 'And you might as well keep it on the main floor for now. No point playing musical chairs with the Incident Room for this one.'

'Fair enough,' Boyd said. 'We'll need to get a diving team to take a look. There's a flooded storage area like a large well.'

'Wouldn't it be easier to just pump it all out? Then Sully could jump straight in and get on with things.'

'The problem is... if we pump it all out, apparently the tower could collapse,' Boyd explained. 'So I'm guessing we'd need to get some scaffolding in to shore it up. Could be more costly.'

'Oh. Right.' Boyd could see Sutherland mentally counting the pennies.

'We could do with the divers checking it out, at least,' Boyd said.

Sutherland wilted. 'Fine. Well, I suppose you'd better go and procure a diver or two, but keep it to a minimum, Boyd.'

Boyd eased himself up out of the chair, his arm muscles screaming. He let out an involuntary old-man *ooofff*.

'You know,' said Sutherland, 'if you're looking to shift that paunch of yours, Weight Watchers is probably the easier way to go about doing it. You could come along with me. Just a thought.'

'Thanks, sir.' Boyd gave him a weak smile. 'I'll give that some consideration.'

6

Boyd's small team comprised the usual suspects. Faces he had grown to trust over the last year: Minter, Okeke, Sully and Warren. He'd have roped in O'Neal too if he'd been around today. Legwork required young and energetic DCs.

Since he'd yet to get his hands on that much desired frothy coffee – Minter seemed to have failed him miserably – Boyd decided to herd them all up to the top floor. As they stepped into the busy canteen, he spotted Minter at the front of a very long queue. He was just about to order.

He sent Warren over with a fiver and instructions to add his, Sully's and Okeke's drinks to the order. Meanwhile Boyd picked out a table far enough away from the rest of the noisy hubbub where they could talk without shouting. It was five to twelve and the early-bird lunch-breakers would soon be turning up. It was only going to get noisier.

Minter and Warren joined them a couple of minutes later with a tray of coffees.

'Cheers,' said Boyd, quickly grabbing his and tearing open a sachet of sugar. 'Right, we can't be arsing about up here for too long,' he began. 'We've got the two blokes we saw earlier this morning coming in any moment now.'

'Knight and Merchant,' Minter supplied.

'And neither were particularly pleased to be dragged all the way to Hastings today,' Boyd added.' He pulled out his notepad to review the notes and to-do lists he'd made while Minter had driven them back.

'Minter, you're my second and action-log gatekeeper. Open up our tab on LEDS. And also get on to operational support for a diving team.' He looked up from his notes. 'Does Sussex have a dedicated diving unit or are we going to have to borrow?'

'Sussex and Kent share a marine policing unit, boss,' Minter replied. 'I'll check their availability.'

'Thanks. Okeke, you're my evidence guard dog.'

She raised her eyebrows 'How charming.'

'Can you take that bone over to Ellessey Forensics?'

'Sure.'

'And rather than just hand it in for them to deal with at their leisure, maybe get an expert to look it over while you're there?' He glanced at Sully. 'Not that I doubt your assessment of it, but they do have a dedicated bone guy over there.'

'None taken,' huffed Sully.

'So, Sully... if Minter can get a diving team over to the tower, can you be on-site to liaise with them when they go down? If they find some more goodies at the bottom, I'd like you there to keep an eye on things. Make sure they're handled and logged correctly.'

'Certainly.'

'So we're calling this a crime scene,' said Okeke. She stirred her black coffee. 'An old, ruined fort with a flooded basement... Surely we're looking at a safe place to dump a body?'

Boyd nodded. 'Let's not assume it's a murder just yet. It could as easily have been an accident.' He was about to test the temperature of his coffee with a cautious sip but paused, musing over this latest case. 'Given how long ago this happened and the age of the victim, it might be tricky finding someone on the mispers register.'

'It might be quite a few decades ago,' cautioned Sully.

'Okeke, can you make a start on that for me, please?'

She gave Boyd a thumbs-up. He turned to Warren. 'I want you researching the tower itself. Previous owners, any events recorded in or near the place over the last forty or fifty years.'

'Yes, sir.'

'And you'll be with me when we interview Knight and Merchant.' Boyd looked at his notes again. 'Stephen Knight's the current owner. Gavin Merchant's the contractor he got in to pump the water out and the one who spotted the bone first.'

Warren pulled a notepad out from his jacket and scribbled that down.

'Boss?'

Boyd looked at Minter.

'We should tape it up as a crime scene, accident or not, shouldn't we? I mean... if the news gets out, we might have all sorts of ghoulish idiots wandering around that tower.'

'Good point,' Boyd agreed. 'Get our CSM over there... Leslie Poole. And you're right, Minter. It's a potential hazard even if it's not a crime scene. Let's get some tape around it, pronto. Can you –'

'On it, boss.'

Boyd glanced down at his pad. There were no further notes, which meant he could finally take a slug of his coffee.

His phone rang. He swore under his breath and put his cup back down onto the table. 'DCI Boyd.'

'Desk sergeant here, sir. Got a couple of grumpy visitors for you.'

7

'And hello again, Mr Knight,' said Boyd. 'How was the drive over?'

'A complete waste of my bloody time,' Knight complained.

He was, thought Boyd, understandably peeved that his whole day would be squandered, not to mention the money he'd paid to have Gavin and his pump sitting idle. Time *and* money wasted.

'How long's this going to take?'

Boyd sat down with his cooling coffee. Warren took the seat next to him. 'We'll be as quick as we can be, Mr Knight. Mind if I record?' he asked, setting his phone down on the table.

'Whatever,' Knight grumbled. 'Who's this?' He nodded in Warren's direction.

'I'm Detective Constable Warren,' Warren said.

Knight sniffed. 'You recruiting them straight from school now, eh, Boyd?'

'Hardly,' Boyd deadpanned. 'DC Warren's got grown kids and he's on his... what is it...?' He glanced at Warren. 'Third marriage?'

Knight looked shocked for a moment and Warren grinned.

'Oh, I see.' Knight shook his head. 'Very fucking funny.'

Boyd hit the red record button on his screen. 'The time is twelve thirty p.m. Today's date is the second of December. Interviewee is Stephen Knight. Interviewing officers are DCI William Boyd and DC Matthew Warren.'

'I thought there was meant to be some big recording machine on the table that beeps first?' said Knight.

'Only on TV,' replied Boyd. 'Anyway, this is just a witness statement. We can do this orally and we'll write it up... or you can write one down yourself if you prefer?'

'This is fine. Let's get it over with,' Knight said.

'Right. So... I gather you own the tower, Mr Knight?'

Knight nodded. 'Bought it a couple of months ago.'

'For what purpose?'

'To restore the poor bloody thing before it collapses.'

'Is it likely to?' asked Boyd.

'My surveyor said it's basically sinking into the ground. It's built on soft marshland, as you know. It's beginning to tilt too. There are stress cracks near the base. So, yes... at some point it'll tumble over unless I shore up its foundation,' Knight replied.

'Which is why you're pumping the basement dry?'

'Exactly. I need it pumped down to the last few feet; we'll quickly install some load-bearing beams in the void, then fill it with concrete as fast as we can.'

'Why the rush?' asked Boyd.

'When the water's removed from the basement, it creates a void... The tower will be weaker. The outside pressure of marsh water pressing against the basement walls of Seventy-nine will cause them to buckle.'

'Seventy-nine?' queried Warren.

'Ah!' Knight snorted. 'The lad can speak! Martello Tower Seventy-nine,' he continued. 'The UKMTPS has given all the towers around the coast a designated number. This one's seventy-nine.'

Boyd had his pen poised over his pad. 'And the UKMTPS is...?'

'The UK Martello Tower Preservation Society. I'm a member of the governing committee.'

'Right.' Boyd jotted that down. 'And they're all about... what? Keeping these things from toppling over?'

'Preserving them where possible. A lot of them have been bought in the past and either knocked down or turned into something else entirely. It's bloody disgraceful.'

Boyd settled back in his chair. 'They're not exactly the most attractive-looking things.'

'They're part of our history!' Knight spluttered. 'They weren't built to look attractive; they were built to defend this country from Napoleon!'

'Right.' Boyd glanced across at Warren. Knight was quite clearly very passionate about his subject. 'So you bought this one to save it? Who'd you buy it from?'

'A man called Ricky Harris.'

The name chimed a bell somewhere at the back of Boyd's mind. 'Why's that name familiar?'

'If you know the name, you must listen to his noisy old racket.' Knight shook his head. 'Nothing but banging and shouting. Ricky Harris was a member of a pop band called Dark Harvesters or something.'

Warren was already on his phone. 'Dark Harvest?'

'Dark Harvest?' repeated Boyd absently. 'They were a big deal in the early eighties, weren't they?'

'Right,' said Knight. 'A bunch of noisy, hairy headbanging idiots.'

'Not your thing?' asked Boyd.

'Not been for a very long while,' replied Knight. 'I'm more Classic FM these days.'

29

'So then,' Boyd said, bringing the interview back on topic, 'you bought it from this Ricky Harris when?'

'At the beginning of last month. November,' Knight said.

'And how long had Harris owned it?'

'Since the start of the nineties, I believe.'

Boyd jotted that down too. 'Have you got any contact details for him?'

Knight laughed. 'Good luck with that.' For a moment Boyd thought the old bugger was going to say he'd died. 'He's impossible to get hold of. Lives on some remote Scottish island in the Hebrides.'

'So how did you manage to buy it off him?' Warren asked.

'Through an estate agent that handles quirky properties.'

'Quirky?' Warren looked confused.

'You know, boy... lighthouses, churches, scheduled monuments... the sort of places your average high-street estate agent wouldn't know where to begin with.'

'And how was Mr Harris to deal with?' asked Boyd.

'Like I said, it wasn't face to face; it was via the agent. I've been trying to buy it off him for the last thirty years. Offering the idiot a pretty decent price. But he wouldn't part with it. No price was ever good enough.'

'Until last month?'

Knight nodded.

'What changed?'

Knight shrugged. 'I suspect he was finally out of money and needed some fast.'

'How much did you offer him?' asked Warren.

The old man glared at him. 'Are you normally so fucking rude, boy?'

Warren's mouth dangled, half open. 'I just...'

'*How much* is my private business.' Knight shook his ruddy face. 'No bloody manners, young people these days.'

Warren's mouth clapped shut and his cheeks pinked.

Boyd stepped in to spare him. 'Why did Harris buy it in the first place? Does he have an interest in history?'

'You'll have to ask him. I expect the fool bought it on a whim because it looked *cool*.' He shrugged. 'You know how idiotic pop stars are. The prat has let it go to rack and ruin over the years. It's a piece of British history that deserves better care than he's ever given it.'

'Right. And you say he bought it back in the nineties?'

'Well, eighty-nine. I think that's what I think it said on the deed.'

'Right.' Boyd noted that down. 'And you said that you bought it November just gone?'

'Yes, I did. Beginning of.' Knight sighed. 'Are we done now?'

GAVIN MERCHANT APPEARED to Boyd to be in his late thirties. He was slouched at the table, his round jaw and thick ginger beard cupped in his hands, and he looked utterly fed up.

'I've lost a day's money, knowing that idiot Knight,' were his opening words. 'So how much longer have I got to wait around before I can get on with the job?'

Boyd set his second coffee of the day on the table and sat down. 'I'm sorry, Mr Merchant...'

'Just Gavin. Or Gav,' said the young chap. 'It's just a chat, right?'

'Yeah,' Boyd said. 'Just a chat. Well, I'm sorry, Gavin, but nothing more's going to happen until we find out what we're dealing with.'

'I can help you out there,' Gavin said. 'It's a bone, mate. Which means it's been there a long fucking while. Could even be a Roman soldier...'

'It's not Roman,' said Boyd. 'Our expert says it looks like it's a few decades old.'

Gavin shrugged. 'So, what...? I'm supposed to just pack up and go home?'

'Unless you want to wait around until we're done. We're sending a diver down to look for the rest of the body. If it looks like foul play, then the tower will effectively become a crime scene.'

'For how long? Will I be waiting two or three days? Weeks? Months?'

Boyd spread his hands. 'I'm sorry, Gavin... I can't say at this point. I don't know.' He looked down at his pad. 'Anyway, you said earlier that you're the one who spotted it?'

'Yeah. I was checking the hose to see what was coming up. I wanted to make sure the pipe wasn't sitting right on the bottom and pulling up sludge.'

'That's bad, is it?' Warren asked.

Gavin nodded, 'It slows things down and puts an unnecessary load on the pump. Well, it's up to Mr Knight to shovel out all the debris that's at the bottom, not me. I'm there to clear the water, that's all. I saw the bone,' Gavin continued. 'Figured it looked human. So we called the police.'

'You? Or Mr Knight?' asked Warren.

'Mr Knight made the call,' he replied.

Boyd scribbled another note, then looked up from his pad. 'Mr Knight said the tower belonged to a Ricky Harris before he bought it. Does that name mean anything to you?'

Gavin Merchant shook his head. 'Why? Should it?'

Boyd shrugged. 'Not really. You're a local, right?'

He nodded. 'Jury's Gap area. Yeah.'

'Do you know anything about the tower?'

'Nope. I didn't know anything about it before Mr Knight hired me to pump it out.'

'So you've lived there all your life and didn't know about it?' Boyd raised his brows.

'I didn't say I didn't know it was there,' Gavin answered. 'I said I didn't know *about* it. History's not my thing. But yeah... I mean, everyone in the area knows it's there. It's just an old ruin, right?'

Boyd nodded. 'Right. Did you ever play there as a child? Explore it? That kind of thing?'

Gavin shook his head. 'No, no. Not really.'

'Not really?' Boyd asked.

'Well, I mean, I messed around in the marshes when I was a kid... visited the beach nearby, you know. But I've never actually been inside Devil's Tower.'

'Devil's Tower?' Boyd prompted.

Gavin shrugged. 'Yeah, it's what some of the kids used to call it.'

'Any particular reason?'

He scratched his beard. 'I don't know. We just did. It's a creepy-looking ruin and you know what kids are like. It was always going to have a creepy nickname.'

Boyd let the silence stretch out for a few seconds, but Gavin seemed to have nothing else to offer.

'Okay,' said Boyd finally, closing his notepad and twanging the elastic band around it. 'Thanks for coming all the way over this morning. We'll be in touch.'

BOYD STOOD by the window with Warren and watched both men walk across to the visitor's parking area. Neither seemed to be talking to each other as they drew up beside their vehicles.

'You okay, Warren?'

He nodded.

'Don't let a person like Knight rattle your cage,' said Boyd.

'I'm not... rattled, sir.'

He clearly was.

'I like to call his type Grumpy Little Jacks,' said Boyd. 'All bark. Like a bloody Jack Russell.'

'Don't they bite too, sir?' Warren pointed out.

Boyd laughed. 'Bad example. But you need to be thicker-skinned in the interview room. Particularly with the arsy ones. Don't let them see they've got to you.'

Warren grimaced. 'Right.'

Boyd nudged him. 'Be a bit more Hard Cop, okay? A bit more Jason Statham,' he added. 'Mr Action Potato.'

Warren smiled. 'What did you make of them both, sir?'

Boyd ran his fingers through his bristles. 'Well, Knight's a pompous prick... and Merchant seems to be as fed up with him as I am.' He paused. 'We'll see what the lab report says, but I think we're probably going to need to look into this Ricky Harris chap.'

'Yes, sir.'

'But first, Warren old son –' Boyd stretched his aching arms and back, which crackled like a bowling ball being rolled across bubble wrap – 'lunch.'

8

Okeke pulled up in the visitor's parking area of Ellessey Forensics, a private forensics contractor that had chosen to turn a Norman church just outside the town of Battle into a small but state-of-the-art facility.

The last time she'd been here it had been sunny, the tidy corporate lawn (previously a graveyard) a cheerful green, the mature trees lush and Turner-esque – all giving the small flint-and-clay Norman church that formed the entrance atrium a chocolate-box-pretty air. Now it looked a forlorn place with the skeletal trees and rain-slicked grass that looked dull and drab. She suspected the groundsman had been using a chemical spray during the summer that had stained the lawn an implausible cartoonish green.

Okeke picked up her shoulder bag and the evidence bag containing the bone. She locked the pool car with a beep and hurried across the gravel, through the glass doors into the entrance atrium.

'Good morning!' The receptionist appeared to be wearing

the same checked shirt she'd last seen him in. 'How can I help you?'

'I'm DC Samantha Okeke, Hastings CID. I called ahead,' she said briskly.

He stared down at the tablet before him and started gently swiping the screen.

'In fact, I think it was you I spoke to,' said Okeke. 'About forty-five minutes ago,' she added pointedly.

The receptionist continued swiping for another few seconds, then finally... 'Ah, yes.'

'Great,' Okeke said with a sigh. 'I'm glad we're all caught up now.'

The receptionist narrowed his eyes briefly. 'You have some forensic evidence you wanted Dr Esquerra to take a look at?'

She raised the plastic evidence bag. 'An arm bone.'

'I'll enquire as to whether he's available.' Once again he began tapping and swiping his glowing tablet screen. Okeke noticed he had a name-block on the counter in front of him.

'Julius? Surely it's quicker just to pick up the phone and call him?'

'We have our system,' Julius replied curtly. He returned to his screen to swipe at a couple more things and then at last picked up the desk phone. 'Please, take a seat,' he said, pointing to some leather chairs that were dwarfed by a giant cheese plant.

Okeke went to sit down and while she waited she admired the giant plant as she had the previous time she'd visited, reaching out and stroking one of the glossy green leaves.

Boyd had been right. It was flipping well plastic.

'Samantha?'

She looked up and saw Dr Esquerra approaching her. He wasn't in his scrubs this time, hidden behind a mask and goggles, but was wearing a smart suit jacket and brown trousers. He could have been in his fifties, she guessed, but had the warm skin tones of a Hispanic South American that hid decades easily. She was about to get up when he held out his hand.

'Please, I will sit with you.' He took the seat next to hers. He looked at the evidence bag on her lap.

'We're hoping to get a gender and perhaps an idea of how old this person was,' Okeke told him.

He took the bag from her and peered at the pale bone through the clear plastic. 'The gender is easy. She's female. Age?' He sucked air in between his teeth. 'Not old. Young adult, perhaps. Where was this found?'

'Submerged in the flooded basement of a ruined tower. I think they're called Martello towers.'

'Yes, I know those,' Esquerra said with a smile. 'They are, in fact, called Mortell-*a* towers.' He pronounced the double 'LL' as a 'Y' – *Morteya*. 'The name became Anglicised to Martello. They were built all over the British Empire, including the Caribbean and Cuba. You say it was submerged?'

Okeke nodded. 'A pump sucked it up from the bottom of the basement.'

He nodded slowly. 'So it has been submerged for some time?'

She shrugged. 'I would think so.'

He nodded again. 'Water leaches collagen from the bone at a steady rate. That is one possible way to determine how long it has been there. If the collagen is completely gone, another way I can possibly date this is to use the dendrochronological process for dating wooden artefacts.'

'Dating wooden...?'

Esquerra seemed pleased to explain. 'One can precisely date a chair leg or a plank of wood by examining the visible growth rings. There is a ring chart, collated from wood fragments found around the world that maps back to biblical times,

I believe. Like a very long barcode,' he added. 'This reflects annual carbon absorption from the atmosphere.'

'Right,' Okeke said. 'I've read something about this.'

'We can do radiocarbon dating on this bone, then curve match the approximate result against the dendrochronological database to get a precise year.'

'To the *actual year*?'

'Oh, yes.' Esquerra grinned, showing a perfect row of small, tidy white teeth. 'Very likely.'

'How long will that take?' she asked.

'A week,' he replied, waggling his hand. 'Maybe ten days.'

Okeke thought she'd better ask, otherwise Sutherland was liable to have a baby when the bill finally landed. 'And how much would that cost?'

Her question was met with a shrug. 'Maybe twenty thousand?'

She managed not to wince. 'Right, okay. I need to make a quick call first.'

Dr Esquerra nodded. 'Of course. Can I have some coffee brought to you? A pastry?'

Okeke looked at her watch; it was gone two. Her stomach was grumbling. 'Yeah, go on, then.' She smiled gratefully as he got up. 'Thank you.'

9

'Is he or isn't he?' asked Sully. 'I mean, it's a pretty binary answer I would have thought.'

'I don't know. I think she – Charlotte, isn't it? – and Boyd are just good friends,' replied Minter.

'They seemed pretty cosy at that barbecue for "just good friends",' said Sully. 'Perhaps they're... what's the phrase...? "Friends with benefits"?'

Minter shrugged. His memory of that afternoon was just as hazy as everyone else's. 'Why are you so interested, Sully?'

They were parked up in front of the Martello tower on a raised spur of land that was surrounded by a swirling crazy-paving labyrinth of low humps of grass and pools of mud.

Sully turned to look out of the passenger-side window of Minter's car to watch Leslie Poole, the crime scene manager, unroll and suspend the perimeter tape round the tower on some traffic cones like bunting at a village fete. The black-and-yellow tape fluttered in the stiff breeze.

'Just a casual curiosity,' Sully replied. 'Call it an anthropologist's interest. I like to think I can interpret the subtle signals of the Homo erectus mating dance.'

Minter looked at him. 'Right, because you weren't at all busy being stoned out of your head and bouncing around the place to Rihanna.' He had a couple of images from that afternoon lodged in his head and one of them was their forensics coordinator, leaping around the bonfire in his burgundy cargo pants and flip-flops like a snagged blue marlin trying to shake itself off the hook.

Sully's expression stiffened. 'I think you're very much mistaken in what you recall. I don't dance. Ever.'

The difference of opinion was spared any further oxygen by the appearance of the marine unit's van on the low horizon, following the meandering dirt track towards the tower. Finally it pulled up beside Sully's CSI van and the team hopped out. Minter counted seven of them as he stepped out into the wind and spitting rain to introduce himself.

'DS Steven Minter, Sussex CID.'

The first one out took a step towards Minter with his hand outstretched. 'DS Thomas, dive team supervisor. Sorry it took us so long; we had a callout in Folkestone.' Thomas looked at his watch. 'Just so you know, it's gone three... It's too late in the day for us to start a dive now. But I wouldn't mind a recce on where you want us diving so we can work out an action plan for tomorrow.'

'Sure.' Minter, aware that Sully was waiting expectantly, introduced him. 'Before we start, this is our forensics coordinator Kevin Sullivan.'

Sully shook the sergeant's hand. 'The search location is the basement storage area of this tower.'

Thomas looked up at it warily. 'The basement?'

'Yes,' continued Sully. 'We believe we're looking at a submerged storage area about thirty feet in diameter and more or less the same depth.'

'Are we talking an open void, or is it compartmental? Is it cluttered?'

'Apparently there's a rotted floor about halfway down, but apart from that we've got no idea at the moment,' answered Minter. 'I'll show you.'

Thomas nodded. 'Lead on.'

Sully and the diving team followed Minter into the ground floor of the tower. Sully had already set up some floodlights on tripods to supplement the dim light leaking in from the arched windows. There was also one poised over the trapdoor entrance to the basement below.

Sully cleared his throat. 'Now, this place is a Mart–'

'Oh, I know about these,' cut in Thomas. 'We've got a few of them still standing in Kent.' He peered down into the trapdoor at the glinting water below, a look of concern on his face. 'They go down quite deep. Lots of storage. They were designed to accommodate a cannon battery and a garrison, and be stocked well enough to withstand a siege.'

'Quite,' said Sully.

DS Thomas nodded at the floodlights spaced around the floor. 'Can you nip those off for me?'

Sully went around and switched them off one at a time, leaving the plank floor of the tower in a gloomy twilight.

Thomas took hold of the rickety ladder posts emerging from the trapdoor hatch and tested the first few rungs with his weight. 'Uh-oh, it's wobbly,' he said, but ducked down anyway to peer into the dark space below as he snapped on a torch.

Immediately shafts of light speered upwards between the planks as he panned his torch around, casting leaping stripes across the low wooden ceiling. The steam of his breath spilled up through the gaps like ghostly apparitions.

'Spooky, eh, boys?' said Minter, trying to lighten the mood. He got nothing back from Thomas's team. They looked concerned at the search area they were being asked to descend into.

'Water's murky as fuck,' Thomas' voice echoed up through

the trapdoor. 'Visibility's going to be a bit of a problem down there.'

He came back up the rickety ladder and sat on the side, his legs dangling below. 'We're probably going to need to treat this like diving on a shipwreck: surface supply set-up, one diver at a time so we don't snarl the lines.' He looked at Minter. 'What are we looking for?'

'Body of a teenager.'

'Skeletal remains only,' added Sully. Then: 'At least one.'

Minter looked at him, surprised. 'You expecting more, are you, Sully?'

Sully shrugged. 'It's a handy place to submerge a body, wouldn't you say? Who knows how many murderers have used this place over the decades...?'

'Nice,' replied Minter. 'Nice thought.'

10

Boyd looked up from his screen to see Warren standing over him, fidgeting to get his attention. 'What've you got for me?' he asked.

Warren handed him a few sheets of paper. 'I've done some digging on this Ricky Harris. He's a bit of a wild character, sir.'

Boyd scanned the top page and recognised a writing style that suggested a sizeable chunk of it had been copied and pasted from Wikipedia. To be fair to Warren, there were additional notes and details that looked as though he'd at least glanced at other sources, including a couple of band photos from Dark Harvest's heyday.

'Jesus.' Boyd grimaced at the images of the five young men in glossy black leather, sporting long poodle perms and bared chests down to their navels. 'Some looks just don't age well.'

Warren grinned. 'Were they a *serious* band?' he asked incredulously.

Boyd looked up. 'You mean... as opposed to what? A *novelty* band?'

Warren nodded.

'Sadly, yes. This, Warren, was what rock music morphed

into for a while back in the day. Young berks dressed up like...'
He really couldn't find a description that honestly did justice to
how ridiculous and self-indulgent this band and their contem-
poraries had looked back in the early eighties. The members of
Dark Harvest were all sporting metal chains, dangling upside-
down crucifixes and belts with leering skull faces on them.
They looked like a parody of a metal band.

'They look like old ladies wearing bondage gear,' Warren
remarked.

Boyd laughed. They really did. Five *EastEnders* Angie Watts-
wannabes dressed up to look like a cross between the Spanish
Inquisition and a bunch of guys in gimp suits.

Beneath the largest photo were details of the line-up. Ricky
Harris was the one at the back on the left: tall and gangly, long,
dark tumbling locks, eyes smudged with black eyeliner, and a
fag drooping from the corner of his mouth.

'Have you managed to find a more recent photo of Harris?'
Boyd asked.

Warren shook his head. 'I don't think they were famous for
very long.'

Boyd checked the Wikipedia snippet, which listed their
discography and tour dates: four albums, several Far East and
European tours and one US stadium tour.

'The band finally split up in 1997,' Boyd said, reading some
of the biography aloud, 'after they'd kicked Harris as a result of
being charged with having sex with a groupie.' He tutted.
Typical arrogant rockers, thinking they could shag who they
wanted without consequence.

Boyd sifted through Warren's notes. He'd found a news clip-
ping from the *Argus* in 1989 that mentioned Harris buying the
Martello tower; there'd been a petition put together by locals
protesting against his plans to turn the tower into the band's
own private recording studio.

Warren handed Boyd another sheet of paper. 'I checked

LEDS and he's registered as living on the Isle of Rum in the Hebrides. He's been a resident there since 1998.'

'And still is?'

'Looks that way, sir.'

'Do you have his contact details? A phone number?' Boyd asked hopefully.

Warren shook his head. 'Just an address. No email. No mobile number. No landline.'

Boyd glanced at the sheet. Even the address looked pretty bloody vague: Dickie's Croft, Isle of Rum, Inner Hebrides, Scotland. He pointed at the *Argus* article. 'Do we know if he came down from Scotland to buy the tower? Did he ever visit the place? How did he even know about it to buy it?'

Warren leant over the desk and pointed at the bottom of the page. 'He was born and raised in Kent, sir. He grew up in Romney.'

Boyd recalled the Romney Marshes had been on a road sign he'd spotted on the drive to Jury's Gap. 'He's a local lad, then,' said Boyd. 'So he'd probably have known about that tower from childhood.'

'I'd say that's a fair shout, sir,' Warren agreed.

'Devil's Tower,' said Boyd. 'I wonder if it was called that when he was a kid.' He settled back in his seat and stroked his chin thoughtfully.

'Well, he's surely going to be a person of interest if this turns out to be a murder enquiry, right, sir?' Warren said.

Boyd nodded. 'I would think so.'

He spotted Sutherland emerging from the kitchenette with a mug of coffee in one hand and a phone, jammed against his ear, in the other.

Sutherland caught Boyd's eye and changed direction, making a beeline towards him. By the time he drew up beside Boyd's desk, he'd ended the call.

'Can I help you, sir?' asked Boyd.

'Before you say anything, Boyd... the answer's an emphatic *no*!' Sutherland said, eyes blazing.

'No to what, sir?' Boyd asked, nonplussed.

'I just picked up a message from DC Okeke about Ellessey Forensics dating that arm bone... I'm not forking out twenty K on a single bloody bone! They are literally taking the piss!' he raged.

'Maybe they're just being humerus?' offered Warren.

Boyd tried his best to hide a grin. Sutherland glared. '*What?*'

Warren blanched. 'It's a joke, sir.'

Sutherland took another few seconds to catch up, then mock-cuffed Warren around the ear. 'Bloody idiot!' He focused his attention back on Boyd. 'I'm running this department budget on fumes at the moment. So the answer's *no*.'

Boyd was a little taken aback at the quoted figure too. 'Twenty K? Why so expensive?'

'She said something about dating it using trees,' replied Sutherland. 'Bloody ridiculous! They must think we're...' He continued to grumble to himself as he turned away and headed back to his office.

Boyd spotted Okeke entering the CID floor through the double doors from the stairwell, peeling her jacket and shoulder bag off. He caught her eyes and waved her over. She weaved her way across the open-plan office, dumped her things on her desk and joined him and Warren.

'All right, guv?'

'Jammy timing,' said Boyd. 'You just missed Sutherland picking up your message. He nearly had a seizure about the arm bone. So, what do we know?'

'Not much really,' said Okeke. 'Dr Esquerra seemed quite sure the bone is from a female. As for age, the best he could give was late teen to mid twenties.'

'Right.' Boyd looked at his watch. 'It's half four. There's a little time left to make use of today. Okeke? Warren?'

Warren's shoulders sagged. 'Mispers?'

'Yup. Mispers, I'm afraid.' Boyd sighed on their behalf. 'Unresolved cases. Female, sixteen to late twenties.' He yawned unintentionally. 'Off you go.'

He went to pick up his phone and stopped. 'Oh, Okeke?' he said.

'Guv?'

'We've got the bone safely back in evidence...?'

Okeke rolled her eyes and he raised a hand in apology as he dialled Minter.

His sergeant answered after the second tone. 'Boss?'

'How's the dive going?'

'It's not,' replied Minter. 'They're starting tomorrow. The team supervisor, DS Thomas, is a little concerned about safety issues and he wants to put a plan of action together tonight.'

'What's the safety issue?' Boyd asked, though he could hazard a guess. He wouldn't want to be the one diving into that murk.

'Clutter, obstructions. Structural integrity.' Warren confirmed his thinking. 'There may be loose or fallen beams down there that could be dislodged and trap a diver.'

'Damn,' Boyd huffed. 'Okay, well, I suppose that's fair enough.'

'The team leader was talking about sending down a remote-controlled thingamajig first thing tomorrow to check it out.'

'Christ, really? He knows we're not diving down on the *Titanic*?'

Boyd expected to hear Minter chuckle, but the line remained silent.

'I think they're really wary about this job, boss. Seriously. The tower's old. It's pretty unstable by all accounts.'

'Right.' Boyd nodded guiltily. 'Okay, safety first. Obviously. Are they heading back to Kent or staying local?'

'Local. They've found a hotel nearby. Thomas wants to know if Sussex Police is settling the tab...'

Boyd suspected it was probably going to be a relatively easy sell to Sutherland, given that he'd just managed to sidestep a twenty-thousand-pound zinger.

'Yup,' he replied. 'You can tell him the rooms are on us.'

11

Boyd pushed the cubed chicken and diced onion around the frying pan. While it browned, he listened to some of Dark Harvest's music on Spotify. It really was dire stuff. If it hadn't already been done by Spinal Tap, he'd have written the band off as a clever parody of the worst kind of heavy metal.

The song titles themselves made for much eye-rolling.

Boyd had heard enough and switched to an easy-listening playlist as he finished cooking dinner. They were having chicken sambal tonight, a recipe his parents had picked up from their travels. Chicken, onion, tomatoes, coconut milk and a little heat from the sambal chilli paste, all served on a bed of white rice. Simple but tasty. It had been a firm family favourite during his childhood and had progressed to becoming a regular much-loved meal with Boyd's own family. Noah had just begun to join them on Wednesday nights, eating his own version (minus the paste), when *it* had happened.

Boyd heard Ozzie barking in the hallway, then a moment later Emma entered the dining room. 'Dad? Are you doing chicken sambal?!'

She poked her head into the kitchen. 'Ohmygod! You really are!' She beamed at him. 'About bloody time!'

He realised she was right to make such a big deal of it. This was a meal they hadn't had in three years. Not since *before*.

'You've remembered how to cook it, I trust?' she said as she dropped her empty Tupperware box in the washing-up bowl and peered over his shoulder.

'Cheeky cow,' he said, swatting her away. 'How was your shift?'

'Long,' she said with a sigh. 'We're starting to get the first of the Christmas work dos coming in. It's an all-hands-on-deck kind of thing.'

He pulled a second wine glass from the cupboard above the hob and waggled it at her.

'God, yes please,' she gasped. 'How was your day?'

'Crime-shaped,' he replied as he poured her a glass of Malbec. 'Someone discovered a bone in the flooded basement of a ruin.'

'Sounds very Hammer House of Horror,' she said.

Boyd sipped his wine. 'Tell me about it. It's got creepiness dripping off every brick.'

She pulled up one of the dining-room chairs to sit in the doorway and watch him cook. 'What is it? Some old abandoned Gothic mansion?'

'No, it's an abandoned fortification. Like a cannon tower.'

'Cool,' she said, putting her glass down and checking her phone.

The chicken cubes were looking pleasingly brown now. He poured in a tin of chopped tomatoes. 'So what's the deal with you and Dan these days?'

'Ummmm...' She paused for a long time and took a gulp of her wine. Then finally: 'Cooling down to be honest, Dad.'

'And that's coming from your side, I take it?' he pressed.

Emma nodded.

'That's a shame. I kind of like Dan,' Boyd said.

'Then *you* go out with him,' Emma replied, shaking her head.

'Ah-haha!' He turned to look at her. 'No, but seriously, Ems, what's wrong with the poor lad?'

She grimaced. 'Maturity. Or lack thereof.'

'He's the same age as you. Why's he got to be mature? Why can't he have a few years of arsing around?'

'You mean, chasing the rock-star dream?' she snorted. 'Like you?'

'It didn't do me any harm. Got a few things out of my system.'

'Such as?'

He shrugged. 'You know, band stuff.'

'Drugs? Booze? Chicks?' Emma leant forward, wrists on her knees. 'That kind of thing?'

'Well... you know, just... *stuff.*' Boyd was wishing he hadn't started this conversation now.

Emma tutted and rolled her eyes. 'Ugh. Boys and their egos. I'm not interested in mothering Dan through this particular phase of his life, Dad. Someone else can do that.'

'Then you should let him know what the deal is,' Boyd replied. 'He's hanging in there, hoping, you know? And trying his best to get answers from me every time I walk into the bloody pub. If it's over, then tell him it's over.'

She sighed. 'It's on my to-do list, trust me.'

Boyd looked at her. 'Then maybe move it to top of that list, Ems?'

She sighed again, looking suddenly twelve again. 'All right,' she replied with a resigned sing-song voice.

AFTER DINNER, Emma went upstairs to have a long well-deserved soak in the bath with a promise that she'd do the dishes later. Boyd took himself and the last dregs of the Malbec into his study to do some noodling on this Martello tower case. Not on the mispers – Okeke and Warren could wade through those – but on Ricky Harris, the apparent owner of the tower since 1989 until recently.

While Ozzie curled himself into a doggie doughnut at his feet, Boyd roused his idling PC and logged into his LEDS account on the remote portal. Given the system was still in a lengthy beta-testing phase, remote access was reserved for DCIs and above. However, his old mate Sunny who had led the training had said that in the fullness of time it would be an all-officers-anywhere-on-any-device system across all forces in the country.

Boyd's first port of call was the criminal database and a check against Harris's name. He wanted to know a bit more about this groupie case. He found the information pretty quickly. Harris had been charged under his birth name, Richard Silas Harris, in early 1997, for sex with a minor.

According to which newspaper you read, he was either a grotesque child molester or a foolish rocker caught out by an underage groupie. One of the tabloids had even made a point of saying he'd been 'dreadfully unlucky' as she was only a few weeks away from 'being legal'.

Nice. Boyd shook his head with disgust. The nod-nod-wink-wink wording of the tabloid's ed-op piece about the incident had made him feel distinctly queasy.

Dark Harvest had made a big thing of kicking Harris out of the band and demonstrating their disgust at his inappropriate behaviour, but Boyd suspected that had been just for show. He was pretty sure that they'd all been guilty of exploiting their female fans in the back of their tour bus without giving a second thought to how old they were or how callously the girls were ejected from the band's hotel rooms once they'd served their purpose.

Dismissing that behaviour as *'things were different back then'* felt like a cop-out to him. It was appalling behaviour, but it had been tolerated because... well... 'lads will be lads and rock stars even more so'. It was almost expected of them, and was even celebrated in some rock and heavy metal glossies – *'Ooh, those crazy, wild guys!'*

Boyd pulled Warren's notes on Harris from his jacket pocket and skim-read them again. Richard Harris was born in Folkestone, Kent, in March 1958. Resident in Romney during his school years. Musician in a number of going-nowhere bands until he formed Dark Harvest in 1979.

The notes were actually more helpful than the LEDS record. The band had enjoyed a few years of success, mostly in the States where they'd joined other more recognisable bands like Iron Maiden and Def Leppard on the stadium and festival circuits. The band had also stoked up some controversy over there – particularly in the Bible belt – with claims that they were all occultists and practised Satanic rituals before every gig. To be fair, it was no worse than Ozzy Osbourne's antics at about the same time.

At least Dark Harvest weren't biting the heads off live bats on stage, Boyd thought.

But there were enough snippets here and there that more than suggested the narrative of five young lads who had suddenly believed they were Kings of the World. Lads in that situation had a tendency to end up believing they could get away with anything.

12

PC Karen Brown was dying for a fag. There was no smoking in the patrol car, obviously. Well, not now anyway. She'd had a caution from her training sergeant for doing that a few weeks ago. So, it was a stark choice between chewing what was left of her fingernails or getting out of the car into the cold, blustery, salty marshland night to spark up.

She looked out of the driver-side window at the tower, taking in the cordon of police tape around the old ruin, snapping and thrumming in the wind. Could she have her ciggy in there?

It wasn't the most appealing idea.

As a local girl, she'd grown up hearing all the ghost stories about this place. Silly stuff that the kids liked to tell each other once they'd grounded their BMX bikes and dared themselves to briefly step inside.

The kids around here had called it Devil's Tower.

But I'm not a kid any more, am I? Karen reminded herself. She was an adult. A plod on probation who was *really* craving a smoke.

'Fuck it,' she whispered, and opened the car door. Immediately the wind tugged a few loose tresses of hair out of her tightly wound bun and she felt the sting of specks of salt water, whipped up off the mud flats, hitting her cheeks.

She hurried over to the tower, stepping over the tape, and pushed the wooden door inwards. Once inside, she snapped on her torch and panned it around. The dive team had unloaded the gear from their van and stacked it neatly on the wooden floorboards – hence her graveyard shift sitting all alone in the patrol car outside.

Karen pulled a cigarette from her crumpled packet of B&H and lit up. She took a long hard pull and then blew out a cloud of smoke that spun and whirled slowly across the large circular space, caught in the eddies of air that whistled in through the small arched windows.

She'd never actually been inside the tower before. Probably because she'd heard the local urban myths and scary stories about child sacrifices. Apparently, 'back in the day' some weirdo devil worshippers had successfully conjured up a demon in the basement of the tower and they'd all been torn to shreds by it. More elaborate versions of that tale featured the footprints of some 'cloven beast' across the muddy flats as it headed out into the night, never to be seen again.

Karen shook her head and took another quick pull on her cigarette before the gusting wind hastened the glowing tip down to the filter.

She glanced at the trapdoor. Apparently if you scooched down low to peer into the basement and listened very carefully, you could just about hear the faint sound of a sobbing child.

A child, waiting her turn to be sacrificed.

'Oh, fuck this,' she whispered, stubbing the cigarette out and hastening back to the warmth and comfort of the patrol car and the reassuring chatter of control radio traffic.

13

'Isle of *what*?'

'Rum, sir. As in what pirates drink,' said Boyd. 'Savvy?' His Jack Sparrow impersonation was pitiful.

Sutherland looked up from this morning's influx of emails. 'And where is this Island of Rum?'

'It's in the Hebrides,' replied Boyd.

'Oh, for Christ's sake. It couldn't just be...' His voice trailed away. 'Right, well that's going to eat into what's left of my budget, I suppose.'

'Yes, sir. But nowhere near as much as the divers.' Boyd realised it was probably unkind to remind the detective super-intendent of the other overheads one single bone had racked up so far... but it did give Sutherland's round face an interesting appearance of mottled corn-beef-like pink.

'Well... how much is a trip up there going to set us back? Have you costed it up yet?'

'A flight to Inverness is about eighty quid,' Boyd said. 'Then there's car hire and a ferry. So barely anything in the grand scheme of things.'

'Can't you get the police up there to bring him to the mainland to interview him?' Sutherland asked hopefully.

'I have asked, and they said no,' replied Boyd, 'unless he's being arrested. Which he's not. Just helping with enquiries at this stage.'

'And you can't just give him a bloody call?' Sutherland groused.

'According to the charming lady I spoke to in the post office there... he lives off grid.' At least Boyd had thought that's what she was saying. Her Gaelic accent had been thick. 'He lives up in the hills.'

Sutherland nodded. 'So, how much is it to take a train up instead of a plane?' he asked.

'Twice as expensive.'

'Oh, for fuck's sake.' Sutherland wilted in his seat. Boyd was tempted to mention that half of the department's budget had been pissed away over the course of the year on Flack's ongoing operation, which, as far as he could see, seemed to have yielded nothing but expense claims.

'Right, Boyd... and you can justify this, can you?'

Boyd nodded. He explained about Harris's past and being ditched from the band. 'But the bit that makes my nose twitch is that he's been hanging on to that Martello tower for the last thirty-three years, even though he hasn't done anything with it. I mean, he could have just forgotten he owned it,' said Boyd, 'or maybe he didn't want anyone else getting their hands on it.'

BOYD APPROACHED WARREN, who was sitting at his desk. Warren had his back to him and some headphones on and had failed to respond when Boyd had thrown a paper ball in his direction. On closer inspection, Boyd could see that Warren was watching a music video on YouTube.

Boyd tapped his shoulder and Warren nearly leapt out of his seat.

'What're you watching?'

'Dark Harvest.' Warren paused the video on an image that showed a young girl in a red anorak being led by a pair of scantily clad 'demons' into the mouth of a dungeon.

'Ah, the golden years of MTV,' Boyd said, shaking his head.

Warren looked up at him. 'This stuff was actually broadcast on TV?'

'Yup.'

Boyd heard Okeke's chair roll back and her footsteps behind him as she came over to take a look. 'Oh, for God's sake. The camera's zoomed in right on their arse cheeks.'

'And that's a child about to be taken down into a torture dungeon,' Warren said, pointing at the screen. He hit play again and the grainy eighties video resumed. The image cut to the band, legs apart, holding their guitars as though they were giant erections and waggling their tongues at the camera.

Boyd whistled. 'I don't remember heavy metal videos looking *that* naff.'

The video went back to the little girl entering the dungeon, then cut to her face. There were tears streaming down her cheeks. Boyd had to give the young actor credit; she looked genuinely terrified.

'Or *that* inappropriate,' added Okeke. 'Jesus... that's just not on.' She reached over Warren's shoulder and paused it. 'It's sick.'

'That was pretty standard fare in those days,' said Boyd.

'Yeah, well, they should've known better,' Okeke muttered.

Boyd stood up straight to stretch his arms out – he was still aching from yesterday's madness in the gym. 'I'm going up to Scotland this afternoon to interview Ricky Harris.' Boyd scrubbed the video back a few seconds and paused on an image of the band. 'That pillock,' he said, pointing to the one waggling his tongue at the camera. 'Warren, you're coming to Rum with me.'

Warren twisted in his seat to look up. 'Seriously?'

'Yeah, you need some more field and interview experience.' Boyd glanced at Okeke, noting the stiff look on her face. 'Okeke, I need you down here as Ellessey liaison in case the divers pull up anything else of interest,' he explained.

'Right,' she grunted.

'Warren, get yourself home. Ask your mum. Pack an overnight bag. Back here no later than midday, all right?'

'Yes, sir.'

Boyd checked his watch. It was 9.23 a.m. He needed to do likewise. He also needed to figure out what the hell he was going to do with Ozzie.

'Oh, well, hello there, officer,' said Charlotte. She looked at the clock on the wall of her office. 'Bit early for walkies, isn't it, Bill?'

'I've come to beg a huge favour,' he said sheepishly. He sat down on the spare chair in front of her desk. 'I've got to go away for a couple of days or so.'

'Ooh...' She looked intrigued. 'Where are you off to?'

'The Hebrides.'

'*What?*' she exclaimed.

'I'm interviewing a person of interest,' Boyd told her. 'Look, I really hate to ask –'

'Is it Ozzie?' she cut in.

He nodded. 'Emma's shifts at the hotel are all over the place. The season of Christmas dos and poor choices with work colleagues has commenced and she's...'

'I'm always happy to mind the old boy,' she said, smiling. 'Do you want me to drop around after work and pick him up?'

Boyd nodded. 'That would be great. You're a lifesaver.' He handed her his spare house keys. 'I've explained to him he's to be on best behaviour and he's to mind his P's and Q's.'

'Oh, Mia will put him straight if he acts up for me,' Charlotte said. 'When are you going?'

'This afternoon,' he replied. 'Train to Gatwick. Plane to Inverness and then a ferry to an island called Rum, would you believe?'

'Rum?' She laughed. 'Seriously? Surely it should be called Whisky?'

'Right. You'd have thought.'

'When will you be back?' she asked.

'Well, if we can actually find the bugger and talk to him – hopefully at the weekend.'

'You'd better wrap up warm, then. Coats, scarves and gloves,' Charlotte said. 'I can't imagine the north-west of Scotland is going to be particularly clement this time of year.'

'I will do,' he said. He was about to smile but it quickly became a frown. 'Uh, look, excuse the state of my house when you go in... I didn't think that far ahead about...'

Charlotte smiled kindly. 'Me wandering in?'

'Right. It's a bit of a tip.'

'There'll be no judgement, I promise,' she said, laughing.

He reached out and squeezed her hand awkwardly. 'Thanks, Charlotte. Shit, I'm really sorry for dropping this on you without any bloody warning at all. I'd have been in a fix if it wasn't for you.'

She sighed. 'Ozzie and I will discuss at great length what your penance shall be.'

14

inter, Sully and the dive team were clustered around the small monitor that had been set up on a makeshift workbench in the middle of the tower's ground floor.

The monitor was displaying a grainy image from the remote-controlled unit descending into the flooded basement below. DS Thomas sat beside the young man piloting it; the rest of the team formed a Greek chorus just behind. The RCU's top-mounted spotlight was doing its best to pierce through the cloudy water to pick out any details.

Minter found it difficult to make much sense of the ghostly greenish-grey swirls on the screen. Every now and then, brilliant white spectral forms flickered across the screen as pieces of debris, caught in the glare of the light, drifted sedately in front of the camera.

'The visibility's piss-poor,' muttered Thomas unhappily. 'We're probably going to get more of an idea of the state of the place if we give it a honk of sonar.'

He nodded at the pilot and the man tapped a button on a keyboard.

'How long does that take?' asked Minter.

'Oh, it's almost instantaneous,' replied Thomas. 'Park it here,' he told the pilot. 'Let's see what the lay of the land below us is. Switch to VGS.'

The pilot took his hand off the controller and hit another key. The screen changed to show an even more incomprehensible monochromatic display of grey splodges.

'This is a void greyscale, looking directly down,' explained Thomas. 'The lighter pixels represent closer objects, the dark ones... further away, obviously. See that dark area on the screen?' The bottom-left quartile of the screen was almost black. 'That's open space below. The lighter splodges here –' he pointed at ghostly shapes at the side of the image – 'that's the tower's wall. See how it grades smoothly to black? That's flat surface.'

He spoke as though it was blindingly obvious.

'You're not getting it, are you, Minter?' said Sully with a pitying look.

'Head over towards that darker bit,' Thomas ordered the pilot. The screen refreshed a couple of seconds later and the dark area jumped towards the middle of the screen and increased in size.

'Hmmm.' Thomas didn't sound particularly encouraging. 'Closer...'

The screen updated again and now the dark area almost completely filled it.

'I think we're looking at a collapsed floor below,' said Thomas, pointing at some straight lines that framed the darkness. 'Those are edges of planks of wood. Floorboards.' He turned back to look at Minter. 'I'm not happy sending any of my lads down into that. Not if there's structure down there that's collapsed; it's too dangerous. There's a risk of getting snagged or trapped.'

'So what does that mean?' Minter asked. 'That's it? You're packing up?'

'It means no one's going down, I'm afraid,' Thomas confirmed. 'But we can keep on scouting with the RCU. If we follow the path that extractor hose took to the bottom, we may well wind up next to the rest of your body.' He nodded at the dark area of the screen, framed by the paler grey planks. 'We're looking at roughly the middle of the floor. The pipe descended through that to the bottom almost certainly.'

'All right, then,' Minter said, nodding. 'Let's go down and take a look.'

The pilot switched the image on the screen back to camera to get a real-time view. The grainy image on the screen began to move again, motes of debris drifting upwards and into the glare of the spotlight as the RCU descended.

The planks of wood hove into view as it passed through the gap in the floor, then disappeared out of sight.

'Watch that the cables don't snag above,' said Thomas.

'Got it, boss.'

'Okay... and let's give it another honk below.'

The pilot tapped a key and switched the view on the screen again.

'It's mostly open space,' said Thomas. 'Those lighter tones –' he pointed at the screen –'suggest an uneven floor. Which will undoubtedly be fallen debris. Let's get down to the bottom there.'

The pilot switched view again and Minter thought he caught a glimpse of some steps in the background as the camera view rotated in a three-sixty as it descended.

'Yep,' said Thomas, following Minter's gaze. 'Those are steps.'

'We're nearing the bottom,' said the pilot.

There were several amorphous humps and bumps that

looked as though they could be mounds of mud or silt, but near the middle, almost directly beneath where the RCU was going to touch down, was something oval.

Thomas had picked it out too. 'Reverse up so that's on the camera when we land,' he said.

The screen image switched back to the grainy camera view. The motes of waterborne debris were increasing now, swirling in random directions like glitter flakes in a snow globe.

'The propellers are kicking up all the crap at the bottom,' explained Thomas. 'It'll clear in a bit.'

The image on the screen jolted slightly.

'Okay, we're now on the bottom,' said the pilot. He released the trigger of his control stick and the swirling blizzard of bright debris fragments began to calm down, gently descending in a unified direction like slow-motion snowfall.

As the view ahead gradually cleared, Minter realised the oval object was a couple of feet ahead of the RCU, perfectly positioned and caught in the full glare of the light.

'That's a holdall bag,' said one of the diving team.

Minter squinted at the screen. As the debris settled down, he began to pick out bold white letters on the side. *B.O.A.C.*

'What's that? Bo-Ack? Is that some sort of brand name?' he asked.

'B-O-A-C,' said Sully. 'British and Overseas Air Corporation. They became British Airways back in the mid seventies, I do believe.'

The image was getting clearer. Everyone's eyes adjusted to the grainy detail, making sense of the starkly lit geometric picture.

'Shit,' said DS Thomas. 'Is that hair?' he said, pointing at the screen.

From the far side of the bag, presumably where the zip would be, a faintly undulating ribbon-like object had been stirred to life by the RCU's propellers, rising momentarily into view to be caught in the spotlight before slowly settling once again to the darkness beyond.

15

'Are you all right, sir?' asked Warren.

No, I'm definitely not. Boyd realised he was clasping the seat's armrest, knuckles bulging with the effort to hang on. 'I'm fine, Warren. I'm fine.'

'It's just a bit of turbulence, boss. Lumpy air, as my mum likes to call it.'

'Right.'

Boyd had climbed aboard earlier this afternoon thinking that he was perfectly fine with flying. It had been a few years since the last time – he'd flown down to Alicante with Julia and the kids to holiday at his parents' hillside villa – and there'd been absolutely no reason to think that he'd been anything but fine as he'd climbed the steps to board the plane.

The take-off had been straightforward. It was the bad weather they'd hit approaching Inverness that had set off this armrest-grabbing behaviour. The phrase 'lumpy air' really wasn't doing it justice.

'You know, sir,' Warren continued blithely, 'my mum says no plane has ever crashed simply because of turbulence. It's usually some component failure rather than the actual weather itself.'

Boyd briefly considered letting go of the armrest and throttling the lad to shut him up, but he was absolutely convinced the plane would suddenly flip over and descend into a nosedive if he didn't continue to keep a firm control of the struggling commercial airliner from here, seat 39A.

'It's an example of people confusing correlation with causation,' Warren continued. 'There's a classic example of that with the jumbo jet that went down over –'

'Warren?'

'Sir?'

'Shhhh... please.'

'Not helping?'

'No. Not really.'

Warren nodded and closed his mouth.

The plane made a bumpy landing at Inverness in driving rain that was on the cusp of becoming sleet. Boyd fought the urge to cheer the pilot out of sheer relief when the plane finally came to a standstill.

They were met at arrivals by a DC Furmor, a tall, lanky man holding up an A4 pad with 'B. Boyle' scrawled across it. He apologised all the way to his parked-up pool car for getting Boyd's name wrong, and for the dreadful weather, which, according to the young man had been brilliantly sunny this morning.

Furmor drove them the remaining hundred and five miles to Mallaig, a fishing port on the north-west coast that described itself as the 'Gateway to Skye'.

'Ye could've taken the Harry Potter train from Fort William,' Furmor said as they neared the marina. 'If ye're into that sort of thing. The train ends up here.'

'And then you have a trainload of confused tourists all asking where Hogwarts is?' Warren asked.

Furmor laughed. 'Aye. And they're none too happy about the answer either.'

He dropped them at a small hotel at the quayside at just after eight. 'Sorry, sir,' he said to Boyd. 'I booked you in under the name Boyle, not Boyd.'

Boyd waved his apology away. 'It's no problem, honestly.'

'Ye're in luck with the ferry. CalMac runs only four days a week in the winter. But tomorrow's one of those days.'

'What time does it leave?' Boyd asked.

'Usually around ten in the morning.' Furmor pointed across the dark marina. 'The CalMac terminal's over there. Ye'll need to check in an hour before the ferry's due to go.'

'Right. Well, thanks for the ride.'

'Aye, s'no problem. Cooperation cross the border, eh?'

Boyd and Warren thanked Furmor, then checked into their rooms and met again five minutes later at a table in the hotel's small bar.

'What're you having?' Boyd asked as Warren sat down.

'Pint of lager and lime, please, sir.'

Boyd raised his brows. 'You're in the Highlands, Warren. Sure you don't want to try something with a little more local flavour?'

Warren shook his head.

'Fine.'

Boyd returned shortly afterwards with a pint of Guinness for himself, the lager for Warren and four bags of crisps, which he tossed onto their table. 'The bar menu closed at eight. We just missed it. It's salt and vinegar followed by cheese and onion for dinner tonight.' He'd been fantasizing in the car about getting some warm, stodgy food in his belly before going to bed – something with gravy and dumplings, perhaps. 'This'll have to do us till breakfast.' He stared wistfully at the packets on the table.

'They start serving breakfast at eight?' Warren asked.

'Yup.' Boyd sighed. 'But the barman said the ferry terminal has a decent café in it. If we get up and head over for nine, we'll have time to grab something decent over there.'

Boyd tore open the first packet and grabbed a fistful of cheese and onion crisps. 'I'm bloody starving.'

Warren sipped his lager. 'Thanks for bringing me along, sir.'

'That's all right,' Boyd said. 'You've done a lot of good intelligence gathering over the last year. But not much in the way of eyeball-to-eyeball interviewing. It's about time you did some real work.' He grinned and took a slug of his Guinness.

'I was doing a bit more research on Ricky Harris on the way up,' said Warren. 'It seems it wasn't just a case of some rock star stepping over the line with an underage fan.'

'What did you find?'

'Well, he was charged with having sex with a minor, a fan who was fifteen. He got eight months suspended. As we know, his bandmates kicked him out; said they didn't want to work with a "pervert" any more.'

'With a pervert? Where did you get that?'

Warren pulled out his phone to check his notes. 'An interview in a magazine called *Kerrang*. I don't know that one.'

'I do,' said Boyd. 'I used to buy it.'

'Well, one of the band said, "He always took things way too far." The band broke up about nine months later.'

Boyd picked up his pint. 'Was there anything more on him taking things too far?' he asked.

Warren shook his head.

In the wake of the Jimmy Savile case ten years ago, Boyd had been expecting a long slew of wrinkly old rockers to be wheeled out into the limelight for the 'crazy' things they'd done twenty, thirty years earlier. For some reason that had never happened, and he'd sometimes wondered whether at some unspoken level the bad old boys of rock 'n' roll had been given a hall pass. Because once that door was opened, it would inevitably become a floodgate.

'What do we know about his life now?' asked Boyd.

'He's lived on a croft since 1998. That's a small holding: a farm big enough to feed yourself,' he explained.

'Thanks for that, Warren. So this ex-rocker's been living on this tiny farm for twenty-odd years? Surely he must have got up to something else.'

'There's only about twenty or so people on the island, sir,' he continued. 'I'm not sure there's that much to do, especially as there's no phone signal or internet.' Warren sighed and tutted. 'I can't believe in this day and age there isn't any internet.'

'That's how they like it on the island, I suppose.' Boyd shook his head. 'Well,' he said, picking up his phone, 'might as well make use of the Wi-Fi while we've still got it.'

There was a text from Charlotte.

VIP GUEST COLLECTED, fed, walked and pooped.

HE TAPPED AN ANSWER BACK.

THANK you so much for that, C. You're a good friend. X

HIS THUMB LINGERED over the X key for a while as he pondered whether two X's would be too much. He decided in favour of moderation.

Warren suddenly jumped up from his seat and pressed his phone to his ear. 'Hullo, Mum. Yeah, we're there now. What?

No, I didn't forget to...' He hastened out of earshot and Boyd couldn't help smiling.

On his own phone there were several missed calls from Minter and Okeke. He dialled his voicemail to hear the message that was waiting for him, wondering which one of them had bothered to leave the message. It was Okeke.

'*Guv? The dive team has just managed to retrieve a body at the tower. FYI, this was definitely a murder, not an accident. Call me back when you get this.*'

He did as she'd asked, but after a dozen rings his call went through to her voicemail. He checked his watch; it was quarter to nine. Which, he knew, was Jay Time: the precious two hours in every twenty-four that Okeke's and her boyfriend's jobs allowed them to actually see each other.

'I've just got your message, Okeke,' he said. 'I'm about to hit the sack myself. I presume Ellessey are doing the autopsy tomorrow morning. I'm going to be incommunicado all of tomorrow until the evening probably. Not planning on overnighting it on the island if we can help it. Will give you and Minter a call when we've spoken to Harris.'

He hung up and returned to his pint. Tomorrow was going to be a long day.

16

Charlotte looked up from her book – a weathered and worn copy of a collection of short stories by John Irving – and slowly realised that the soft buzzing noise that had permeated the story she'd been reading was her phone vibrating on the side table. She picked it up, saw OLD BILL on the screen and smiled.

She glanced at Ozzie, who was curled up with Mia beside the wood burner. 'I think your dad's ringing to see how you're getting on,' she told him.

She answered the call. 'Good evening, Charlotte Kennel Services.'

'It's Bill,' he replied, unnecessarily. 'How're things with Ozzie? He's not being a pain, is he?'

Charlotte smiled at the view before her: Ozzie and Mia in a cosy huddle, staring blissfully at the flickering flames in the grate with glazed eyes. 'Oh, he's fine. He's bagged the best spot in my lounge and Mia's loving the company. How're you doing? Are you where you need to be yet?' She could hear what sounded like a pinball machine in the background.

'I'm on the mainland still,' Boyd said. 'We're getting a ferry across to Rum early tomorrow morning.'

Charlotte chuckled at the name once again. 'Oh, I do love that.'

'I always want to do my Captain Jack Sparrow imperson-ation when I say it,' Boyd said.

'Who's Jack Sparrow?' she asked. 'Does he work with you?'

She heard him laugh. 'You really have bypassed the last twenty years of popular culture, haven't you?'

'I've had better things to do with my time,' she replied haughtily. 'Anyway, how was your flight?'

'A little bumpy. Nothing I'm not used to, though,' he lied.

'A worldly wise jet-setter, huh?'

'That's me.'

She took a sip of her coffee. 'So it's a ferry over, a quick interview, then a ferry back?' she asked.

'That's the plan,' Boyd replied. 'Although, if it's too late in the day, we might get a hotel room here tomorrow night and fly back Saturday.'

'Well...' Charlotte said, not wanting to draw the conversa-tion out too long; Bill sounded tired. 'Don't you worry about Oz; he's decided he's the man of the house this evening and he's absolutely fine.'

'Don't let him boss you around.'

'Oh, I think Mia and I can handle him,' she said, smiling. She was enjoying having this part of Boyd here in her house. She heard him try and stifle a yawn. 'Look now – off you go, Mr Detective. Get some sleep so you're bright and ready to tackle your bad guy tomorrow.'

'All right. Look, Charlotte, thanks again for –'

'Shh. It's okay, really.'

'Right. Okay,' he replied, dutifully chastened. 'Night night, then.'

'Goodnight, Bill.' She ended the call and set the phone back down on her table, pleased that she hadn't sounded too clingy. Just the right amount of warmth and friendship, and nothing more than that. She didn't want to scare him away.

It was a damned tightrope: you couldn't be too keen nor too standoffish either. At her age, opportunities to find someone to grow old and happy with were increasingly hard to find. Particularly someone as lovely as Bill. She still had no clear idea what his feelings were for her – whether he saw her as just a dog-walking friend or whether he saw more possibilities in their friendship. She found herself reviewing his last few texts: friendly, warm, grateful for minding Ozzie, but there was nothing in them that hinted he wanted to develop their companionship further.

He lost his wife just a few years ago. Slow down. What the heck do you expect?

She seemed to be telling herself this more and more regularly recently. She knew that happiness wasn't guaranteed with someone else. A relationship didn't necessarily ensure good company. Bill was the perfect friend. Would he be a perfect partner, though?

Ozzie suddenly leapt to his feet and unleashed a deafening volley of barks. He padded from her front room to the kitchen and fired off another steady burst of deep chesty barks at the back door.

'Ozzie!' She got up and followed him through. 'What's the matter, boy?'

He looked at her, then the door. At her, then back at the door again.

'Do you need the loo?' She unlocked the door and let him out into her small yard, wet with the steady drizzle. He shot out into the darkness and down to the far end, towards the wheelie bins and the gate to the alley outside.

'Oh, I see.' She sighed. 'A cat is it, eh?'

He jumped at the gate several times, sending it clattering against its post, then he snuffled and snorted noisily along the bottom of it. Mia joined him.

'It's just a cat or a fox,' she said, walking over. 'There's no reason to go potty, old boy.'

She shooed him up the yard to the door, then, as an afterthought, she closed Ozzie and Mia in the kitchen and went back to check that the gate was properly secured. The bolt was slid across, just as it should be.

Definitely a cat.

She took a deep breath to calm herself down. Ozzie was a lovely old boy, but his sudden barrage of ear-splitting barks was enough to jolt anyone's nerves.

It's just a cat, she told herself again, as she listened to the steady hiss of the drizzle against the paving slabs in her yard.

But then she heard something else. A very subtle but unmistakable noise: the scrape of a shoe on the cobbles on the other side of the gate.

'Hello?' she called softly.

Silence.

Charlotte held her breath to listen more closely. The sound of footsteps moving away would be unsettling, but better than this perfect stillness, which suggested that someone was standing, stock still, barely a couple of feet away from her. Separated by nothing more than a flimsy wooden gate.

'I'd piss off if I were you,' she said, adopting the most menacing accent she could. 'I've got two German shepherds in 'ere... mate.'

Her mockney accent was Dick Van Dyke at his very best.

She thought she heard a soft snigger through the wooden slats. She took a step back and looked up at the space above the gate. A street lamp two doors down cast a sickly amber sheen across the overgrown alleyway and threw a permanent orange glow across the ceiling of her back bedroom.

Tonight, though, the fizzing light had picked out something else... the gentle rising and fading curl of someone's breath ascending into the night.

17

From the warmth of the passenger cabin, Boyd watched Warren dry-heaving over the safety rail. Most of this morning's Big Breakfast Bap was on its way down to the bottom of the sea, or already lining the bellies of the gulls that seemed to be chasing the ferry away from mainland Scotland.

Boyd shook his head. The poor lad had gone large for breakfast at the ferry terminal's café, as he'd woken up this morning absolutely starving. Boyd had done likewise and was grateful that the large froth-covered swells that were making the ferry wallow aft to stern weren't having the same effect on him.

He watched Warren wipe his mouth, check his coat, then his jacket and tie, and stagger back from the aft deck into the ferry's passenger lounge, which was pretty much two rows of orange plastic seats and a snack vending machine.

'Better?' asked Boyd.

Warren collapsed into the bucket seat beside him, groaning wretchedly.

'I thought you were going to cough up a kidney out there.'

Warren doubled over, elbows on his knees and gazed at the scuffed wooden floor between his feet. 'Oh God, oh God,' he mumbled to himself.

Boyd couldn't help but feel sorry for him, slightly paternal even. He patted his back gently. 'At least it's all out now, sunshine. All done.'

'I didn't... I didn't know I got seasick, sir,' Warren muttered. 'I'm really sorry.'

'Don't worry about it. You never been on a choppy sea before?'

Warren shook his head. 'Never been on a ship before.'

Boyd nodded and huffed a laugh. 'I suppose it makes us even, doesn't it? I was a bit of a muppet on the plane up.' He patted the young man's back again. 'I won't tell the others if you don't.'

The trip across the Sea of the Hebrides took an hour and a half, and they had the passenger's lounge to themselves.

At quarter to twelve, the ferry pulled out of the sluggish swells and into sheltered Kinloch on the Isle of Rum. The bay was little more than a horseshoe-shaped bite out of the island, peppered with a few single-storey wooden buildings on either side and an old brick castle in the middle.

The pilot brought the ferry up alongside an unmanned pier on the left-hand side of the bay and, with the help of the only other crewmember, secured lines fore and aft.

'Aye, just hop over, lads,' the pilot called out. 'Ye'll be fine.'

Boyd let Warren go first. The relief on Warren's face as he stood on steady ground once more was a picture.

'Where do we find the community ranger?' Boyd asked the pilot.

'Carol's normally at the visitor's centre,' he said, pointing at the hut at the start of the pier. 'Ah, hang on, no. It's a Friday. She's not there; she'll be working in the post office right now. Past the castle.' He pointed at a hut on the far side of the bay. 'That's about twenty minutes on foot. Lovely walk, it is.'

Boyd looked up at the heavy grey sky, spitting mean-spirited stinging drops of freezing rain down at him. *On any other day, maybe.*

He hopped off the ferry with his and Warren's overnight bags slung, one on each shoulder. The ferry was already untethered with its engine roaring impatiently by the time he'd passed Warren's bag to him and turned to wave thanks to the pilot.

Already feeling the cold, Boyd pulled the scarf and beanie out of his pockets. 'Right, it looks like a brisk walk to the post office, then,' he said.

The walk took them twenty-minutes, just as the pilot had said, and they arrived outside a building that looked like a cross between a scout hut and a chirpy well-used community hall: the Isle of Rum General Store. There was an old-fashioned red telephone box standing proudly outside it.

Boyd instinctively reached for his own phone and checked for a signal. Nothing.

'If we need to phone home, that's it, then,' said Boyd, pointing to the box.

He led the way inside the building and found presumably the only shop in the world that stocked a single item of virtu-ally everything ever made by man. There was a young woman behind the counter ticking items off a clipboard, a pair of glasses pushed up above her forehead into an untidy nest of auburn hair.

'Are you Carol?' Boyd asked.

She looked up. 'Aye.' Then, after a brief confused frown, she gave them a friendly smile. 'Ah, you must be the coppers from England.'

Boyd offered her his hand. 'I'm DCI Boyd and this is DC Warren.'

Carol turned and reached for a notepad on a shelf behind her. She tore a page from it and passed it over the counter to him. 'Message for you.'

He looked at the scrap of paper. It bore Minter's name and a message: '*Call me ASAP.*'

'I believe ye're over here to have a chat with our Dickie?' Carol asked.

Boyd nodded. 'Yeah, we are.'

She looked concerned. 'Now what can the poor old boy have done wrong to bring ye all the way over here?'

'I'm sorry, I can't really talk about that. It's a police matter,' he said. He held the note up. 'Have you got a phone I can use?'

She nodded at the entrance to the shop. 'There's a call box outside.'

'Ah... well, you see, I've not got any cash,' Boyd said. 'Not since the nineties anyway. Warren?'

Warren shook his head.

Carol spread her hands. 'Well now, lads, I have a shop full of goodies... and change in the till.'

18

Okeke watched Dr Palmer as she silently studied the small corpse on her examination table. The cadaver was still tucked into the foetal position in which they'd found her inside the holdall.

The vinyl BOAC bag had been carefully cut away from her; the zip had rusted solid and in several places her flesh had fused with the inner lining of the bag. They had a possible name for the girl already: Patricia Hemsworth. A label bearing that name had been stitched onto the collar of the blue denim dress she'd been wearing. A printed name label this old suggested the girl had been from some institution. Perhaps a foster home or maybe even an orphanage.

Okeke texted the name to Minter: *Possible victim name – Patricia Hemsworth. Anything on mispers?* She was hoping he'd get a quick result on LEDS and was expecting her phone to vibrate in her jacket pocket at any moment.

She turned her attention back to the work going on next to her, trying not to look at the girl's skeletal face. Her flesh had darkened to a wrinkled, leathery reddish-brown that reminded Okeke of dried-out, hardened conkers. The girl's long blonde hair was spread out across the green vinyl cover of the examination table like a Japanese paper fan. It was the only part of Patricia that hadn't been corrupted by the decades she'd spent down there underwater – her hair was still fair and untangled as if it belonged to a child who'd just stepped out of the bathtub.

'Cause of death was probably blood loss,' said Dr Palmer. She pointed to a ragged tear in the leathery skin located just below the collarbone on the girl's right side. 'This puncture runs all the way through to her back. The trajectory of it, I would say, might have nicked her lung, but almost certainly severed an artery.'

'Any idea what could have caused it?' Okeke asked.

Palmer shook her head. 'Something irregular. It wasn't knife-sharp. I've seen wounds like this caused by idiots clambering over spike-topped park fences and slipping.' Dr Palmer pulled a lens down and inspected the wound more closely. 'Okay, so I can see some splinters of... wood, it looks like. So perhaps a wooden spike of some sort.' She looked at Okeke. 'You said she was retrieved from a ruin?'

Okeke nodded. 'A tower.' She couldn't think of the name for them right now. 'Over near Romney. There's wooden planking on the floors inside.'

'A tower? Okay.' Palmer nodded. 'There are signs of perimortem bruising. There may well be some broken bones in there too. I'll need to do an X-ray first.'

'What're you thinking?'

'My first thought is that she fell,' Palmer replied. 'Perhaps onto a wooden spike or some jagged bit of wood,' she said, pointing at the wound. 'If she was impaled, then blood loss would have finished her off relatively quickly, but...'

'But what?'

'Her eyes.'

'What about them?' Okeke asked.

Dr Palmer looked up at her. 'They're gone.'

'I thought... don't they just break down pretty early in the decomposition process?' said Okeke.

'They do, but they'll leave behind a dried membrane. These are actually gone.'

'Rats?' Okeke wondered.

Palmer pointed at the bag. 'She was zipped up in that, right?

'It wasn't completely zipped up. The diving team said her hair was out.'

'I suppose something could have got in and had them. I'll need to do some closer work on the eye sockets.' Palmer looked up again at Okeke over the rim of her glasses. 'There is, of course, the far more obvious issue, though, isn't there? How did she end up in that bag?'

'Well, the obvious answer is foul play,' Okeke said. 'Especially given the other arm bone that we found down there. But then there's always room for the possibility that the death was accidental and the body was hidden.'

'Oh, I see, a passing Samaritan?'

Okeke shook her head and shrugged. 'Any signs of sexual assault?' she asked.

Dr Palmer's eyes wrinkled behind her glasses. She could have been smiling or grimacing; it was hard to tell. 'I don't know if I'll be able to get that kind of detail out of this one. However, it's highly suspicious that there was no underwear beneath the dress. If there's vaginal or anal tearing, it might show up. But this is essentially mummified flesh.'

'DNA?'

Palmer pulled a face. 'You're thinking semen or saliva traces?'

Okeke nodded.

'I can swab, but, honestly, don't hold your breath.'

Okeke's phone buzzed in her pocket. 'I'll go and take this outside,' she said, relieved at the opportunity to take a break.

Dr Palmer nodded.

Okeke stepped out of the dungeon-like gloom of studio three into the brightly lit corridor outside. She answered the phone.

'Patricia S. Hemsworth was aged eleven when she was reported missing in 1971,' Minter began. 'She was on a camping holiday nearby with a large group of kids. Police searched the beaches, the marshes, the tower, but presumed after a couple of days that she'd been caught by a riptide and pulled out to sea.'

'And that's it? They just gave up?'

Okeke heard him sigh. 'Seventies policing, right? Plus, she was a kid from a care home. So I suppose there were no distraught parents to plead for the police and public to keep looking for her.'

'Shocker,' she whispered. 'So a token effort, then?'

'It looks like it,' Minter replied.

'You said they searched the tower?' Okeke said.

'I've just been going through the notes. One of the PCs said that they checked the main floor and the floor below...' Minter paused. 'Which was obviously above water back then.'

'That's the floor that you said was caved in?'

'Partially, yeah,' replied Minter. 'There's a caved-in bit in the middle. I don't know for certain how many wooden floors the basement area had. It looks like just one at the moment, and a stone or brick floor at the very bottom.' He paused. 'How's the autopsy going?'

'She's pretty much mummified,' Okeke told him. 'So far cause of death looks like a penetration wound through her upper right chest. We're thinking she could have fallen on a wooden spike.'

'Well, that's plausible,' Minter said. 'There's a *lot* of jagged wood down there.'

'But we're missing eyes,' said Okeke. 'And there's the fact she was stashed in a bag.'

'Hang on a minute... You said *no eyes*?' Minter said.

'As in not decomposed but gone. Possibly eaten by rats or removed.'

She heard Minter whistling air softly. 'Look, gimme a sec, Minter. Signal might go.'

She made her way out of the building and shook a cigarette out of her packet. She lit up, took a long pull, then blew out a cloud of smoke. 'So, we have one child victim from seventy-one. And one teenage or older victim from...'

'Yet to be determined,' completed Minter.

'Uh-huh. And the arm bone, according to the bone expert, is about twenty years old, so we're looking at a murder in the late nineties or early noughties. Patricia's body dates to about fifty years, which matches up with the LEDS misper database,' Okeke said.

'An eleven-year-old girl and a teenager or young woman, potentially decades apart? That's enough of a gap to suggest a different killer,' Minter suggested.

'You twitchy about calling it a serial killer case, Minty?'

'I'm just being cautious, Okeke. Not jumping to conclusions. We've got a spare bone, that's all.' Minter paused. 'Of course, there's always the possibility someone accidently left their arm behind after a visit.'

Okeke let out another cloud. 'Ha.' She wasn't sure what sounded less likely: two killers using the same place to dump their bodies, or a serial killer returning to his dumping ground thirty years later. 'If it's one killer, then he'd have to be pretty old by the time we get to victim two.'

'Maybe sixty? Seventy?' Minter replied. 'That's not *that* old. Anyway, it's too early to be making a call on this. The boss can make decisions on next steps when he gets back, eh?'

'Two bodies in the same remote place? It's very coinciden-tal, don't you think?' she mused.

'Ah, well, it's actually quite convenient?' His Rob Brydenlike Welsh intonation lifted that last statement into an unintended question. 'It's close enough to several camping sites. It's remote and it's flooded. Maybe we've found a murderer's fly-tipping site?'

Okeke winced. He really wouldn't be so flippant if he was here, if he'd just seen what she had. 'Have you managed to get through to Boyd yet?' she asked, changing the subject. 'You should try and –'

She heard him exhale heavily through his nose. 'Is there any remote chance you could stop project-managing me, Okeke?'

She rolled her eyes. 'I'm just reminding you.'

He sighed. 'I left a voicemail just now, and a message with the community ranger for when he arrives on the island. I'm sure he'll be in touch when he can.'

19

Boyd shoved a fistful of coins into the slot in the hope that he'd have long enough to talk without the pips going, if that was even a thing these days. He dialled Minter's number, which was picked up after a couple of rings.

'Ah, is that you, boss?' he asked.

'Yeah,' Boyd said. 'I just got your message from the ranger. What's the latest?'

'We found a whole body at the bottom of the tower,' Minter said. 'So now we have a complete skeleton… plus a spare arm bone, just in case.'

'What?' Boyd said, momentarily confused.

'Two victims. We've got *two* victims now, boss.'

Boyd mouthed *Shit* through the glass at Warren. The DC's brows locked together into a question mark. Boyd held two fingers up for him to see. 'All right, then,' he said. 'Tell me all about the *new* one.' As Minter started to fill him in, he pushed the door of the phone box open with his foot and beckoned Warren to join him.

Warren stood awkwardly at the entrance to the phone box, pointed inside and mouthed, *In there?*

Boyd rolled his eyes and beckoned again.

Warren squeezed in carefully beside his boss and they stood with the phone nestled precariously between their faces.

'Okeke said Ellessey puts the arm bone at roughly twenty years,' Minter continued.

Boyd twisted around to put another coin into the slot, almost pushing Warren back outside in the process. 'That's a big gap for the same killer,' he said. 'Unless we're going to find more victims in between.'

'Okeke and I hypothesised another possibility, boss,' Minter said. 'We could have two killers using the same dumping ground. It's a bloody good place to lose a body, wouldn't you say?'

'Two killers using it but not knowing about each other?' Warren asked sceptically.

'All right, Warren mate,' said Minter. 'Well, you wouldn't, would you? If you knew some other twat was fly-tipping bodies in the exact same place, you'd stay well clear, right?'

Boyd wasn't a huge fan of coincidences. They tended to loom large in badly argued prosecution cases, or soap operas that had jumped the shark.

The payphone finally began beeping annoyingly in his ear and Boyd realised he only had enough change to chase it away for another minute. He shoved Warren back outside and fed another couple of fifty-pence coins into the slot. 'Okay, so how are the divers getting on?'

'They've gone, boss,' Minter replied.

'What?'

'They said it was too dangerous to send someone down. They sent a remote unit down and that's what hooked the body.'

'Bollocks.' Boyd let his forehead bump gently against the phone booth's glass window. 'Right, then – I guess the only other option is to go ahead and have that tower pumped out.

Okay. Tell Sutherland that's what we're doing to do next, will you, Minter, and that the place will need to be made safe?'

Minter took in a deep breath. 'Sutherland won't like that.'

'Well, that's tough,' replied Boyd as he patted his pockets for any more loose change. 'Tell him we need to get that started ASAP. It's going to take a while to empty that basement I'd have thought.'

'Will do.'

'All right, Minter, thanks for the update.'

'Oh, boss?'

'Yeah?'

'Be careful –'

The call disconnected before Minter could finish, but Boyd had a pretty fair idea of what he wanted to say. It was quite possible that 'Poor old Dickie' as Carol had fondly referred to him... was a serial killer.

20

'Are you sure she said two miles?' Boyd huffed.

'Yes, sir,' Warren replied.

'Maybe she meant vertically?' He stopped on the side of the track and leant against a flint wall. 'Fuck me, this is killing my legs.' He sighed. 'Bloody Minter.'

'It could be worse; it could be raining, sir,' Warren chirped.

They were on a dirt track that seemed to be one relentless uphill ramp towards the middle of the island. It was the only 'road' on the island that linked Kinloch to Kilmory, the island's only other settlement, which, according to Carol, had been deserted for more than a hundred years and was only occasionally occupied by researchers studying the wild red deer on the island.

'Ye'll not get lost. There's only the one road. Dickie's place is the only woodland ye'll come across while ye're on it.'

Warren scanned the bare and craggy slopes either side of them, a jagged moonscape of rock and moss that seemed to sternly discourage any foolish notions of wandering off-piste.

'There are trees up ahead,' he said. 'I'd say just another kilometre... or so, sir.'

'Trees?' Carol had distinctly said the word 'woodland'. On this barren-looking landscape of moss, rocks and tussocks of hardy grass it seemed inconceivable that something as exotic and ambitious as a 'wood' might exist.

'Yep, there's definitely more than a few trees, sir,' Warren promised. 'Another ten minutes or so and I reckon we'll be up there.'

Boyd followed Warren's gaze and spotted an irregular hairbrush of treetops on the smooth peak ahead of them.

They reached the island's one and only wood beside the road just before half twelve and found a path that branched off the road to their right and into the trees. From the lowest bare branches dangled decorations made from twigs and twine – the kind of meaningless figurines that horror filmmakers seemed compelled to linger on as grim portents lying ahead.

'I guess this must be Harris's place, then,' said Warren, eyeing them warily. 'Jesus, that's scary.'

Boyd eye-rolled and shook his head. There seemed to be a generation out there brought up on found-footage slashers who lost their minds as soon as they lost sight of tarmac. He led the way down the muddy path into the wooded area and immediately caught a whiff of smoke. 'Good,' he said, 'It smells like Dickie's home.'

The path was little more than a deer run, and thick gorse and spiky bushes spilled into the space, scratching their shoulders and elbows. Finally they emerged into an open area. Ahead of them was a grubby-looking Portakabin surrounded by an encrustation of extensions and lean-tos constructed from a mixture of properly lumbered wood, corrugated iron and branches from the trees around the clearing. There a chicken coop with hens wandering around a wire-mesh enclosure, a pair of goats in a more robustly fenced enclosure, and several raised beds with bamboo frames and withering runner-bean plants clinging to them.

Boyd heard a dog barking from behind him. The noise startled a dozen crows out of the skeletal branches above them. He turned round to see a black Rottweiler standing in the middle of the path they'd just walked along, blocking their way back out.

'Hello there, boy,' Boyd said, trying to sound as unthreatening as possible. He noticed Warren shuffling behind him. 'Easy boy.'

'Lilith!' A thin high-pitched voice echoed out from among the trees. 'Be NICE!!'

'Easy *girl*,' Boyd corrected. The Rottweiler sat down on her haunches and settled for lifting her lips and showing her teeth while she rumbled unpleasantly.

A moment later, Boyd caught sight of a figure moving cautiously through the woodland towards them: a man with long grey hair pulled into a scraggy ponytail and a thick Grizzly Adams beard that was several shades paler. He stepped out of the undergrowth, one arm clutching a bale of twigs and branches, the other hand holding a machete.

The grey sky rumbled above and Boyd felt a few stinging droplets of icy rain bounce off his head.

'Can I help you, gentlemen?' the man inquired.

'Are you Ricky Harris?' asked Boyd.

The man stopped in the path beside his dog. 'Yes,' he replied warily. 'And who wants to know?'

'I'm DCI Boyd from Sussex CID and this is DC Warren.'

Harris's face stiffened. 'What do you want?'

'We've just discovered a body in your Martello tower,' Boyd said conversationally.

Harris shook his head. 'It's not mine any more.'

'It dates back several decades,' said Boyd. 'And it's been your tower, until recently, since 1989 if I'm not mistaken?'

For a moment it looked as though Harris was either going

to drop his kindling and run or command Lilith to rip their throats out. Eventually, though, he let out a long-suffering sigh.

'I bought that fucking thing when I was high on coke,' he informed them. 'Never even bothered to look at it. Biggest mistake ever.'

Boyd glanced up at the darkening clouds. The sleet was getting too heavy to ignore and, now that he'd stopped walking uphill, he was starting to feel the bitter cold. 'Any chance we can talk to you inside, Mr Harris?'

Harris seemed hesitant, but, after the briefest of pauses, flipped on a smile. 'Since you've walked all the way up the hill, I s'pose I can make you a cuppa.'

He and Lilith led them into his cabin. Inside it was cluttered with a random assortment of tools, half-finished projects, boxes of tinned food and items of memorabilia from his heavy metal days.

Boyd couldn't see a kettle, or a stove, or anywhere to sit even.

'Ah, this is just my garden shed,' Harris said, seeing Boyd's confusion. He set the machete down on a workbench. 'We have to go via this to get to my home.'

At the far end of the cabin was a curtain on a pole and Harris pushed it aside to reveal a dark passageway beyond, lined with planks of wood. It looked almost as if they were entering a mineshaft.

'I like to think of this as my version of Bag End,' said Harris. 'Piled dirt and compost over a rubber membrane which lies over a timber frame. Perfect insulation for the long winter months.'

The passageway widened into a surprisingly large round room with a sloped, conical ceiling that peaked with a smoke vent. The floor was made up of more wooden slats, softened with rugs. The sloping walls were lined with velvet drapes. A lava lamp was sitting on a coffee table, and they could hear music playing.

'You've got electricity?' Boyd said, surprised.

Harris pulled a face. 'Of course. I've got a couple of turbines out away from the trees. We're never short of a stiff breeze here on Rum.' He turned on a couple of lamps around the room to brighten it up. 'So what do you think of my hobbit hole, eh?'

He turned on a tap, which protruded from between two planks, and filled a battered and blackened kettle with water. 'I've got a water tank above. It's all plumbed in, as you can see.' He set the kettle down on a wood burner and prodded around in the grate, stoking up the embers and adding another couple of dried logs on top.

'It's very cosy,' remarked Boyd. 'It's a bit like one of those posh festival yurts.'

Harris grinned. 'Right. That's the vibe what I was goin' for – Glasto, 1979. Before it got overrun with bloody yuppies.'

Warren was looking around for somewhere to sit.

Harris pointed out a hammock. 'It's my bed. Don't you worry, son – you'll find no bodies in there.'

Warren carefully sat down on it, legs and arms braced in case it flipped over and dumped him onto the ground. Lilith came over to sit right in front of him.

'So, um... are you totally self-sufficient?' asked Warren, keeping his eyes firmly on the dog.

'You mean foodwise?' Harris asked.

Warren nodded.

'Nah, that's not working out so well. I get eggs and milk from my girls outside, but trying to grow anything here is a fuckin' ball-ache. Not worth the effort. I get everything else from the general store.'

'Do you... barter the eggs and milk?' asked Warren, trying not to fall off the hammock in case that triggered Lilith to lunge for his throat.

Harris snorted with laughter. 'It's not still the Stone Age here, lad. I've got a running tab with Carol and Dennis. When the royalties come in twice a year, they take what I owe out of that.'

The kettle began to hiss on the stove.

Boyd found a wooden seat – a section of tree trunk with an 'L' roughly carved into the side and topped with a cushion. He sat down. 'So,' Boyd said. 'We're here to chat to you, Mr Harris, because –'

'Because the world never forgets a paedo?' finished Harris. He looked Boyd in the eye. 'Let's be honest... that's why you're up here, isn't it?'

21

Minter rubbed his hands together to get some warmth back into his fingers. 'Buggeringly cold today, isn't it?'

Sully shrugged as he peered down into the dark void below. 'The cold never really affects me.'

Minter wondered how that could possibly be true. 'There's no insulation on you at all, Sully.' The man was just bone wrapped in skin and a paper-thin forensic suit. Even the hair on his head was little more than a spectral outline of fine blond follicles. More halo than hair do.

'I generate heat with the sheer horsepower of my intellect,' the forensics coordinator replied. 'That's why I don't have to jog ten miles every day to keep trim; the sheer calorie burn of my brain is enough to keep me lean and mean.' He got to his feet. 'Whereas you, detective sergeant, have to punish yourself with God knows how many hours of pointless self-flagellation every day.'

'Ah, but it's not pointless if I enjoy it, is it?' Minter countered.

Sully sighed and snapped on his torch. 'Well, if the

modern-day equivalent of moving boulders from one side of a quarry to the other and back again keeps you a happy chappie, who am I judge?' He looked back down into the open trapdoor. 'The water's going down quickly. I can almost see the floor below now.'

Minter joined Sully beside the trapdoor and panned his own torch around. The beam picked out items of debris that were breaking the surface now. Mostly dislodged bricks and banks of built-up silt. The top of a post on the far side had turned out to be the handrail for a set of wooden steps that hugged the wall and descended into the water.

Just outside the tower, they could hear Gavin Merchant's pump chugging noisily away. He'd been more than happy to return to the job as soon as he was satisfied that Sussex Police were going to pay up if that grumpy arse Knight refused.

'Mr Knight will be well chuffed if you mugs end up footing his bill,' Merchant had said, chuckling.

'Yeah, well, we're not pouring the concrete as well, if that's what the cheeky bugger's hoping for. It can collapse around him as far as our boss is concerned,' Minter had told him.

Earlier this morning, Minter had watched the young man ease the thick extraction pipe back down through the trapdoor, jostling and jiggling it to make sure it sank down into the brackish water as far as it could go, wondering if it was going to land right where it had the first time and suck up another bone.

'It's a bit like going back in time,' said Sully thoughtfully. 'Don't you think, Minter?'

'Huh?' Minter looked over at him.

'The water level going down? That basement storage area has been slowly filling up, I suppose, for the past hundred years or so. Gradually concealing the past an inch at a time. It's fascinating.'

'Christ, Sully!' Minter laughed. 'Next you'll be telling me you go metal detecting on the weekends.'

Sully looked up at him sharply. 'And what if I do?'

Minter closed his eyes and shook his head. 'Oh, Jesus...'

'Well, it makes more sense than the ridiculous escapade you're up to this weekend. What is it called? The Iron Gland Challenge?'

'*Man*,' Minter corrected, then realised he hadn't needed to.

Minter's phone buzzed in his jacket pocket and he fumbled it out, nearly dropping it into the glistening water below.

'Don't drop it,' offered Sully helpfully.

It was Okeke. 'Hello, Minty,' she said. 'Are you and Sully having fun?'

'What've you got for me?' he asked, ignoring the question.

'Ahh, okay.' She chuckled. 'Well, I have for you a big win, hopefully.'

'Go on.'

'I'm still at Ellessey... I'm heading back to the station now, but I wanted to catch you because they found some pretty useful things in the grot at the bottom of that BOAC bag.'

'Such as?' Minter asked.

'A time capsule of sorts...' She paused for effect. She sounded as pleased as punch with herself and was obviously waiting for him to nudge her along.

'Explain...' Minter finally relented.

'There was a Tupperware lunch box. Sealed. Completely dry inside. With a fossilised apple core, a Dairylea triangle wrapper. And a Batman *Pez dispenser*.' Okeke chuckled again. 'Yep, me too. I had to look that one up. Thing is, it was all perfectly sealed and perfectly dry inside. Dr Palmer is pretty sure we'll get some viable DNA off what's in there.'

Minter had to rewind that. 'A Pez dispenser?' He actually remembered those. 'So this is what... a *child's* bag? A kid? You're saying a kid did this to another kid?'

'Possibly.'

'Jesus.'

'But that doesn't explain the other humerus bone. Don't forget we have a second victim. Did this kid grow up and kill someone else?' Okeke sighed. 'Maybe I'm getting ahead of myself. Anyway, Dr Palmer's going to fast-track the DNA work. We should get a result tomorrow. If so, we might get a hit on the NDNAD. So, even though it's the weekend, I'm booking in a shift for tomorrow.'

'Dammit. You go ahead. I can't,' Minter said.

'What?' Okeke exclaimed. 'You *have to*...'

'It's my Ironman Challenge,' he reminded her.

'Fuck that, Minter! We could have an actual name by the end of tomorrow!'

'No, Okeke, I can't. I've been training months for this.'

'Do it another time!'

Minter suppressed a spark of irritation. 'Excuse me? You're not the boss of me, Okeke. Don't make me remind you I'm the DI.'

'Fine,' she replied huffily. 'I'll go in alone, then.'

Minter was actually torn. Surprisingly so. A gem of evidence like this lunch box could, if she struck lucky, lead her right to the front door of some child murderer who must have long thought he'd got away with it. Solving a case like that and having your name stamped on top of it was a bloody career gift.

'In fact, Okeke,' he said, 'this case is decades old. It can wait till Monday. We'll do it –'

'I'm coming in tomorrow... *boss*. Just saying.' She hung up on him before he could say anything more.

'Bloody typical, that is,' he muttered to himself. 'Bloody typical.'

22

'Christ above, it was one slip-up, one error of judgement,' said Harris. 'And I'm tellin' you everyone was at it back then, shagging the groupies. It was part of the whole rock-'n'-roll thing. Sex, drugs, booze, right?'

'But the fact remains that she was a minor,' said Boyd.

'She was one of a bunch of chicks who crashed our after-gig party and went back to the tour bus with us. Shit like that happened every single night.' Harris leant forward in his creaking rocking chair. 'Every single fuckin' night. So no, man, I did not check the date of birth of every eager fan who rushed to get on the party bus with the band.' He settled back again, a wiry, old, desiccated figure, sitting in his rocking chair, glinting eyes sunken into their sockets. 'But there it is... The shit always sticks. Ricky Harris the paedo. The sex offender.'

'And that's why the band kicked you out?' asked Warren.

'Yeah. Because, despite that Bad Boys of Rock image we had, they were scared that some other groupie – or groupie's mum – would point the finger at them. They wanted to put as much distance between themselves and me as they possibly could. Those wankers just threw me under a bus, man.' Harris chuckled to himself. 'Of course, the satisfying bit is when they came to record their next album, they couldn't come up with anything even half decent. Those idiots chucked out the one member of the band who could actually write a decent fucking song.'

'You were the main creative driving force, then?' asked Boyd.

'Yeah. All the big ideas. The lyrics, the album covers, the videos...'

'Those videos that feature young girls being abducted and tortured?'

Both men turned to look at Warren. Boyd raised his eyebrows.

'Your pop videos were basically abuse porn,' Warren added.

Harris rolled his eyes. 'It's what sold records back then, sunshine. I know things are all woke and wonderful now, but back then...'

'The same laws on sex with a minor existed back then,' countered Warren. Lilith rumbled menacingly at Warren as he leant forward in the creaking hammock. He managed not to flinch and kept his eye contact with the old man. 'That hasn't changed, Harris.'

Boyd couldn't help the slightest smile. *Good lad.*

Harris shook his head. 'Jesus, boy. Things weren't all politically correct in those days, okay? It wasn't all wall-to-wall do-gooders whining about everything! Heavy metal was the Wild West of showbiz for God's sake! Anything went! Throwing TVs out of hotel windows, trashing nightclubs, snorting coke off a chick's tits, drinking Jack Daniels in pints. Fuck... it's what the record company *wanted us to do*. What the music press wanted us to do – act "bad"!'

'But not sexually assault a child,' said Warren.

'I didn't "assault" her. And she wasn't a fucking child!'

'She was under sixteen,' snapped Warren. 'That's the definition. And it's there for a reason, Harris.'

Boyd nodded. Christ. How many times had he heard grown men claim they couldn't tell or that that the girl had said she was older.

'I don't recall her fighting me off,' said Harris. 'Bloody hell... Those girls were queuing up to get in!'

'A minor is legally unable to give consent,' said Warren. 'Which, in fact, makes it rape.'

'Oh, piss off, man,' Harris snorted. 'They knew exactly what they were doing. Christ... what the fuck do you know about the eighties? You weren't even born then, sunshine!'

'The fact is, Harris,' said Boyd, stepping back in, 'there's a law and you broke it, knowingly or otherwise. And that comes with a consequence.'

Harris nodded slowly. Ruefully. 'Oh, and don't I bloody well know that.'

'In interviews with the press –' Warren glanced down at his notebook – 'the band said they kicked you out because you "took things too far". What did they mean by that?'

'Like I said... they were trying to distance themselves. Scared shitless that they'd be accused of the same thing. The next to have their lives ruined.'

'Nick Priest, the singer, said that –'

'Fuck that prick.'

'– said that you were into "creepy occult, ritualistic shit". What exactly did he mean by that?'

Harris sighed. 'That was just the band image. It was no different to the nonsense Black Sabbath and the others were peddling at the time. It sells, okay? Millions of teenage boys – mostly American – rebelling against their Bible-bashing parents by buying a piece of vinyl with a picture of the devil on the front. Nothing more than that.'

'Did you believe in any of that occult stuff at the time?' asked Boyd.

Harris turned to look at him, then cracked a grin. 'You shitting me?'

Boyd waited.

'No, of course I fuckin' didn't! It was just... what was *cool* at the time, man.' He chuckled. 'Flowers in the sixties, drugs in the seventies, devil in the eighties... right?'

'Occult imagery,' Boyd added. 'Which included images of child abuse, execution...'

'For fuck's sake!' Harris snorted. 'Here we go again. The world's full of that shit. Paintings, movies, books, videos –'

'But not *celebrating* it,' cut in Warren.

'We weren't fuckin' *celebratin'* it...'

Warren checked his pad again. '*Burn the witches. Roast them black. Or drown the bitches, like pups in a sack.* The lyrics from one of your songs?'

Harris sighed. 'Yeah, from "Kill Your Darlings". For fuck's sake. It's not literal. It's, like, an allegory, man. A fucking metaphor.'

'For what?'

He shook his head. 'All the things that pissed me off. Record company execs, shitty managers, NME journalists, bootleggers, mainstream radio DJs...'

'All of them summed up as a little girl to be ritually slaughtered?' Warren said.

'That album was called *Slaughter Your Innocents*. It was all part of the album's riff, man. And it was meant to be fucking ironic, because none of those music biz types were innocents.'

Boyd stepped in again. 'So, 1997, you're turfed out of the band. What did you do after that?'

'My wilderness year,' Harris responded sullenly. 'It wasn't a great time to be honest. I did a lot of drugs, booze... felt pretty sorry for myself. It cheered me up no end that the band fell apart nine months later. I mean, metal was pretty much dead then anyway.'

'Did you visit your Martello tower at all?' Boyd asked.

'No. Like I said, I've never even seen the bloody thing.' He shrugged. 'It seemed a kinda cool place to have a studio when I bought it. Should have figured I'd never be able to do anything to it because of a bunch of history-mad Nimbys.'

'You'd known about that tower since your childhood,' said Warren. 'Is that correct? You grew up locally?'

Harris looked at him. 'Sure. I was born and raised in Romney. Every kid around there knew about Devil's Tower.'

'Why was it called that?' asked Boyd.

'Ahh.' The old man's face creased with an impish smile. 'Because of the Aleister Crowley story. You've heard of *him*, right?'

Warren shook his head.

Boyd had. 'He was a famous occultist from the turn of the century, wasn't he?'

'Bit later,' said Harris. 'Between the war years, actually. He was a crazy motherfucker. Into all kinds of weird Wicca and satanic crap. The story associated with the tower was that in the forties, just after the war ended, he and some acolytes performed a ceremony in the basement... Summoned the devil, as you do, and the devil tore them all to little pieces, except for Crowley; it then stormed out of the tower and across the marshes, leaving a trail of hoof prints behind him... which, if you look closely, can still be found today.' Harris laughed. 'It's a load of complete crap, obviously, but kind of a cool backstory, right?'

Under other circumstances, Boyd mused, it probably would be.

'And you say you've found a body down there, eh?' Harris grinned. 'So maybe that satanic voodoo shit wasn't a load of crap after all?'

23

Sully couldn't help himself. Sitting down on the recently laid-out sheets of plywood – for safety – here on the upper basement floor, he waited for the water to recede. It was like waiting for Christmas. Frustrating. Worse than that, he mused, it was like waiting for the 'Okay then' from his mother to unwrap his presents beneath the tree, which eventually came *after* lunch, pudding and the sherry when every other kid in the world had already unwrapped theirs.

The water was now a foot or so below the upper basement floor. He got up and carefully went over to the ragged hole in the middle of the wooden deck through which the RCU had descended, and now the pump hose, which disappeared into the abyss. It looked as if it had collapsed a long time ago.

His torch picked out a monochrome environment of dark-green algal slime on the surrounding wall. It glistened on every surface and where it wasn't present the surface glistened black with silt.

'*Holding back the years,*' he sung out loud, tunelessly, to himself. He hummed the rest of the melody, not knowing the words, or even the band. That's what it was like, though, wasn't it? Time rewinding, revealing the hazy past? Already, he'd noted graffiti etched into the brick walls. Not the usual *Joe Sucks Ballz* graffiti, but carvings left by bored soldiers who'd once been stationed in the tower, waiting for invasions that had never quite happened.

Pvt Peter Buffin, 1799: Stationed in this wretched place, plucked from Hookey's Nose.

Sgt J. P. Weston: 'Yanks, Go Home!

Sully loved these little indelible pieces of carved historical memories. History viewed from the muddy boots, rather than history viewed from the lofty height of a distant historian's pen.

In the gunk of silt and algae, there were forensic clues of more recent visitors, their place in the timeline evidenced by the rubbish they'd left behind: green glass Coke bottles from the sixties, Bazooka Joe gum wrappers from the fifties, rusty Chesterfield tobacco tins from the forties.

The racket made by the pump and generator was distant down here, almost absent. The only sounds were the echoing of lapping water, the gurgling of the pipe and his own careful footsteps on the wet, creaking boards. There was not even the squeak of a rat.

Which was a blessed relief. Rats made Sully run headlong into other people.

He wandered back over to the wooden post and the bannister that slanted downwards into the slowly descending water. He could see four steps now. Ten minutes ago there had been just three.

Time rolling backwards.

The fifth step was revealed every now and then as the water sloshed around. Not for the first time, Sully carefully descended the first three steps, placing his feet as close to the brick wall as he could so as not to challenge the sodden wood too much.

The fifth step was clearly wider than the others, and he suspected it was a support platform for the staircase, which wound its way down round the inner wall of the tower. Presumably there'd be a post beneath to hold it up, or, more likely, a thick support beam sticking out from the central brickwork. He watched as step five gradually revealed more and more of itself, a slick uneven carpet of algae, and gaps between the slats.

Despite the fact that scaffolding was due to be going in later today to shore up the wooden steps – safety first, of course – he stepped down onto the fourth stair and heard it creak unhappily beneath him.

He squatted and aimed his torch at the next few steps.

Yes, number five was definitely supported. He felt a little bolder and squatted down to peer between the wooden slats of the steps as the water's height slowly receded. He aimed his torch directly down into the gap, and the black water flickered light back at him. The gap between the next two planks showed no flickering reflection. There was no water there.

'Ah, a wall-support beam, then,' he muttered smugly. 'Thought so.'

He aimed his torch along the gap, towards the wall where the thick support beam emerged from the old brickwork.

It wasn't a snug fit. There was a fair bit of space either side of the beam. The bricklayers had left deep cubbyholes for the carpenters to later place their beams, but clearly neither group had discussed with the other how much space would be needed.

Sully dared to step down onto the as-yet-unseen sixth step and was relieved to feel it was nice and firm there. He squatted down to peer into the cubbyhole.

The light from his torch picked out something wedged firmly beside the old oak beam. Something that glistened blackly. Something that glistened like a bin liner.

He felt his heart give a little skip. Not out of fear – inappropriate as he knew it would be to admit in company; it was the thrill of discovery. The same little adrenaline ping he got when his metal detector passed over a submerged hunk of metal.

24

'You hung on to that tower for over thirty years,' said Warren. 'Why?'

'I didn't exactly hang on to it, man,' Harris pointed out. 'I couldn't fucking sell the bloody thing. It's also a scheduled monument, which meant I couldn't do a thing to it either.'

Boyd recalled Knight had said he'd made several 'decent' offers over the years. Either Harris was lying or he had unrealistic expectations for what the tower was worth.

'And by the way,' Harris continued, 'if that wasn't bad enough, being the owner meant I was liable for any of the idiot kids coming to harm if they broke a leg or something.'

'Kids?'

Harris nodded. 'Bloody teenagers. There was an illegal party, or what do they call them – raves? – held in my tower a while back. For fuck's sake. I was lucky nobody fell off the roof, or broke an arm or a leg, man. I'd have been sued into bankruptcy. Not only was the tower a fucking waste of my money... it was a liability. I ended up havin' to hire somebody to fucking watch the place!'

'Who did you hire?' asked Warren, glancing at Boyd.

'Some security company...' Harris shook his head. 'Can't remember the name. I cancelled that contract in 2009, 2010, I think.'

'Why?'

'Money,' he replied with a shrug. 'As in, I was running out of the stuff. Not sure if you two are up to speed on music royalties, but since that greedy green bastard Spotify turned up on the scene... you either gig for a living, or you give up.' He picked up his mug.

While Harris slurped the last of his tea, Boyd looked around his hobbit hole. There were a few token reminders of Harris's band years: an electric bass guitar with the body shaped like a V... *naturally*. Some album covers were lined up on a shelf, displaying images designed to provoke and enrage conservative Christian parents: upside-down crosses, penta-grams, obscure pagan and Wicca glyphs.

'But then you finally managed to sell the tower last month?' said Boyd. 'Talk me through that.'

Harris finished his tea and set his mug down on the wooden floor with a heavy clunk. 'Yeah, there's another bloody story.'

Boyd checked his watch. The ferry did a return run to Mallaig in the afternoon, stopping at Rum at about half five. 'We have time,' said Boyd.

'Well, when I first bought the tower in eighty-nine, no one was bloody interested in it. And then, when I planned to develop it, suddenly everyone was up in arms about it. There was all this crap about it being turned into a millionaire's night club. Fucking stupid...'

Warren leant forward. 'What were your –' Lilith growled and Warren slowly settled back again. 'What were your plans for it?' he asked, eyeing the dog warily.

'A recording studio. That's all. No fucking night club or drugs den or satanic bloody temple! Anyway, the locals got all shitty about it, man; they put a petition together and lodged a complaint against my plans while they campaigned to have that pile of rubble turned into some protected national monument. They even gave themselves a bloody name!'

'UK Martello Tower Protection Society?' said Warren.

'That's them!' replied Harris. 'Fucking ridiculous. Bunch of stupid...' Harris' voice trailed off. 'I've had to deal with those silly bastards for the last twenty years. They wouldn't let me develop it so I offered to sell it to them over and over but they didn't want to buy it either.'

'Who did you deal with? Can you remember any names?'

'Course I can. Two arseholes who go by the names of Arnold and Knight. They knew they had me over a barrel –'

'Stephen Knight?' said Boyd.

'Yeah. That tight shithead finally took it off my hands. Not exactly the asking price but a decent amount, I suppose, given there's nobody else out there dumb enough to buy it.'

'So you're saying you were *trying* to get rid of it? Not hold on to it? Because we heard different,' said Boyd.

'Well, whoever told you that was talking bollocks. I've been trying to offload that thing ever since I got fucked over. I've needed that money.' He nodded at his surroundings. 'I live cheaply here. A couple of hundred every month for teabags, tobacco, some food, but that's still money, right? I'm not living on fresh air, man.'

'But you and Knight finally struck a deal last month?' said Boyd.

'Yeah.'

'What changed?'

'Dunno, guess the time was right.'

'And what does that mean?' Boyd asked.

'Shit just lined up.' Harris grinned. 'The Dark Gods approved the deal, man.'

Warren sat forward. 'The Dark Gods?'

'Heh, heh.' Harris chuckled. 'Nah, got a call and decided the price was right.'

'So you *do* have a phone?' said Warren, surprised.

Harris reached across to a dusty crate that stood for as a coffee table and picked up a Nokia that looked about twenty years old. 'I do. But it only works on the mainland.'

'So,' Warren said, looking at him, 'you're not on this island all the time?'

'I go across to the big smoke every now and then, sure,' Harris said, shrugging. 'When I need something Carol and Dennis don't stock in their shop.' He glanced at Boyd. 'And, no, I don't mean drugs or booze. I've been clean for the last ten years, man. Anyway... Knight gave me a figure I could be happy with, and the deal was done.' Harris laughed. 'To be honest, I was well pleased.'

'How much did Knight offer you?' asked Warren.

Harris tapped the side of his nose. 'Enough to tide me over for a lo-o-ng while, given that I'm not exactly living in Vegas.'

'But more than previous offers?' tried Boyd. He watched the old man's bony hands fidgeting restlessly.

Harris nodded. 'I suppose he and his conservation buddies had more money than usual to fart around with.'

'And did he mention their plans?' asked Boyd.

'He said the thing was sinking into the marsh, that he needed to pump a concrete foundation into it before the base collapsed,' Harris said. 'But you say you found a body down there, eh?'

'Yeah,' Boyd confirmed. 'The foundation work's on hold. Obviously. Until we've concluded the investigation.'

'Good.' Harris chuckled. 'I hope the whole fucking thing collapses.' He slowly reached down behind a box of tin cans and pulled out a packet of tobacco and some Rizzlers. 'Best thing for that bloody ruin. To just fucking disappear.'

'What else do you think we'll find down there?' asked Boyd.

'Who knows? Dozens of sacrificed children? The countless bones of headless fair maidens?' Harris chuckled sardonically. 'Maybe even the dismembered remains of Crowley's unlucky acolytes, eh?' He licked the Rizzler and finished rolling his cigarette, sparked a lighter and pulled on it until the end glowed brightly and crackled softly. 'Do let me know what you find... I'd be very interested.'

'Oh, we will be back in touch, Mr Harris,' said Boyd. 'Now that we know where to find you.'

25

It was already getting dark as they made their way back down the island's only road to Kinloch. Boyd was finding the downhill journey a much easier one.

'So what was your take on that, Warren?' Boyd noticed that he kept looking back uphill towards the silhouette of the receding wood. 'Relax, he's not going to come charging after us with a chainsaw.'

'I know,' Warren replied.

Boyd puffed out a cloud into the freezing cold air. 'Well?'

'I don't know. He's what I was expecting. Creepy as hell. What about you, sir? What do you think?'

'I don't know if he's our man,' Boyd mused.

'Why do you say that?' asked Warren.

'Well, I can't believe he'd have sold the tower if he was responsible for and knew about a couple of bodies sitting down at the bottom, can you?'

'Maybe he thinks Knight's just pumping down concrete?' said Warren. 'Maybe Knight didn't mention anything about pumping it dry first? So he thinks it would be safe enough to let it go?'

'A calculated risk?'

Warren nodded. 'You heard him... He said he needed the money.'

'Well, that's a big risk to take if he was aware of what was in the tower, given that his music and videos seemed to be about killing darlings and innocents. If a body turned up, he must have realised he'd be the first person we'd come and talk to.'

'Maybe that's his angle, sir? ... *If I dunnit, why would I frame myself, ma-a-an?*'

Boyd chuckled at Warren's impersonation. 'That's possible, I suppose. It's a tactic that's been used plenty of times before.'

If Harris had anything to do with the body in the bag, then that was a first-class performance, Boyd thought. He'd managed to put on a convincing show of not actually giving that much of a crap.

'Jeez...' hissed Warren.

'What?'

'Harris would have been, what, thirteen? A kid... killing another kid?' Warren looked at him.

Boyd shrugged. 'It happens, Warren. Those two boys that killed Jamie Bulger weren't any older.' He puffed another plume of air out into the gathering darkness. He remembered how sick the whole nation had felt over that one.

Boyd tugged his beanie down. It was getting ridiculously cold now. 'Well, Harris is definitely a person of interest until we know more.'

'What's the next step, sir?' Warren asked.

'Hopefully by now Sutherland's given permission for the pumping to restart and the water's coming up and out as we speak. We've also got that other arm bone to explain. I'm presuming we're going to find at least one other body at the bottom of this Devil's Tower.'

'Shit,' whispered Warren, glancing over his shoulder once more. 'Devil's Tower *is* a good name for it.'

Boyd huffed out another cloud as he chuckled. 'All that Aleister Crowley crap, eh?'

'Is that worth looking at?' asked Warren. 'I mean, not summoning the actual devil and everything, but if some ritualistic things were done down there in the... past?'

'I'm pretty sure vinyl BOAC sports bags weren't a thing back in Aleister Crowley's time.'

'Oh, right.'

'Muppet,' said Boyd with a smile. 'You did a good job today, by the way.' Honestly, he'd been impressed with the lad.

'Really?' Warren asked.

'Yeah. You asked some good questions and didn't let him off the hook despite Lilith.'

Boyd reckoned that Harris had the Rottweiler 'guard' Warren because he could see it was throwing Warren off balance. Or maybe Harris had just thought that was funny.

They stopped at the post office to collect their overnight bags. While they were there, Boyd asked Carol how often Harris came down to the shop for things, and how often he took the ferry to the mainland.

'Dickie's in every few days for something or other. And he takes the ferry to Mallaig, I think, every couple of months or so for a curry,' she replied. 'He does love a hot madras.'

Boyd was tempted to ask her if she knew who he was: namely, an ex-rocker and sex-offender. But he decided to let it go. She probably did. The internet meant there were very few secrets these days, even in remote places like this.

He and Warren made it around the bay to the closed-up visitor centre and the unmanned ferry stop with an hour to spare. As soon as he was no longer walking, Boyd quickly began to feel the cold. He pulled out a spare jumper from his overnight bag and layered up. Warren pulled a cagoule out and huddled inside it. There was a wooden hut like a bus-stop shelter and they sheltered inside as they waited for the boat.

While they waited, Boyd had time to reflect on Harris, his crime and its consequence. To be on the sex offenders register was to share company with a broad spectrum of convicted men who ranged from the predatory and dangerous to fossilised old rockers like Harris.

Harris – despite his unconventional past, the *appalling* music (in Boyd's opinion), exploitative lyrics and sickening imagery – had paid a hefty tariff for what *might* have been a crime committed unknowingly. However, borderline legal age or not, an adult having sex with a teenager was not, in Boyd's mind, a symmetrical exchange. It was weighted heavily against the younger person with false promises and, in many cases, life-damaging consequences in the aftermath.

If *fame* was the facilitator for that kind of behaviour, then *shame* would be the minimum consequence.

The ferry turned up, bang on time. Given that it was battling a headwind coming into the sheltered bay and riding a lumpy sea, that was no mean achievement. Warren was better on the return leg of the journey to Mallaig, not having just had a full breakfast this time and, as they pulled into the harbour at seven in the evening, he congratulated the grey-faced lad for not feeding the trailing gulls again.

26

On the way back to the airport at Inverness to catch whatever flight was available back down south, Boyd's phone finally decided to wake up to the fact that there'd been several missed calls from Minter and Okeke.

Boyd dialled Minter's number and after a dozen rings it clicked over to voicemail. He tried Okeke and she answered almost immediately. 'Guv? Are you back from the savage outer islands?'

'I'm on the way to the airport. You and Minter both called me. What's new?'

'We've got *another* complete body,' she said.

'Have you found the rest of the body that belongs to the humerus bone?' Boyd asked.

He could hear raised voices and music in the background. Okeke muttered something to someone and a moment later the noise was gone, replaced with a steady rustling sound of a crosswind and the ever-present faint cry of gulls. 'Sorry, guv, post-work pint.'

'So come on, then,' Boyd said, thinking he could do with a post-work pint about now. 'Give me the gist.'

He heard her spark up and take a pull on her cigarette. 'Not the rest of the body. I mean, they've found a second complete body. Adult female, early twenties, according to Dr Palmer.' She puffed out. 'So that's two bodies and a bone. Let me do the maths for you... That'll be *three* victims now, guv.'

Boyd let out a low whistle and held three fingers up to Warren. 'Have you resumed pumping yet?'

'Yeah. And this one was revealed about an hour after the water started pumping out. She was stashed in a gap in the basement wall. In a bin liner.'

'Christ. Maybe you and Minter were bang on.'

'About it being a dumping ground?' she said.

'Yeah.'

'It'd make sense, guv.' She paused. 'How was Ricky Harris?'

'He's a slightly-more-with-it Ozzy Osbourne,' Boyd told her.

Warren leant in towards Boyd's phone. 'Barely!' he yelled.

Okeke snorted. 'You think he's our man?' she asked.

Boyd explained the summation of his thinking. 'Harris is either completely innocent or guilty of a single incident. I'm really struggling to see him as a serial killer, though.'

'Right. So... it could be him for Hemsworth, and then somebody else for the arm and this new one, guv?'

'That's feeling more likely... Have Ellessey done an autopsy yet?'

'No, that's on Monday morning, guv. Dr Palmer's away over the weekend.'

'Isn't there someone else who could do it?' Boyd asked.

'The whole practice is closed, guv. They're having a Christmas do somewhere.'

'What. Really! For God's sake. What is it with...?' He took a breath and let it out slowly. 'Okay. So what's happening with the tower? Is the pumping going to continue over the weekend or is Merchant off for a few beers too?'

Okeke laughed. 'No, he's happy to finish it. The sooner it's done, the sooner he can move on to another job.'

'So who's supervising over the weekend, then? Minter?' Boyd asked.

'Uh, no. He's doing that Ironman Challenge of his.'

Boyd shook his head. Yes, of course he was... 'Well, we need someone there in case something turns up. Is the contractor pumping right now?'

'No. He'll be back again tomorrow at eight in the morning,' Okeke said.

'Well, we'll need to rota someone to get over there before he starts –'

'I'm on it, guv. I'm taking an extra shift tomorrow,' said Okeke. 'I'll be on site. I imagine Sully will be keeping me company most of the time as well. He's as happy as a pig in a mud down there in the basement. Honestly, you should see him.'

'Good. Good job, Okeke.'

'When are you back, guv?'

Boyd sighed. 'I'm going to see whether we can grab a flight back down from Inverness tonight. If not, it had better bloody well be first thing tomorrow.'

'Okay,' she replied. 'Shall we touch base then?'

Boyd grunted an affirmative and hung up.

Warren looked up from his phone. 'Did I get that right, sir? There's another body?'

'Yeah.' Boyd tucked his phone back into his coat. 'Against the balance of probability,' he said, 'it looks as if we might have more than one killer.'

27

They managed to catch the last scheduled flight of the day heading back down to Gatwick. It was, to Boyd's immense relief, a much smoother return flight.

Boyd drove the pool car to Hastings, while Warren slept in the passenger seat throughout the entire journey. They arrived at his house at just gone one in the morning. Boyd parked up and shook his shoulder.

'We're home, sleepyhead,' he said, nudging him again for good measure.

Warren blinked at him, confused for a few moments. Boyd nodded at the steamed-up car window on Warren's side and the porchlight winking on outside. He caught sight of Warren's mother peering out from the open front door. 'C'mon, mate – Mum's waiting,' he said, chuckling.

He wound his window down. 'I've got your son here, Mrs Warren!' His breath formed a plume in the cold, billowing back into the warm fug of the car.

'Oh!' She gave him a quick wave as she hurried across the drive in her slippers and dressing gown. 'Thank you for looking after him, Mr Boyd,' she said, as she opened the passenger-side door. 'Come along, Snore-a-saurus,' she said as she cajoled Warren to gather up his things and climb out of the car.

'Oh, hey, Mum,' he said drowsily. 'What're you doing up so late?'

'Will you have a cup of tea, Mr Boyd?' Mrs Warren asked.

'No, thanks,' Boyd said. 'I'm going to dump him and run, if that's okay? But thanks for the offer.'

Mrs Warren looked a little relieved. 'Was my Matty well behaved on your field trip?'

Boyd fought the urge to smile. She was perfectly serious.

'Yes. He was very well behaved,' he replied solemnly.

'Night, sir,' said Warren, still blinking sleep out of his eyes as he got out of the car.

Boyd watched him shuffling into the house like a kid who'd spent the longest day ever at Disneyland, with his mother firing question after question at him as they stepped inside. The only thing missing, Boyd thought, was a Mickey Mouse cap on his tufty head and a goodie bag clasped under one arm.

Boyd drove home and parked the pool car on Ashburnham Road right outside his house. It looked dark and empty.

He dragged his overnight bag off the back seat, locked up and fumbled with the front-door keys by the light of his phone as he walked up the path to his door.

No barking? Then he remembered Ozzie was with Charlotte. He unlocked the front door, stepped into the hallway and flicked on the hall light. He hung his coat on the hook and left his bag by the door.

I'll deal with that tomorrow. He was too bloody tired to even put it out of the way. He climbed the stairs, with the intention of having a pee before hitting the sack – then he was damned well signing out for twelve hours.

His thoughts were interrupted by the sound of a thump on the floor upstairs.

He paused mid-step and waited, perfectly still in the dark for a few seconds.

There was another soft bump, then the sound of a muffled voice.

Emma's voice.

The tone was... his best description of it was *whiny*. The same tone she'd used as a kid when she didn't want to do something. He slowly took another creaking step up the stairs, holding his breath to listen more closely.

Maybe she was dreaming. Having a nightmare?

But then he heard another voice, deep and male, sternly chastising his daughter.

Boyd hurried up the remaining steps, crossed the hall and kicked open his daughter's bedroom door.

Her bedside light was on. She was hunched up on the floor, wearing only a T-shirt and a pair of pants. Standing over her, completely naked, was a man, his hands wound into her hair tightly and roughly jerking her around by it.

The man spun round as the door crashed open and Boyd saw it was that coifed jerk Patrick who Emma worked with. His eyes bulged with horror as Boyd grabbed hold of him by his quiff and yanked him backwards and off balance.

'GET THE FUCK OUT OF MY HOUSE!!' He dragged the flailing Patrick out of Emma's room to the top of the stairs. 'OUT NOW!!!'

He swung a kick at Patrick's bare arse as he scrambled down the stairs, but his toe merely grazed a buttock. Patrick was too quick on his feet.

Boyd switched on the hall light so the bastard could find the front door more easily, then went back into Emma's room, pulling her into a hug 'Emma! Are you okay?!'

'Dad!' she wailed explosively. 'Dad, what the fuck!?! We're just messing around. DAD!'

He gathered up Patrick's discarded clothes on the floor and threw them down the stairs. 'Get dressed and fuck off!'

He returned to Emma and helped her up off the floor. 'Jesus, Emma! For Christ's sake...!'

She shoved him away and then curled up into a foetal ball on her bed, sobbing.

'Emma, what the hell –?'

'OUT! OUT! OUT!!!' she screamed at him.

'Did he hurt you? Did he –'

She leant over, picked up a shoe and threw it at him. 'GET OUT!!!!!'

Boyd backed up, out into the hallway and closed the door, utterly confused and unsure as to what his next move should be. He could hear Patrick staggering around in the hallway, grunting as he struggled to get himself dressed.

Boyd took several steps down the stairs, not entirely sure what he was going to do when he got to the bottom, but the sound of his heavy steps made Patrick change his plans. Boyd heard him fumble with the front-door latch and by the time he'd reached the bottom step the door was wide open and he could hear the receding patter of Patrick's bare feet slapping down the pathway and into the night.

Boyd picked up a balled sock and a trainer and tossed them out into the darkness after him, then slammed the front door shut.

Shit. He realised he was trembling from head to toe. Not with rage... but... with the sudden flood of adrenaline in his blood stream. And, yes, maybe a bit of fear. Fear that he'd got it badly, *badly* wrong. And fear that maybe he hadn't... that another ten minutes and she might have been roughly forced into doing something that she really hadn't wanted to do. Something that would haunt her, damage her.

He hurried back up the stairs again, lingered outside her door and listened.

She was still sobbing.

He rapped his knuckles against her door softly. 'Emma? Emma? Can I come in?'

'No!' her muffled voice came back. 'Go away!'

'Please!' he replied. 'Let me just...'

'Go away!' she cried.

He gently cracked the door open and began to step in. 'Honey, Ems... I...'

'DAD! FUCK OFF!!!!' she screamed.

He backed out of the room. He heard her feet hit the floor, take two steps and the door thudded shut, almost trapping his fingers. Her lock *snicked*.

'Emma? Was he assaulting you? Was he –'

'Dad,' she whimpered through the door. 'Just go to bed!'

'I can't just –'

'It wasn't rape!' she replied. 'Okay? If that's what you were about to... Just... just leave me alone...! You've ruined my life enough for one night!'

He lingered by the door for a moment, horribly unsure as to what to do.

'Go!' he heard her call out. 'I know you're still hovering there.' He was relieved to hear that her voice had some of that normal Emma Attitude to it now. 'Dad, I said GO!'

He went.

28

He didn't get a wink of sleep that night. His mind kept turning over and over what had just happened, with Julia whispering cautionary caveats in his ear. His first thought, in the middle of the night, had been that he'd just walked in on a home invasion and sexual assault. That was why he'd behaved the way he had.

Initially.

But then, of course, as he grabbed the man by that ridiculous bloody quiff, he'd realised it was her work colleague Patrick. Not that that for one second ruled out home invasion. Or rape.

Just messing around, Emma had called out. *Just messing around!*

But he'd already been committed to throwing the arsehole out of his house.

Maybe Patrick had told her it was just a bit of fun... but Boyd had spotted the red welts on her shoulders, Patrick's fist in her hair, and he'd heard her pleading voice through the door. Maybe it was a game *he* wanted to play, but Emma had not sounded particularly keen.

Boyd lay awake in bed, listening in the stillness of night for any sounds coming across the hallway from her bedroom – the muted sound of sobbing, the soft murmur of a conversation over the phone. There was nothing.

Daylight slowly leached into the sky along with the sound of gulls and the electric whine of an early-morning delivery cart. That sound always took him back to his childhood: it was reassuring, the whine of a milk cart and the clink of bottles.

Morning fully formed and he waited for Emma to make the first move and get up for breakfast. But she was obviously doing the same... waiting for him to get his breakfast, then go to work. She was clearly avoiding him.

She's still pissed with me.

He got up, got dressed and went downstairs – noisily, so that she would hear that he was up – and put the kettle on. Maybe, he thought hopefully, his clinking and clanking around the small kitchen would stir her into coming down.

He wanted this upcoming conversation over and done with as soon as possible.

He'd rehearsed in his head some opening lines about how there was always room for a little 'messing about' in a relationship... which only confirmed that the whole thing was going to be mortifying for both of them.

What he had seen (and he wished to God he could scrub that image from his mind) had looked to him more like *control* than messing around. If Patrick got his rocks off that way, then he was probably going to wind up being a complete bastard of a boyfriend. Boyd was, he reassured himself, doing Ems a favour. Maybe she'd think twice about dumping Daniel when she came to her senses.

She's not going to see it that way this morning. Julia's voice. God he missed her. She would have known exactly what to say to get through to Emma. She would have known exactly how to smooth things over.

It was ten o'clock before he finally decided to go and get Ozzie. Emma was quite clearly planning to wait in her room until he'd left the house. He texted Charlotte to say that he was on his way over. He'd have to drop the pool car back at the station and pick up his Captur before collecting Ozzie, otherwise the vehicle manager was liable to moan about dog fur all over the back seat.

He arrived at Charlotte's front door at five to eleven and rang the doorbell.

29

Okeke congratulated herself on remembering to bring her wellies this morning. She crossed the upper basement floor towards the wooden stairs that hugged the brick wall and descended into the dark depths of the tower.

Sully was down below on the steps to the lower floor. 'Careful there!' he called out. 'Step on the stairs right up against the brick wall. And also, Okeke, you might want to hold on to the scaffolding in case a whole slat goes under your weight, no offence.'

'Wow. Thanks, Sully.' She shook her head. 'None taken.' She panned her torch into the water below. 'Okay, so it's gone down a fair bit.'

Sully looked up at her. He aimed his torch past her to the top of the stairs. 'The holes in the wall for the support beams appear to be staggered downwards at regular intervals, located at every forty-five degrees,' he said cheerily. 'So there's the first one behind you, where I found the body. Let's call that twelve o'clock.' He swung the torch round to another cubbyhole just behind him. 'So, going anti-clockwise, there's ten thirty. It's empty.' He panned the torch ahead to where the steps descended into the ink-black water. 'There's nine o'clock.' The beam of light pierced through the foggy water and lit up several slimy green bricks just below the surface. 'Another half an hour of pumping and I reckon we'll be able to have a look into it.'

'You sound hopeful,' Okeke said with a poorly veiled look of distaste on her face.

'Yes, actually, I am. If we get another *complete* body, we might start to get a more consistent victimology. At the moment we have a young girl stuffed into a bag, a young woman stuffed into a hole in the wall... and a spare arm bone. It would be helpful to know if we have three murderers or whether it's all just one man with a broad range of hobbies.'

'For fuck's sake, Sully,' Okeke hissed. 'Are there any red lines you won't blunder over in the hunt for a laugh?'

'Somebody got out of bed on the wrong side this morning,' Sully commented. 'It's a coping mechanism, Okeke. Either you desensitise or you derail.' He looked up at her again and shrugged. 'The dead are nothing more to me these days than meat-and-bone puzzles.'

Okeke could see why family liaison and crime scene forensics were departments that were kept on entirely different floors.

Sully sighed. 'I can't believe Ellessey aren't taking a look at the *last* victim to be stashed here until Monday.'

'Last? What makes you so sure she's the last?' Okeke asked.

'It stands to reason,' Sully said smugly. 'Victims number one and two were dropped to the bottom. One in a bag and another in pieces. Then he, or they, got wiser and started stuffing bodies into the support-beam slots, presumably from the bottom up.' He aimed his beam to the top of the steps where he'd found the most recent body. 'That was the last decent storage nook to disappear beneath the water line. There are no other bodies in the tower above... therefore, I'm presuming she was the final victim to be stashed here.' He spread his hands. 'Easy.'

'Do you think there are many more support-beam holes below?' Okeke asked.

Sully shook his head. 'A few more steps, then we're down to the next floor. Which, I'm thinking, *has* to be the bottom. This next one is our last chance.'

Okeke shook her head. He really did sound excited at the prospect. 'How long ago do you think she was stuck in there? The last victim?'

Sully shrugged again. 'It might be easiest to determine that by judging the rate at which the water level's been rising over the years.'

'Only if it's been flooding at a constant rate,' Okeke pointed out.

Sully nodded. 'True.'

'But what's your best guess from the state of the body?'

Sully puffed his cheeks. 'Fifteen to... twenty, twenty-five years?'

'*That* long ago?'

He nodded. 'The water's cold down here pretty much all year around. There are no currents to disturb and break down the soft tissues. There's no wildlife in here to pick at the body.'

'What about rats?' she asked.

'Only if they had scuba equipment.' His smile quickly faded. 'I didn't see any gnawing distress marks, Okeke. I could be wrong. The body could have been down here even longer than that.'

She nodded at where the water level was about to reveal another wooden step and another hole in the wall. 'So we might find one final body at this nine o'clock position.'

'Hopefully,' he replied.

She shook her head again. Sully was like some kid playing around in an escape room: every nook and cranny, every scrap of bone and tangle of leathered flesh, another exciting clue to slide into place.

Sully glanced down, then up at the two support holes above the water. 'If it had been dry dirt hiding the bodies and not water, I could give probably give you the precise year from the layering, but water is tricksy.'

'We'll just have to let these girls tell us themselves, then,' said Okeke.

30

'Hey there!' Boyd offered Charlotte a little wave as she opened her front door. 'I'm back from the Hebrides.'

He thought he noticed a look of relief on her face, which she quickly replaced with a flickering smile.

'Come on in,' she said.

He stepped inside. 'So how's the old lummox been?' he asked her, looking around. 'Is he still here? It's very quiet...'

'He's been as good as gold,' she replied.

On cue, Ozzie appeared in the doorway that led to Charlotte's sitting room. He barrelled up the hallway and into Boyd's legs as soon as he recognised him. Boyd hunkered down and rough-housed him for a few moments, bonking foreheads accidentally.

'He's really missed you,' Charlotte said a little flatly.

Boyd looked up at her. 'Are you okay, Charlotte?'

She nodded. 'I'm a bit tired, that's all. I didn't get very much sleep last night.'

'Was it Ozzie? Was he being a pain?'

She bent over to ruffle his head. 'No, it's been lovely having such a gentleman stay with us ladies. How was your trip?'

'Not the best. We had a bumpy flight and a bumpy ferry there. I came a cropper on the first, Warren on the second,' he explained. 'We were just about as bad as each other, I think.'

'Did you get to interview your man?' she asked.

'Yeah. We may well have some more questions for him later.' He looked at her more closely. 'You *do* look tired.'

She nodded. Not only did she look tired, she looked stressed. Her eyes appeared red and puffy, as if she'd been crying. 'Is everything okay at the theatre?' he asked.

'Yes, work's fine,' she answered.

Boyd was dimly aware that he knew little more about her life in general other than her job and the fact she walked Mia on the beach a couple of times most days. Oh, and she went to dance classes. He was also aware he owed her a huge thank you for stepping in at such short notice.

'Can I take you out for a pint tonight? Perhaps some fish and chips? My treat?'

'I'm not sure. I...'

She really didn't look right. Her default setting was an awkward and curiously old-fashioned chirpiness. Bridget Jones meets Jane Austen. She normally had a twinkle in her brown eyes and a mischievous upward corner to at least one side of her mouth.

Not this morning, though.

'Charlotte, has something happened?'

'Look... it's nothing. I'm honestly just a bit tired, that's all.'

He would have pressed her further, because the change in her manner seemed to him to be more than having lost a little sleep, but the phone in his jacket began to buzz insistently. He pulled it out.

It was Okeke. 'What's up?' Boyd answered.

'I'm at the tower. We've got another body, guv. Same as the last two, wedged into the brickwork.'

'Shit. *Another?* Is Sully with you?'

'Yeah, he's called in some more of his SOCOs to help. It's going to take a few pairs of hands to get the body out in one piece. It's well and truly rammed in. There's something else, guv.'

'What?'

'There's graffiti. Symbols... carved into a few of the bricks beside the hole.'

'I'm coming over,' said Boyd. He hung up. 'Further developments,' he said to Charlotte, by way of explanation.

Charlotte nodded. 'You'd better go.'

'I'm coming back later,' he said as he unhooked Ozzie's lead from a coat peg and clipped it onto his collar. 'And I'm taking you out for dinner. My treat. My thank you and I'm not taking no for an answer.'

She nodded meekly. 'All right.'

'I absolutely insist.'

She nodded again and opened the front door for him to step back outside.

31

B oyd pulled up on the dirt track outside the Martello tower and found a place to park at the end of an increasing line of vehicles: Gavin Merchant's truck, two SOCO vans, Okeke's battered old Fiat, a patrol car, a Land Rover and now his Renault Captur perched at the end. There was no more available firm ground to park another vehicle as the hummock of land descended on all sides into a swirling labyrinth of silt pools and grassy berms that extended to the horizon.

Boyd had decided to bring Ozzie along with him. He could visit the crime scene and walk Oz along the beach nearby if there was time – two birds with one stone, so to speak. He looked around. The place seemed deserted save for Gavin holed up in the cab of his truck, listening to something that sounded like Coldplay. Presumably everyone else was sheltering inside the tower from the icy wind.

He led Ozzie over towards the entrance and was about to step in when typically Ozzie dropped his anchors and did a must-poo-now right in the middle of the doorway.

'Oh, for fuck's sake,' Boyd muttered as he fumbled in his

coat pockets for a poo bag. These days most of his coat pockets contained a roll of bags on the go. But not this one apparently.

Shit.

Literally.

He did his best to kick the two nuggets Ozzie had deposited into the long grass but only managed to roll them to the side of the doorway.

Good enough.

He stepped inside and saw there was a small 700-watt generator set up in the middle of the main floor, humming loudly and powering a floodlight beside it. From the rays of light spearing up between the floorboards, it looked like there were floodlights set up on the floor below too.

He headed over to the open trapdoor and the ladder emerging from it and was relieved to see there was some reinforced flooring and scaffolding down there too. He could hear voices echoing up from beneath. A woman's voice – not Okeke – arguing loudly with a man.

'... you need to leave the tower now, please, sir!'

'It's MY FUCKING TOWER!'

'I understand that, but this is meant to be a secured...'

'Jesus Christ... You people can't just pull this place apart like this... It's bloody vandalism!'

He could also hear Sully's voice, giving instructions to his colleagues. 'Careful... careful... *puh-lease!* Mind that strut, you clumsy ape!'

Boyd found an old rusty iron hoop on the far wall, presumably something to do with hoisting or lowering supplies back in the day, and he secured Ozzie's leash to it. 'You okay to hang out here for a while?' Ozzie cocked his head and Boyd took that as permission granted. He returned to the trapdoor and climbed down.

The newly revealed floor had been completely covered with sheets of plywood to protect the individual planks beneath by spreading the load from any ill-judged, heavy footsteps.

Where he'd spotted the top of a post a few days ago, there was now a handrail and steps leading down, hugging the curved brick wall. He could see a figure in a white forensic bunny suit reversing up the reinforced steps, holding one end of a light-blue body bag.

Another figure emerged carrying the other end; this one was Sully. 'Let's just set her down over there for the moment,' he said, pointing at a sheet of plywood close to the wall.

Okeke emerged behind him. She spotted Boyd and smiled. 'Ah, there you are.'

'What's with all the shouting down there?' he enquired. It was loud and still going on.

'It's Mr Knight,' she replied as if that explained everything. 'We had to remove some of the brickwork to get her out.' Okeke had her nitrile forensics gloves on and was holding a wet brick in each hand. 'Speaking of which...' She held them out as she approached him. 'These are the two that have carvings on them.'

Boyd led her over to the nearest spotlight and she slowly angled them in the light so that he could see the grooves.

'There's a pentagram,' she said, 'and also a swirly thing and an upside-down crucifix thing with a blob at the top. I'm presuming standard devil-worship crap, right?'

Boyd nodded. 'Nothing that wouldn't look out of place on an Iron Maiden album cover,' he replied. 'You said these bricks were next to the body?'

'In the wall beside the nook. We had to take some bricks out to get into the gap and...'

'Knight threw his toys out of the pram?'

'Right. How was Ricky Harris?' she asked.

'The Prince of Bloody Darkness?' he said in a poor Brummy accent.

Okeke looked puzzled.

Boyd shook his head and pressed on. 'He was pretty much what I was expecting. The love child of Keith Richards and Ozzy Osbourne.'

'Is he of interest still?'

'Very much so. I mean he was giving us the old "*spent most of the eighties totally off my face on coke, man*" shtick. He confirmed he bought the tower when he was with Dark Harvest because he thought it looked "kinda cool".'

Okeke rolled her eyes.

'But... he knew all about the Devil's Tower name.' He summed up the Aleister Crowley story – well, it was more urban myth really – and she looked back down at the bricks she was holding.

Boyd peered more closely at them too. 'Any local kid with a penknife could have carved those, though,' he said.

'Probably,' she replied, 'but probably not without seeing this body as they were doing it. These bricks were under the steps, right beside the hole in the wall. The body was stuffed in head first, wrapped in a blanket. But the feet were virtually sticking out.' The bricks were getting heavy in her hands. She set them gently down on the plywood. 'Whoever stuffed the body in there could have also carved these symbols.'

Boyd rolled his eyes. 'Or the bricks could have been carved first, Okeke.'

'True.'

Leslie Poole, their CSM, emerged at the top of the steps, coaxing Mr Knight to follow her up. They were still sniping away at each other.

'– like I've already said, Mr Knight, this is now a crime scene, not an –'

'You clumsy vandals knocked a huge fucking hole in the side! You DO understand this tower's structure is fragile. You can't just –'

'Half a dozen bricks being removed won't make a blind bit of difference, Mr –'

'Mr Knight?' Boyd straightened up and walked over. 'Our crime scene manager is quite right; you shouldn't be down here. In fact, you shouldn't have stepped past the crime-scene tape in the first place.'

'How long are you lot going to be poking around down here?' Knight snapped. 'I've already explained that with half the water pumped out now there's increased pressure on the basement walls, right? Your bloody scaffolding or not, my surveyor says we need to get this empty space filled in urgently. Because it's also sinking!' Knight said. 'And tilting. The longer we fanny around, the more unstable it'll become. You lot are at risk too! How much longer are you going to need down here?!'

Boyd looked around. The pumping had been going constantly as far as he was aware for a couple of days and so far the water level had dropped about twenty feet. 'At the current rate I don't suppose too many more days. Three... four?' he guessed.

'Then what?'

'We'll want to do a fingertip search across the floor. Maybe another couple of days.'

'So a week, then?' Knight huffed.

Boyd shrugged. 'Perhaps. But that's not something I'm prepared to guarantee. *If* there are any stability or safety issues here, we'll get our own structural surveyor back in and shore it up some more.'

Knight shook his head. 'This is a piece of national heritage. And it's sinking into the bloody marsh! If you screw up, it'll be lost forever.'

'What's the big deal?' muttered Sully. 'Fifty years from now, most of Sussex will probably be underwater anyway.'

Knight glared at him.

'Look, Mr Knight,' Boyd said in what he hoped was a

calming voice. 'We'll be as quick and as *careful* as we can. Another week or so and it'll be all yours to... preserve, conserve or whatever you call it to your heart's content, okay?'

Knight looked as though some of the wind had been robbed from his sails. 'A week?'

Boyd was about to add 'or thereabouts' but instead just nodded. 'Now, if you'll let Leslie escort you up and out, perhaps we can crack on with processing this body?'

Leslie Poole began to coax Knight towards the ladder and, as he went, Boyd almost called out to warn him about the dog turd in the doorway.

32

He spotted a lone figure standing further up the beach. Another boy. He was throwing pebbles into the waves, trying to make them skip.

He descended from the grass-tufted dunes across the windy beach and made his way cautiously towards him.

Closer, he could see the boy was a little younger. Perhaps just a couple of years.

'Wotcha,' he said.

The younger boy spun round, taken by surprise. 'Oh, hello.' He sounded posh.

'How old are ya, mate?' he asked. An important question.

'Eleven,' said the posh-sounding boy. 'And what about you? You're really tall.'

'Thirteen. Lanky, me mum calls me. Where you from?'

'Kent. I'm on holiday with my grandparents. At the caravan place.'

'I live round 'ere,' said the lanky one. 'Nuffin' much to do most of the time.'

Posh Boy nodded. 'It is a bit boring.' He had a large blue holdall on his back, arms through the handles like it was a backpacker's bag; B.O.A.C. was stencilled on the side.

'What's in your bag?' asked Lanky.

'Spare clothes. In case I get wet.'

'Oh. Right.'

'And a packed lunch. Marmite sandwiches. Orange juice. I've got Dairylea triangles too and some sweets.'

Lanky shrugged. 'I got nuffin'.'

'You can share if you like,' offered Posh. 'Later, when it's lunchtime.'

Lanky smiled. 'Cheers, mate.' He bent down and picked up a pebble and tossed it at the surf of a retreating wave. 'That's 'ow you do it. When the wave's goin' back.'

'Ah...' Posh smiled. 'Thanks.'

'Want to hang out?' asked Lanky.

Posh smiled again. 'Sure. Is there anything to do?'

Lanky shrugged. Then a thought occurred to him. 'I know a cool place we can go.'

'Yeah? Where?'

'It's a ruin.'

Posh cocked his head. That sounded interesting.

'They call it Devil's Tower,' said Lanky.

33

Boyd noticed that Charlotte had barely touched her seafood linguini. He'd taken her out to Brodie's, a place near the mall that Okeke had recommended. Charlotte had made a token effort; she'd plucked out a couple of mussels and pushed the pasta around her plate a bit. Boyd, however, had successfully demolished his gourmet burger and was now halfway through a side of onion rings.

'Charlotte,' he said finally, 'there's definitely something up. What's happened?' It had to be something that had occurred while he'd been away, he reasoned. She'd been perfectly fine when he'd dropped Ozzie off. 'You're not right,' he persisted. 'Even I can see that. And I'm going to keep on at you until you tell me.'

She looked up from her plate. 'I think someone's watching me.' Her brows flexed momentarily as if she was annoyed with herself for actually voicing her worry.

'*Watching?*' Boyd let his fork clatter to the plate. 'What do you mean... Peeping Tom watching?'

She shook her head. 'No. Not that...'

'Stalking?'

Her eyes widened slightly. 'I... I don't know what the definition of that is,' she said, 'but... someone's been standing outside my garden. Last night and the night before.'

'Are you sure?' he asked, mentally kicking himself the moment the words left his mouth. 'I mean...'

'I'm sure,' she replied confidently. 'There were footprints in the back alley. I saw his breath.' She forced a smile. 'Ozzie heard him too. The clever boy sent him packing the first night.'

'And he came back the next?'

She nodded. 'I spent the night in my back room with both dogs, watching the fence.'

'What did you see?'

'His breath, Bill. Just... one cloud after another... like a smoke signal.' Her voice wobbled at the end. She took a sip of her wine.

'How long was he there for?' Boyd asked.

'I don't know. A while, though.'

'Then?'

'He moved off down the bin alley.'

'Could it have been some, I don't know, dealer? I know there's been quite an uptick of that in the area.'

Charlotte shook her head. 'I think it's someone –' her voice fluttered again – 'someone who *knows me*.'

Boyd leant forward so that he could keep his voice low. Brodie's was a wine bar that doubled as a boutique restaurant in the evenings; it was small with closely placed tables bearing dripping candles in wine bottles, soft folksy music and softly spoken table conversations. *Intimate* was how Okeke had mischievously described it.

'How do you know that? Could it be one of your colleagues at work? Have they been behaving differently around you?'

He'd met a couple of them. Bernard shared her office on Wednesdays when he did the accounts, rotas and payroll. Hugh managed the White Rock Café. Neither of them seemed like men she couldn't handle with a firm word if they stepped over a line. To be honest, neither seemed like the type to stand out in the cold for a couple of hours either.

Charlotte shook her head. 'It's someone I used to know. Someone from my past.'

Her past was a place that thus far had remained a locked box. He'd tried on a few occasions to prise it open over the last six months, but with little success. Charlotte had been able to firmly, but gently, dissuade him from pressing the matter.

'Who do you think it is?' he asked.

She shook her head. An unreadable little gesture. Was she berating herself for having given this much away or telling him she wouldn't answer?

'Who?' he pressed. 'Charlotte, this is important – you must let me in.'

She looked at him and took a deep breath before replying. 'It's Ewan.'

Boyd waited patiently and after a minute she continued.

'My ex-husband.'

He did his best not to react overtly. He'd been pretty certain she'd had a significant relationship in her past. There had been markers. She'd shared anecdotes from her youth, from her school days and then funny stories from recently, her time living in Hastings and working at the theatre. But there had been a noticeable scarcity of tales from the period in between.

'Yes,' she added. 'I was married for twenty years. About ten of those –' she took a large sip of her wine – 'were the most *terrifying* years of my life.'

Boyd pushed the remaining onion rings to one side. 'Charlotte... was he –'

'Abusive?' she cut in, then shook her head. 'More... *possessive*, after the honeymoon period when you're both putting your best foot forward, being the best possible version of yourself. That only lasted for a few years. And then...'

'What?'

'I don't know what the correct clinical term is, Bill, but... for want of a better word, he went completely insane.'

'Insane,' he repeated. 'How do you mean?'

'He became obsessed.'

'With you?'

Charlotte stared at her food. 'With a girl. He kept painting her over and over.' She looked at Boyd. 'I mean, she resembled me. She looked a lot like me, and sometimes he said it *was* me, but...'

'What?'

'I'm sure it was someone else. Someone he was trying to get out of his head and onto the canvas.'

'So... what happened? Where is he now?'

'I thought he might be locked away by now,' Charlotte said. 'Either in prison or some kind of mental institution.' She paused. 'Or perhaps even dead.'

Boyd could hear her voice faltering again. He reached out and took her hand. 'Charlotte... tell me about him.'

THEY WERE one of the last couples to leave Brodie's, and Boyd stated firmly that she was not going to walk back home nor call a local taxi. She was going to stay in his spare room for tonight at least.

'I can't. I need to go back for Mia,' Charlotte said.

'We'll walk back up to mine, and then I'll go and get her,' he insisted.

'But you've had too much to drink.'

He'd had two large glasses of Malbec with dinner. He could still be technically over the legal limit, but by the time they'd walked back up the hill to his house and had a coffee, he reckoned he'd have metabolised at least one unit away. And, after the story she'd just told him, he suspected his heart rate was already up a notch or two.

She accepted his offer and they walked back to Ashburnham Road. He made them both a strong coffee, which he drank quickly, took her door key and made his way to the car.

'Bill,' she called from the front door. 'Be careful.'

Boyd gave her a cheery salute and climbed into his Captur. He closed the door and now, finally out of earshot, he let out his first unguarded response to what she'd told him.

'Fucking bloody hell.' He took a deep breath, started the engine and headed back down Ashburnham Road, replaying her story as he drove. She'd met Ewan in 1985 when she was just eighteen. Thinking back to last night's traumatic events, she'd been a few years younger than Emma.

In his mid twenties, Ewan had been a charismatic artist. When she'd first met him, his star was on the rise, catching the attention of esteemed collectors like Charles Saatchi, and in proper rock-'n'-roll style they were married just six months later.

His art was traditional, as opposed to installation art, a term Boyd had come to associate with people who could neither paint nor sculpt. Ewan used actual oil paint on actual canvas. Charlotte said she'd been his muse, not just an artist's typical chat-up line but genuinely; all his paintings seemed to feature her likeness in one way or another, as either the central subject or a shadowy figure in the background.

Ewan's work, she'd said, was fashionable for about five years, until the likes of Saatchi turned their attention elsewhere, then his bankability had plummeted.

She'd told Boyd that the obsessive behaviour had begun around that time. His frustration with his waning career had been directed her way. Small things at first. Barbed comments and bouts of jealousy whenever she left the house without him.

When she'd gone out to work and become the breadwinner, it had got steadily worse.

Towards the end, she'd told Boyd, Ewan had become scary. Delusional. Paranoid.

Boyd pulled up outside Charlotte's place. There was a light on in the hallway and a lamp on in the front room, presumably left on for Mia. He noticed that her car was parked on the road outside, which made it look, he thought, to any passing stalker as though she might in.

'He was getting really frightening, Bill, before I finally managed to escape him,' Charlotte had explained. She'd said that eventually she'd been frightened that he might actually kill her; she'd managed to grab a bag and get away from him. That had been seventeen years ago, and she'd been hiding from him ever since.

Boyd climbed out of the car into the soft amber glow of the street light. He looked up and down the road. Saturday night glowed from the houses in her street. Their windows flickered with wall-mounted TVs downstairs and computer screens upstairs.

He spotted Mia's silhouette perched on the back of the armchair in the front room as she peered out into the darkness, her dangling Brittany ears swinging as she studied first one direction, then the other.

He took Charlotte's keys out of his pocket, unlocked the front door and stepped cautiously inside. 'Mia?' he called softly.

He heard her jump down from her perch in the lounge, and her nails click-clacked across the wooden floor into the hallway. Boyd reached up, pulled her lead from a coat hook and clipped it onto her collar. 'Do you want to come for a sleepover with Ozzie, eh? Do you?'

Mia stood on her hind legs and looked at him before

twirling in an excited circle. Charlotte often called Mia her little meercat. He smiled as he finally saw why.

He had no intention of lingering. If Charlotte's ex-husband really was as delusional as she said and had somehow managed to locate her, then it probably wasn't a good idea to hang around.

'Right, off we go, then.' He led her back to the car and onto the back seat.

He was about to open the driver's door when he had a second thought. If she really was being stalked by her ex, then there'd need to be *some* evidence presented for the police to initiate any action.

Given that the only thing that Charlotte had seen was someone's breath on the far side of the fence, it could actually be anyone: a dealer, a teenager having a fag...

Since I'm here...

He opened the car door and grabbed a torch from the glove compartment. Then, after locking Mia in, he made his way up the narrow street until he found a cut-through between the terraced houses: an overgrown footpath that looked as though it would be a minefield of dog crap hidden among the fallen leaves. The only illumination came from an amber light halfway down, crowded by bare branches and casting a flickering sulphurous monotone glow of shifting zebra-stripe shadows.

He carefully picked his way down the path – testing the ground for the inevitable soft squelch – until he came across the opening to her bin alley.

Boyd paused and listened for a moment. Again, it was silent save for the murmuring of TV sets and the gentle rustle of bushes and nettles stirred by the breeze. He could just step in, snap on his torch and see what happened. If he bellowed 'Police!' at the same time, anyone there would most likely bolt like a rabbit.

But if it is Ewan...? He did a quick hazard assessment. If this bloke was twenty-five in 1985, he'd be in his sixties now, so, if it came to a scuffle, Boyd was probably going to have an advantage. But what if he was carrying a knife? Well, that was every man's equaliser, wasn't it? He suspected that if it was a career burglar or drug dealer, of any age, waiting there, the most he'd see of them was a flash of trainers and the back of a hoodie as they made a hasty exit.

Or... it could be a crazy old painter with a sharpened palette knife.

He pulled his phone out and unlocked it.

He decided the '*Boo! It's the police!*' approach was probably the smart way to go. He raised his long-handled torch to his shoulder, stepped into the narrow alleyway and snapped the light on.

The stark beam picked out several wheelie bins running down the length of the fencing. The only movement came from a cat hopping up onto the fence and off into someone's backyard. Other than a few plastic bags and escaped recycled rubbish, there was nothing.

Boyd let out a little sigh of relief.

I should probably check out Charlotte's gate.

He took several steps into the alleyway, panning his torch into the gaps between the bins to make sure no one was hiding there. 'Police!' he called out. 'If there's anyone down here up to no good, now's probably a good time to fuck off.'

The cat yowled, whether in confrontation or support, he wasn't certain.

Boyd continued down the alleyway until he found himself standing beside the gate marked with Charlotte's house number: 37.

He panned the torch down at the ground, not sure what he was hoping to find. The ground was a mush of rotting fallen leaves, escaped rubbish and cat shit on a bed of old cobblestones. And, yes, there were footprints, plenty of them. Most likely from the bin men or her neighbours wheeling their bins out or in on collection day.

He aimed the torch back up onto the gate and her fence. There was a hole in the fence. A wood knot that had either fallen out or been pushed out. He stepped closer and peered through the hole to see her small backyard.

More than that, there was a clear view into her kitchen and the door to the hallway. He could even see a sliver of the front door and its stained glass.

He scrunched down and peered upwards. He could see her bathroom and her spare bedroom. A Peeping Tom using this little knothole in the fence had a pretty good view to the front downstairs and would also have a tantalising glimpse upstairs.

A Peeping Tom, then?

A potential burglar?

Or worse?

He decided he'd get her ex-husband's full name from Charlotte and take a look on LEDS first thing Monday morning.

34

Boyd surreptitiously watched Charlotte as she threw the tennis ball, for both dogs, down the shingle beach towards the retreating surf. Mia pursued it only ankle-deep into the freezing cold water, while Ozzie plunged the rest of the way in rather than let the sea, his evil roaring nemesis, claim the prize.

'You know I'm not doubting you saw someone...' Boyd said.

Charlotte smiled. 'The poor young lady has simply *lost her mind*,' she pronounced in the style of Maggie Smith.

'But...'

She looked at him. 'There it is... the *but*.'

'*But* there's nothing to verify it was your ex out there. I mean... you know there's a handy spyhole in the fence at the end?'

She looked at him. Apparently she hadn't known.

'Charlotte, you can see into the kitchen, up the hall to the front door. And up into the bathroom.'

Her eyes rounded. 'Thank God that window's frosted glass!'

'Well, that's something. But... and I'm not sure this is something you'd *want* to hear, but it could simply be that you have a neighbourhood perv.'

She raised her brows at the *simply*.

'Sorry, that came out sounding flippant. What I'm saying is this: stalkers tend to want to let their victims know that they're being stalked. That's half the buzz for them. The fear they can inflict, the sense of control.'

Ozzie deposited the ball back at his feet, slimy and wet. Boyd tossed it back down the beach and continued: 'You haven't received any anonymous texts? Had any letters or notes posted through your door?'

She shook her head.

'And nothing at work?'

She shook her head again. 'The thing is, Bill, Ewan wasn't – isn't – your average stalker, if there's such a thing. There was something –' she paused – 'almost destroying his mind from the inside. Maybe from his past. I don't know.'

'You can't excuse what he did like that,' replied Boyd.

'He was sick,' Charlotte said. 'Collapsing mentally. At first, when I started to go out to work, I was worried I'd come home to find he'd done himself in. Then... as *things* got worse, I started worrying that he'd want to take me down with him. So that's when I left him.' She sighed. 'I... We separated. I wish I could say that one day I'd had enough and told him to his face I was leaving. But I didn't. One day I went to work and just didn't go home.'

Boyd said, placing his hand on her back, 'Where did you go?'

'I went to stay with a female colleague. I couldn't stay with my parents or my grandparents. And it was lucky that I didn't. Ewan went round to their homes looking for me. My friend helped me to hide from him. It was...' Her voice faltered. 'Terrifying. I really thought he was going to end us both...'

She waved a hand at Boyd to indicate that she'd talked

enough. 'Change of subject, please.' She cleared her throat. 'Let me just say thank you,' she said firmly, recomposing her face but unable to hide the tremor in her voice. 'Thank you for putting me up. And,' she added with a smile, 'for putting up with me.'

'Hey, that's okay,' he replied. 'I've got more rooms than I can use. It's just me and Ems rattling around in there.'

'Speaking of Emma...' She retrieved the ball from Mia's wet muzzle. 'You're going to need to talk to her about the other night.' Ozzie let off a volley of barks and she tossed the ball back down the beach.

He'd given Charlotte a detail-lite version of what he'd walked in on last night when she'd asked where Emma was.

'Arghh... she's still avoiding me,' he grumbled. 'She won't answer my texts, my calls.'

'She's probably embarrassed, Bill. And angry with you. You walked in on a... private situation.'

He ground his teeth and his jaw flexed. 'She might have been going along with that bastard but not willingly.'

'You don't know for sure what was going on,' Charlotte replied. 'But you *do* need to find out.'

'I'm bloody well trying to!' he groused.

'Or perhaps *someone else* needs to talk to her?'

He looked at Charlotte hopefully and she nodded. 'I'm happy to, Bill. It might be better... with me, you know? With someone who's not too close. And perhaps with someone who's female?'

He nodded. 'Christ... would you?'

'Of course.'

He squeezed her shoulder lightly. 'Thank you, Charlotte. That's really good of you.'

'Just paying my rent,' she replied.

'You do know you can stay as long as you like,' he told her.

'Thank you. Another night would be good, if that's okay?'

she said. 'But I don't want to be intimidated into keeping away from my home. It's my space. My home. My sanctum sanctorum. It might not be much but it's mine.'

She took another deep breath.

'And I'm not giving it all up simply because of some Peeping Tom... I've *earned* my home.'

35

Boyd shoved a pot of Oats-So-Simple into the kitchenette's microwave and slapped it on. He and Charlotte had polished off two bottles of Malbec through Sunday afternoon and into the evening, and both had emerged from their respective bedrooms this morning late and with sore heads.

Charlotte had decided to take a flexi-day since Mondays were slow at the theatre anyway. She'd said she'd walk the dogs and promised Boyd she'd try to have a chat with Emma when she came back in from her night shift.

'Hey-ho, boss! And how are you this mighty fine morning?'

Boyd turned to see Minter in the doorway, looking very pleased with himself. 'Ahh. I take it your Ironman Challenge was an epic win?' he said.

'I was well into the bottom half of the entries, to be honest,' he replied. 'Not so good. I was hoping to do much better.' He grinned. 'Didn't need my recovery day after all, though.'

'Why are you looking so bloody chirpy, then?' Boyd asked. The detective sergeant *did* look ridiculously pleased with himself. Puzzlingly so.

'Well, boss... a funny old thing happened to me just after I crossed the finishing line.'

'You collapsed? You needed a paramedic? You had an out-of-body experience?' Boyd said.

Minter stroked his immaculately clipped beard. 'No, boss, but I was approached by a modelling talent scout.'

The microwave pinged beside Boyd. 'You what-the-what?'

'A talent scout from one of those modelling agencies stopped me and gave me her business card.' Minter absently straightened his back, pushed out his pecs and ran a hand through his glossy dark hair.

Boyd pulled his pot of oats out of the microwave. 'You might want to be careful, Minter,' he said with a straight face. 'Did she say what kind of modelling?'

'Well, not exactly, no. But she said I had just the right look for their agency. She said they pay their models a fortune. She said they're after the athletic type. That's why she was lingering around the finish line.'

Minter pulled a business card out of his waistcoat pocket and held it out.

Boyd took it and looked at the card. '*HardMen*'. The name was in a bold burgundy font set against a dark green background. Very masculine, with a hint of online casino about it.

'You might want to give them a call before you think of a career change,' he said, pulling a face. 'I mean... it looks a bit, you know...'

'*Hard* Men,' Minter read the name aloud. 'As in masculine fellas. Totally ripped blokes, so to speak.'

'No, I get that, but...'

'What?'

Boyd grinned and gently slapped his shoulder. 'Nothing, Minty, my man – I'm sure you'll be great.'

He took the piping-hot bowl of oats back to his desk, sat down and logged himself into LEDS. There was work to be done following his trip up to interview Harris, of course, but top of his list was the name he had written down on a slip of paper.

Ewan Lester Jones.

Not officially police business just yet, but it might well become police business if Charlotte's stalker did turn out to be him.

He tapped the name in. He'd also managed to get a date of birth out of Charlotte, which meant she'd guessed he was going to do a little unofficial digging, even though she hadn't asked him to.

Ewan Lester Jones. D.O.B.: 14-02-60

Bingo. Ewan Jones had a criminal record. Boyd was about to open it when the LEDS 'help system' interceded and splashed a message box across the whole screen.

Essential Database Section Maintenance In Progress: We apologise for any inconvenience.

His head flopped back and he found himself gazing in frustration at the polystyrene ceiling tiles. 'Oh, for Christ's...'

He ate his porridge and tried his luck again, but to no avail. The perky apologetic message popped up once more.

Okay. Fine. There was, of course, always Google. He tapped Jones's name into the search bar, along with 'artist' and got back a cluttered page of results. There were a couple of pictures of a willowy young man with wavy hair, standing proudly before a painting in a gallery, beside a tweedy-dressed older man who had an arm around his shoulders. It could have been his father or his agent.

Boyd clicked through to one of Ewan Jones's paintings. He had no idea what the fine art terminology would be for the man's painting style – but to his eyes it looked loose and energetic. He could see broad brushstrokes that could have been applied with a paint roller, then in other places the tiniest of details had been applied with care and a fine tip.

The next image pulled a breath out of him. It was Charlotte. Unmistakably her. Younger, of course; younger even than she would have been at the time, he guessed. The portrait made her look as though she was twelve or thereabouts. Jones's style was the same – careless splashes of paint for the background, broad confident strokes for her body, but the finest attention reserved for her face.

Particularly around her hazel-coloured eyes. He had her likeness nailed in those eyes.

There was something about the portrait that set it apart from chocolate-box art. The colours were muted, like a Polaroid left too long on a windowsill. The background was dark.

Clutched in one of her pale hands was a piece of scarlet material. A handkerchief, maybe. And that was the only bold splash of colour in the entire composition.

He clicked back to LEDS. Miraculously it was up and running once more. He typed in Jones's details again and the man's criminal record popped up.

The face in the top-right corner of the screen was that of a man in his late forties, the photo taken back in 2005. He still had a full head of wavy hair that had largely gone grey and was sporting a scruffy salt-and-pepper beard with some flecks of auburn still hanging on in there. Boyd looked at the docket. He'd been arrested and interviewed over an allegation of a violent assault on his wife, Charlotte K. Jones.

Boyd scanned the interview transcription. Jones's contributions were all 'no comment', but the interviewing officer's questions filled in most of the details. The allegation was that he'd followed Charlotte to work one morning and had spotted her getting a coffee with a male work colleague. That night, when she'd come home, he'd confronted her about it, accusing her of having an affair, then he'd punched her in the face.

There was a photo attached that made Boyd wince. Charlotte – in this picture she was nearly twenty years younger but somehow looked older, drawn and haggard. One eye was slightly puffed up and discoloured. The case appeared to have not been taken any further and Boyd spotted a tacked-on note that Charlotte had refused to press charges.

He involuntarily slumped back into his seat. He could imagine an all-too-familiar scene playing out across a kitchen table. A tearful Jones pleading with her that he'd never hurt her again. That he loved her beyond words and he had no idea what had come over him. And Charlotte nodding, perhaps forgiving... certainly hoping she could believe him.

Boyd scrolled down to the next entry and his heart stopped.

From the look of things, Charlotte had had a *very*, very lucky escape.

'Guv?' Okeke was standing in front of his desk.

Boyd looked up from his screen. 'Yup?'

'We've had some results back from Ellessey on the DNA swabs.'

It took him a moment to switch gears back to the Martello tower case. 'DNA swabs?'

'From the lunch box? The apple core. The wrappers, the Pez dispenser?'

'Ah, right.' He checked his watch. It was twenty past ten. The last hour and a half had shot past him. He'd meant to call the team together for an update before lunch but had allowed himself to get sidetracked.

'Let's grab the small conference room and rally the troops, then,' he said.

Okeke nodded. 'In ten?'

'You going up for a coffee?'

She nodded again. 'Do you want the usual?'

36

Boyd returned from visiting Sutherland's goldfish bowl to find the four of them assembled in the small conference room and deeply involved in a discussion about Minter's potential career change.

'... O'Neal nearly wet himself when I told him,' Warren was saying. 'Said you were probably going to end up in a porno.'

'Yeah, well...' Minter tried not to look irritated. 'He's just jealous.'

'So what aesthetic was it that they were evaluating you on?' asked Sully. 'The ability to adopt an upright walking posture? Opposable thumbs?'

'Was it the monobrow?' Okeke chuckled. 'Or the permanently grazed knuckles?'

Minter slow-clapped. 'Bravo – hilarious stuff, guys. Bloody hilarious. I'm pissing *myself* here, I am.'

'I read somewhere there's an agency that hires out stunt torsos,' continued Okeke. 'You know, for those close-up shots of Mark Wahlberg or Tom Hardy?'

'Or Putin,' added Sully. 'You could end up being Vladimir Putin's stunt belly?'

Boyd sat down at the table. 'All right, kids, that's enough. Leave our poor supermodel alone please. The D-Sup's joining us in a second.'

'Does Sutherland know?' asked Okeke hopefully.

'If O'Neal knows,' said Warren, 'I'd say everyone in CID knows by now.'

Sutherland appeared outside the glass door, summoned like a genie by the mention of his name. He stepped in. 'Good morning, everyone.'

'Morning, sir,' they chorused.

He grabbed the spare seat, sat down with them and looked expectantly at Boyd.

'Right,' Boyd began, 'first things first... we've got some DNA results back from Ellessey. Okeke, what's the news?'

She looked down at the email she'd printed out. 'They got two distinct DNA profiles off the apple core.'

'Apple core?' repeated Sutherland incredulously. 'An apple core survived fifty years?'

Okeke nodded. 'Uh-huh. It was in a totally dry, sterile environment. The lunch box was completely sealed and, excuse the pun, bone dry on the inside. The apple core looked like an old conker.' She glanced back at the email. 'So, two distinct profiles. Profile Alpha has no matches or familial matches on the NDNAD, but Profile Beta gave us a hit.' She gave Boyd a broad congratulatory smile. 'It's our man Ricky Harris.'

Warren let out a gasp, then punched the air. 'I knew it. I knew it.'

Sutherland ran a hand across the smooth skin under his chin. 'That's a relief. So it was money well spent, then,' he said as if the trip up north had been something he'd championed all along.

'Is that going to be enough to charge him and bring him down here?' asked Warren.

'I doubt it,' said Minter. 'CPS will want more than that.'

'We've got forensics that put him with the girl,' said Okeke. 'He's got form: we've got suspicious behaviour – buying the tower and hanging on to it for so long. And then there's all that awful music and the videos, those sick album covers...'

'Unfortunately the law doesn't allow us to convict a man for poor taste,' said Sully. 'If it did, then half of CID would be in jail.'

'Nor for making a poor property purchase,' added Boyd. 'Plus, there are two DNA profiles. I presume they've ruled out Patricia Hemsworth as the other?'

Okeke nodded.

'If we can't identify the other one, or we do and the other profile belongs to someone who is now deceased, then Harris's defence becomes as simple as "the other guy did it",' said Boyd.

'What about joint enterprise?' asked Sully.

Sutherland shook his head. 'CPS don't like using that so much these days. It's acquiring a bit of a reputation for bouncing at trial.'

'We'll definitely need more before we can make an arrest,' said Boyd. 'Otherwise all we're doing is warning him. And I suspect he'd do a good job of going to ground somewhere else.'

'We've got the two complete bodies that were stuffed in the tower's wall going on the slab this afternoon,' said Okeke. She checked her watch. 'In a couple of hours' time actually.'

'Can you sit in on those?' asked Boyd.

'Yep, I'm already on it,' she replied.

'I can go too,' said Sully. 'If you want?'

Boyd shook his head. 'I want you back at the tower. Who's there now, by the way?'

'Leslie Poole and a couple of uniforms,' answered Sully. 'They're pumping water again.'

'Good.' Boyd nodded thoughtfully. 'Poole handled Knight pretty well. Read him the riot act and kicked him out of the tower,' he said with a smile. 'I like her a lot.' He looked at Sully.

'We're expecting at least one more body down there with that arm bone... It's going to happen sooner or later. How close are we to the bottom?'

'We're nearly there,' said Okeke. 'Another couple of days by the sound of it.'

'Okay, so best that you're on hand, Sully, in case something else gets sucked up or revealed.'

Sully shrugged. 'Okay.'

'If we get lucky on one of those two bodies... and, by that, I mean Harris's DNA is on them, *then* we can issue an arrest warrant to get him parcelled up and sent down here.' Boyd looked at Sutherland. 'Joint enterprise on Patricia Hemsworth would probably stand a chance then. Not bad for the money spent, eh, sir?'

Sutherland nodded. 'Indeed. Happy days.'

'Warren?'

'Sir?'

'I've been thinking about the symbols that were carved on the bricks pulled out from the wall... Do some digging on the album covers for Harris's band. I'm pretty sure I saw some similar swirly symbols in his grotto.'

'Yes, sir.'

'Harris was super keen to mention he was the creative driving force of the band. Maybe there's a link, motif or theme running through their stuff that can add weight to our next interview with him?'

Warren nodded.

'Minter?'

'Yes, boss?'

'I need to update the action log with you. And then, I'm afraid, once Okeke has the initial results on the two bodies, we're probably going to have to start trawling mispers to see if we can ID them.'

'Would you like me to go and grab O'Neal?' Minter asked.

'Flack's roped O'Neal into Operation Rosper,' cut in Sutherland. 'He made a request to have him swapped into his team.'

'Swapped? Who's been tossed out?' Boyd asked.

'DC Lawrence.' Boyd knew nothing about him. 'Personality clash,' added Sutherland.

'What...? Is this Lawrence a pain in the arse, then?'

Sutherland made a non-comital shrug.

'All right, well, let's not have him here.' Boyd looked across the table at Minter. 'In that case, I guess it's just you and me hitting the mispers... you stud-muffin, you.'

37

While he was waiting for news from Okeke and Ellessey, Boyd took the opportunity to have a look at the rest of Jones's criminal record.

In 2008 Ewan Jones had been charged with violent assault and the abduction of a woman in Canterbury, Kent. He'd been working as a security guard at the time.

According to the file, he'd used his uniform and ID lanyard to convince a woman walking home at night that he was a policeman. The woman had realised at the last moment that something was wrong, but it had been too late; she'd been overpowered and bundled into the back of his van.

Jones had driven her across Kent and into East Sussex. The woman, however, had managed to escape him when his van had careered off the road and into a ditch. Apparently Jones had been over the legal limit, but he'd also had significant traces of synthetic cannabinoids – Spice – in his blood at the time.

The woman had fled and managed to flag down a car and the police had been called.

There had been no big, dramatic manhunt. The arresting

officer had found Jones sitting beneath a road sign out in the Romney Marshes, about a hundred yards away from his totalled van. The officer had said that 'he almost seemed relieved to have some company out there'. What made for chilling reading, though, was the fact that in the back of his van was what was essentially a murder kit: duct tape, plastic bin bags and a kitchen knife.

It was clear that he'd intended to kill her, then dispose of the body.

Boyd dug his earbuds out of his bag, put them in and clicked on the first of several interview videos – made just hours after Jones's arrest. The camera was the usual corner-mounted one with a wide field of view that encompassed the small room. Jones was sat in the corner and there were two detectives on bucket chairs, almost boxing him in.

Jones looked tidier, his wavy hair now a closely clipped silver sheen. His scruffy beard was a tidy little white goatee. He'd put on some weight too. A far cry from the willowy young art prodigy with a golden future ahead of him.

'Okay, recording on. The time is 3.15 a.m. The date is September the fifth, 2008. Interviewee is Ewan Lester Jones. Interviewing officers are Detective Inspector Sutherland, Sussex CID, and Detective Sergeant Ross, Kent CID.'

Boyd leant in closer. He'd thought he'd recognised that perfectly round head of Sutherland's.

'Now then, Ewan,' started Sutherland, 'you were arrested for violent assault and abduction. I'm going to repeat the caution for the video record. You do not have to...' Boyd scrubbed the video forward twenty seconds. '...so why don't you explain to us what happened. Why did you grab this woman? What was your intention?'

It was the kind of question guaranteed to draw out a 'no comment', but it looked as though Jones, still wearing his security guard uniform, was keen to engage. 'I had to,' he replied. 'I really had to do something.'

Jones's accent was neutral. Boyd had been half expecting a slightly more *earthy* accent. Something a bit *geezer*. But instead he had plummy vowels and the all-present-and-correct consonants of a Radio Four theatre critic.

'Do what exactly?' pressed Sutherland.

'I had to take... care of the matter once and for all,' replied Jones. 'She was getting angry with me. Getting really angry.'

'Who was? The woman you abducted?'

'No, Lottie. My Lottie.'

'Who's *Lottie*?'

Jones chuckled, then muttered and shook his head. He seemed to be engaging with someone else in the room.

'Ewan?' prompted the other copper, Ross. 'Who is Lottie?'

It took Boyd a moment to twig. *Lottie? He's talking about Charlotte, isn't he?*

'I really let her down,' said Jones. 'I really...' He started to sob.

'Ewan,' said Sutherland. 'Tell me some more about Lottie. Come on.'

Ross handed Jones some water in a plastic cup. He accepted it gratefully, took several sips and tried to compose himself again.

'I promised her,' he said softly. 'I promised her I'd do better.'

'Lottie?' prompted Sutherland.

Jones nodded. 'She deserved much better.'

'Who is Lottie?' asked Sutherland. 'A friend? A girlfriend?'

Jones looked up from his lap. 'My angel. My guardian angel. She's done so much for me and I treated her so badly...' He began to sob again.

'What did you intend to do with the woman you abducted earlier?

'She looked so much like her. So much like her. I... had to.'

Like Charlotte?

Boyd paused the video, then scrolled down through the record until he came across a picture of Jones's victim. There were bruises and scrapes on her face. She'd been beaten, presumably as Jones attempted to wrestle control of her. Scabs and bruises aside, the likeness was unmistakably there. She bore a strong resemblance to Charlotte. It made the hairs on the back of his neck stir.

Jesus. Ewan Jones had found himself a lookalike. Because he couldn't find his Charlotte, he'd been trawling for a surrogate. Boyd returned to the interview video and hit 'play'.

Sutherland looked down at a page of notes. 'So, it says here, you're married to but estranged from a woman called Charlotte Jones?'

Jones nodded.

'Is that who we're talking about, Ewan? Charlotte? Your wife?'

'She was so beautiful,' he whimpered. 'So beautiful. I can't believe what we did to her.'

'What did you do to her?'

Boyd paused the video and scrubbed it back.

'...can't believe what we did to her...'

We? It sounded a lot like he'd said 'we'. But then it could've been 'he'. He played the video again, hoping that the younger DI Sutherland had picked up on it.

But he hadn't. 'What happened to Charlotte?' Sutherland was focusing there. 'What did you *do* to Lottie?'

Ewan Jones had his head in his hands and was sobbing. 'I wanted to say sorry,' he wailed. 'I wanted to make it all right.'

There was a beep and the two detectives turned to look over their shoulder. Sutherland sighed and wilted. 'For the record... it's 3.19 a.m. The duty solicitor has entered the room. You are?'

'Sebastian Graves. Has Mr Jones been cautioned?'

'Yes, of course,' replied Sutherland irritably.

A young man in a dark suit stepped into view, steered himself past the detectives and sat down next to Jones. 'I'd like this interview to be terminated until I've had a chance to talk to my client.'

Sutherland leant in towards the recorder. 'It's 3.20 p.m. – the interview has been suspended.'

The screen went black.

∾

STAYING SEATED, Minter wheeled his chair over to Boyd's desk and parked himself at the corner. 'Boss, I had a quick chat with Okeke to get the basics about an hour ago and I've got some mispers that look promising. Are you okay to review them now?'

Boyd closed the tab on Ewan Jones and looked at the print-outs that Minter had placed on the corner of his desk. 'Yeah, go for it.'

'So, first up, we've got Laura Kahn, aged twenty-three. Reported missing in 2003. She was living in Hounslow at the time.'

Boyd picked up the top printout and found himself looking at the photograph of a smiling, young, dark-haired woman.

'What made you pull her up?' he asked.

'Her mother said she had an interest in haunted houses, urban legends, visiting ruins. She was part of a forum called Undercover Explorers. People who go breaking into old, abandoned buildings to take spooky photos or "ghost-reading" measurements.' Minter shrugged. 'Scooby-Doo types.'

'Right.' Boyd looked at Laura's picture. She had a vaguely familiar look to her. Something about her eyes.

'Her mother said that Laura used to arrange trips online with other forum members and she didn't like it, because, well, they were strangers that Laura was going to meet in person in remote locations. That's any mother's nightmare, right, boss?'

Boyd nodded. 'Can we get access to the forum? Is it still running?'

Minter shook his head. 'It's a four-oh-four – that page is missing, boss,' he added, seeing Boyd's confused look.

'Right. And what about identifying features?'

'Nothing useful. No birthmarks, tattoos, scars.'

'Okay, that's not enough for a positive ID. So who else have you got?'

Minter passed him another printout. 'Chloe Hunter, aged nineteen. Reported missing 1999. She was more local. From Romney in Kent.'

Boyd looked at the photo. Another smiling face. He hated that: the pictures that heartbroken mums handed over always seemed to be ones like this. A freeze-framed moment of happiness that would inevitably be compared to a discoloured face on a slab. Chloe had thick make-up on, and purple hair. A look that used to be called 'goth' but was now – at least the last time he'd checked – 'emo'.

'Her parents said that she'd broken her left leg a few weeks before she went missing,' said Minter. 'That would show up as recently knitted bone,' he added, 'if she's one of our bodies.'

Boyd jotted it down to remind him to mention to Okeke when they were done.

'Boss,' said Minter. 'There's something else...' He flicked through some of the other printouts he'd brought over. 'Here... the investigating officer took photos of some of the things in Chloe's room: her diaries, journals, her pinboard. Take a look at this...'

He handed over a photograph of a corkboard. It was cluttered with all the things Boyd expected to see: photo-booth strips of her with a girlfriend pulling daft faces, concert-ticket stubs, essay assignment reminders, postcards, some dried flowers, drawings and doodles.

'Shit,' muttered Boyd as he stared at a scribbled image pinned to Chloe's board. He looked up at Minter. 'Why the hell didn't you give me this one first?'

38

Okeke watched as Dr Palmer made a slow and steady toe-to-head visual assessment of both bodies laid out on the two examination tables.

She had placed a Post-it note on each table: the nearest to Okeke had 'Jane Doe' scrawled on it; the furthest away said 'Judy Doe'.

'Jane looks fresher by a few years,' said Dr Palmer.

Okeke nodded. 'We found her further up the tower's stairs. So we're presuming she's the more recent of the two.'

Palmer checked her notes on an iPad. 'Ah, yes. And she came in...?'

'Last week,' Okeke said pointedly. '*Before* your Christmas party.'

Palmer looked up from her tablet, noting Okeke's tone. 'It was our annual conference.'

Okeke answered that with a sceptical bounce of her brows. 'Right.'

'And both these bodies have been underwater practically the whole time?'

'We presume so. We're running with the assumption that

the killer tucked them into holes in the wall that were just above the surface of the rising water. Places he knew would be submerged relatively soon.'

Palmer nodded. 'And they weren't sealed up in any way?'

'Not like Patricia Hemsworth, no. The first one was wrapped in a bin liner, but it was torn, so completely water-logged. The second one –' Okeke glanced at Jane – 'was just jammed into the hole.' She shrugged. 'Our man was obviously getting lazy.'

Dr Palmer bent down to look more closely at Jane's head. 'The eyes are gone, just like the girl in the bag,' she said.

'Patricia Hemsworth,' Okeke noted.

'But also I see the tip of the nose and lips have gone.'

'Is it possible rodents got to them?'

'That's what I'm thinking. I can see gnawing striations on the nasal cartilage and the flesh here along the philtrum has the same marks.' Palmer peered more closely at the empty eye sockets. 'But if you look very carefully you can see uniformly spaced striation, which suggests to me...'

'A serrated blade?' offered Okeke.

Palmer nodded. 'The eyes were popped out with a knife.' She checked her iPad again. 'Which, by the way, I also noted on Hemsworth.'

'So the same killer, then,' said Okeke.

Palmer looked up. 'Not necessarily. Same knife, though. Or rather the same *kind* of knife.'

Okeke flipped a page on her notebook, pen at the ready. 'What kind?'

'There's a thicker groove here, which suggests the handle-end of the blade grinding along the orbital ridge. Making it a very small blade. The kind you'd fold out from a penknife, I'd say.'

Okeke jotted that down. 'Could we match those striations to a make of knife?'

Palmer nodded. 'If you can provide me with a range, I can see if we get a match on one.'

Okeke's phone buzzed in her jacket pocket. She fished it out.

'Is that your squeamish DCI?' asked the pathologist. She was smiling.

Okeke grinned and answered. 'Guv?'

'Okeke, I've got a quick question for you.'

'Go on.'

'Can you ask if either of our cubbyhole bodies show signs of a recently knitted broken leg?'

'Any particular leg?' she asked.

'Left. Lower leg, shin bone, whatever that's called.'

'Tibia,' said Okeke.

'Right, well done,' Boyd said. 'You win a lollipop.'

Okeke lowered her phone. 'Dr Palmer, have you done the X-rays on these bodies yet?'

Palmer nodded. 'First thing this morning.'

'DCI Boyd wants to know if either girl showed signs of having a recently healed broken left tibia.'

Palmer picked up her iPad and swiped through several pages of details. 'Let's see...'

Okeke put the phone back to her ear. 'She's just looking that up. Why? Do we have a decent misper candidate?'

'We may do,' said Boyd. 'If there's signs of a mended shin, then almost certainly. Did I hear her say they've already X-rayed?'

'Yeah. She's checking through her slides now.'

Palmer looked up from her tablet, then turned to point at the other body behind her. 'Judy Doe,' she said. 'Left tibia, you said?'

Okeke nodded.

Palmer made a thumbs-up sign. 'There's a clear indicator of

a healing callus along her left tibia. And enough of a bump present to indicate it was a recent break.'

'Did you hear that?' said Okeke.

'Yes!' Boyd exclaimed. And hung up.

'You're welcome,' Okeke muttered to herself.

39

'Just wander in, Boyd, why don't you?'

Boyd sighed and paused just inside Sutherland's office with a folder under one arm. He reached back and rapped his knuckles on the wide-open door.

Sutherland sighed. 'Take a seat.'

Boyd sat.

'Could you shut the door first? Please?'

Boyd got up, shoved the door closed and sat back down. 'Sir, I think we've got enough now to issue an arrest warrant for Harris and have him brought down.'

Sutherland's eyes bloomed behind his Penfold glasses. 'That was quick. What have you got?'

Boyd talked through the sequence of evidence: one of the bodies had been identified as Chloe Hunter – a familial DNA swab would confirm that. Chloe had been a heavy metal fan, and Dark Harvest was one of her favourite bands. Boyd showed him the picture of the corkboard in her bedroom and pointed at a symbol that was a musical note upside down with two crossbars near the bottom.

'That's a symbol used on several of the band's album covers.'

'What does it mean?'

'Nothing, really. Warren's done some research. It's just a pretentious squiggle that Harris came up with.' He pulled out a printed image from the folder he'd brought with him and set it down on Sutherland's desk. 'This is one of the bricks that was pulled out from beside Chloe Hunter.'

The same design had been etched into the brick's side along with several others.

'Hmmm.' Sutherland stroked the tip of his nose. 'That's helpful of him.'

'Moronic... if Harris is our man. It's as good as carving *Ricky Woz 'Ere*.' Boyd cracked a tilted smile. 'Obviously the muppet thought the water was never going to go back down again.'

'Well, it's certainly interesting... if... that symbol's unique. If it's Harris's design.'

'Warren did an image search. He couldn't find it anywhere other than links that tie with the band.'

'It could have been carved by a fan?' said Sutherland.

'That's possible,' Boyd conceded. 'But we've also got Harris's DNA sitting alongside Hemsworth. The girl in the holdall.'

Sutherland nodded. 'Do you have a theory that ties Hemsworth with the other victims?'

Boyd sat back. 'Harris killed a child when he was just a young teenager – possibly with the assistance of another person. That's the unidentified DNA I'm referring to. Harris buried her in the tower's basement. Later, when he becomes successful and makes his money, he buys the tower to make sure that no one can knock it down or do it up. But... he also realises, having done that, it's a bloody good place to carry on dumping bodies.'

'You're saying you think this old rocker is a serial killer?'

Boyd shrugged. 'We've got two very plausible mispers that fit timeline-wise with Harris owning the tower. Plus, the MO also links all three.'

'Which is?'

'Their eyes were plucked out.'

'Christ.' Sutherland huffed.

'I reckon we've got enough here to make a CPS-sanctioned case. And we might be able to get him to give us something on the other DNA in the lunch box. A childhood mate? A school friend?'

Sutherland sat quietly for a moment, looking at the pictures in his hands. Finally he nodded. 'All right, then – that passes over my red line.' He smiled. 'Good work, Boyd. I'll get on to the Scottish police to arrange the warrant and they can pick him up.'

'Excellent, sir. Thanks.' He went to get up, then hesitated. 'Oh... there's something else, if you've got a moment?'

Sutherland was still smiling, which Boyd took as a yes.

'There was a case you were SIO on going back a few years.'

'How many years?'

'In 2008.'

Sutherland eyes rolled up to look at the ceiling. 'That's going back a bit.'

'Ewan Lester Jones? Do you remember that one?'

Sutherland scowled. 'I vaguely recall the name.'

'He abducted a woman from Kent. Drove her into Sussex and was almost certainly taking her somewhere to kill her and dispose of her, but he ran his van off the road into a ditch. She got away.'

The detective superintendent suddenly nodded. 'Oh, blimey, yes. I remember that. He was a bloody strange charac-ter. What do you want to know?'

'What was your take on him?'

'Complete nutter, if I recall correctly,' Sutherland replied. 'I think he was a sculptor or something?'

'An artist.'

'Oh, that's right, yes... I remember those god-awful weird paintings of his.' Sutherland's forehead rumpled with effort as he cast his mind back. 'Depressing paintings of the same depressing person again and again, I believe.'

'Did he say what drove him to abduct that woman? What his intentions were?' Boyd asked.

Sutherland frowned as he fumbled through his old career memories. 'Nothing coherent that I can recall. I mean... he was under the influence of drugs at the time he was arrested, and then later, when he'd sobered up, he was all "no comment". If I remember rightly, the defence tried to get him a softer sentence on the grounds of diminished responsibility, but the judge wasn't having any of that. And I quite agree.'

'You don't think he was mentally incap–'

'Mad? No. I think he was a sexual predator that we got lucky with and caught before he could rape and kill that poor woman.'

'But do you know why he went after that particular woman?' Boyd pressed.

Sutherland shook his head. 'Sorry, I honestly can't remember the case in great detail. It was quite a while back. Look, Boyd, what's this about? Is it linked to the Martello tower?'

Boyd shook his head. 'No, it's not related. It's just...'

'What?'

'Somebody I know... She's, well, she actually used to be married to him.'

'Good grief!'

'Yup... it's a small world.'

'Someone you know?' asked Sutherland pointedly. 'A friend? Or –'

'Just a friend.'

Boyd felt uncomfortable asking what he wanted to ask. It was a bending of the rules, but still... 'I want to interview Ewan Jones.'

'Why?'

'I need to know what was going on with him when he abducted that woman. Maybe he'll be a little more talkative now that he's done his time.'

'Why the interest?' asked Sutherland. 'If it's nothing to do with the Martello tower?'

'I need to know if Jones is still fixating on his ex-wife, my friend Charlotte.' He explained about her past with Jones and the concern she had that someone had been loitering outside her back garden.

Sutherland narrowed his eyes. 'Jones would have been psychologically evaluated before he was given parole. If he's out on licence, it's because he's been deemed a no-risk and behaved himself inside.'

'But if he's stalking her...'

'And do you know that he is?' asked Sutherland. 'Does Charlotte wish to report him? Does she have any evidence? Letters? Texts? Phone calls? Social media posts? Has he made any vocal threats?'

Boyd didn't answer; he had nothing to back up his suspicions.

'That's an uphill struggle, Boyd, without any evidence. If there's no justifiable reason for you to bring him in for interview... and then he makes a harassment complaint?' Sutherland sat forward. 'Add to that, the personal connection? It's going to look very much like you were looking to settle an old score.' Sutherland shook his head.

Boyd nodded. 'Right.'

'If she has concerns... she needs to ring 999 and report it. If she has evidence, by all means bring it to me. If she's scared, maybe she could stay with a friend for a while. But please, Boyd, don't go and do something you might regret.' Sutherland checked his watch again. 'I better get a wriggle on with this warrant if you want Harris down here.'

40

Charlotte heard Emma's bedroom door open and her light footsteps coming down the stairs and along the hall.

She got up off the sofa and followed her into the kitchen. 'Hello, Emma.'

Emma almost jumped out of her skin. 'Oh, shit! I thought you were at work!' She let out a gasp as she put the kettle on. 'You made me jump. Fancy a brew?'

'Ooh, yes. Tea, please,' Charlotte said with a smile.

'No probs.'

Charlotte watched her as she bustled around the small kitchen. 'Are you working at the hotel this afternoon?'

'Uh-huh,' she replied. 'My shift starts at four.' She pulled a couple of mugs out of the cupboard. 'So... how come you're here? Are you staying over for a while?'

Boyd and Charlotte had concocted a story that her combi-boiler had broken down and her house was without heating and hot water until a replacement valve could be fitted.

'Hopefully I can head back home tonight,' she replied. 'I do really miss sleeping in my own bed.' She watched Emma as she pulled a carton of soup out of the fridge and then went to the sink to rinse a Thermos flask. 'I hope you don't mind me asking, Emma, but why aren't you talking to your dad? He's quite upset about it, you know?'

Emma turned round. 'I presume you heard what happened?' she said, colouring slightly.

Charlotte decided to downplay what she knew. 'I heard that your dad threw some chap out.'

'By his hair,' said Emma. 'Literally... by his hair!' She shook her head, clearly struggling to make sense of it. 'I mean, that's physical assault, isn't it? By my dad? For God's sake... by my dad. The policeman!'

'Your dad's not a thug, Emma. Why would he do that, do you think? It doesn't sound like something he would do for no reason.'

Emma started to vigorously dry the flask in her hands. 'Dad walked in on us... okay? Patrick and me. He didn't knock first. Just...' She puffed her cheeks out, then blew. 'Jesus.'

'He said he heard you saying no,' replied Charlotte. 'He was worried about you.'

Emma's face flushed brightly. 'He told you, didn't he? He told you what he –'

'He told me that Patrick was hurting you. That you had bruises.'

Emma clamped her eyes shut. Mortified. 'Oh, God.'

'And he's not just a lad, is he?' added Charlotte. 'He's a bit older?'

Emma turned her back and mumbled. 'He's thirty...some-thing. So what? It's over now, anyway. He doesn't want anything to do with me.'

Charlotte could see Emma's shoulders shaking. She stepped forward, then touched her back lightly. 'Emma,' she said gently, 'I was in a relationship like that once. He was a lot older, worldly wise, charming. I fell for him completely. He was my world. And it started out so wonderfully but...' She trailed off.

Emma wiped her cheeks and turned to look back over her shoulder. 'But?'

Charlotte sighed. 'But the relationship changed over time. It became unbalanced. I became more of an object to him than a person. It wasn't nice.'

Emma turned round completely. 'You were in an abusive relationship?'

Charlotte nodded. 'A terrifying one. I ended up having to hide from him.'

'Oh, God,' replied Emma. 'I had no idea.'

'I don't know the details of what your dad saw, but he did tell me that Patrick had you by the hair...'

'It was a... a game,' Emma muttered. 'God. I can't believe we're having this conversation.' She put her face in her hands.

'Me neither.' Charlotte smiled ruefully. 'And I can't believe I'm admitting this,' she continued, 'but I know about those sort of games. I wasn't always as – how shall we say? – as prim and proper as I appear now.'

'He said it was just a bit of fun. A little role play. I'll admit I wasn't keen – but I wanted to please him.'

Charlotte tutted. 'Isn't it funny how some men confuse role play with coercion.' She reached for the kettle and snapped it off. 'If you have a man in your life who can get you to do something you don't want to in order to keep him... that's a big warning sign, Emma.'

41

Boyd looked up from his screen to see Minter, Okeke and Warren pulling on their coats and getting ready to join the general end-of-shift migration towards the double doors.

'You working late, guv?' said Okeke.

He looked at his watch. It had gone five thirty; the day had whizzed by while he'd been shuttling back and forth between his desk and Sutherland's office, assembling an evidence portfolio that ticked enough boxes for one Chief Inspector Alasdair McBain of the Western Isles force to get off his arse and mobilise a couple of plods to go and arrest Harris.

Given that the operation would be ferry-dependent, they needed the paperwork sorted today so that the detectives would be ready first thing tomorrow morning at the terminal in Mallaig to catch the damned bloody thing.

'Hopefully not too late,' he replied. 'I'm just making sure all the red tape is in place, or cut... or whatever, so we can get Harris over here ASAP.'

Okeke pulled a face. 'Good luck with that.'

Minter paused beside his desk. 'Is there anything I can do to help, boss?'

Boyd shook his head. 'No, I'm only waiting on confirmation that they're good to go tomorrow. Off you go, Derek Zoolander.' He watched the puzzlement on Minter's face slowly resolve as he and the others made their way across the main floor. Just before he disappeared through the double doors, Minter turned and stared back at Boyd, then pulled the perfect Blue Steel pout.

Boyd laughed and raised his hand in salute. Then, as the door closed behind them, he turned back to his screen. He grabbed his phone and dialled the number he'd tracked down minutes earlier.

The phone rang a couple of times before someone picked up.

'Sarah Shah speaking. Who's this?'

For a heartbeat he toyed with giving the woman a false name. But then, he figured, that was just asking for trouble down the line.

'I'm DCI Boyd, Sussex CID,' he said. 'I believe you're the supervising probation officer for Ewan Jones?'

'Yeah, he's one of mine.' She sighed wearily. 'What's he done?'

'Nothing. Yet. I only want to get your take on him.' What Boyd actually wanted was the man's address so that he could go and talk to him himself. But, as his gatekeeper, his parole supervisor was unlikely to give him that without just cause and a lot of paperwork.

'My *take* on Jones?' She drew in a long breath. 'What're you asking for exactly? Whether I think he's going to be a difficult client? The short answer is no. So far he seems to be behaving himself. Why the call?'

'Has he been following his licence conditions?' Boyd asked.

'Yes. I've got no complaints there. He's been calling in once a fortnight.'

'What about a home visit?'

'As in, have I conducted one yet?'

'Yes,' replied Boyd.

'Of course. As soon as the accommodation's arranged and they've moved in, there's one, then a follow-up visit once a month.'

'Where's his accommodation?'

'I can't give you the exact address, but it's in Dover, if that helps. That's all I can tell you.'

Boyd realised, belatedly, that he hadn't really planned this conversation out. He'd sort of hoped he could wangle the address or at the very least her take on whether Jones had been properly assessed before being let out on licence.

'And when was your last home visit?' he asked.

He heard paper rustling as Shah looked it up. 'A few weeks ago.'

'And?'

Shah sighed again. 'And what? What is this?'

'Well, I assume you look around, right? Evaluate how they're adjusting on the outside – whether they're coping. Whether they're breaching any specific licence conditions.'

'Yes, of course. There were no indicators of drug-taking or alcohol abuse. No indicators that he's broken curfew.'

'Does he have an ankle monitor?'

'That's not one of his licence conditions.'

'So he *could* have broken curfew?' Boyd pointed out.

'Yes. I suppose it is possible. But... from what I could see he's been keeping himself busy enough with his painting. To be honest, he's quite a good artist. He enjoys watching *Portrait Artist of the Year*... Said he was hoping to submit one of his self-portraits.'

'That sounds encouraging.'

'Yes. I mean... I'm not sure the show would allow an ex-con

on, but it's good that he's making plans. Finding a harmless displacement activity to fill their time is one of the biggest problems we have. It's almost impossible to find them jobs, particularly clients like Jones. Boredom's often a real problem. They have too much time to dwell on the past... It's easy to slide back into old habits.'

'But you're not seeing that with Jones?'

'No, he's been a busy little bee. His room's like a gallery, pictures plastered all over the walls. I warned him the landlord might give him some stick if he carried on using pins. He said he's switched to using Blu-Tack now,' said Shah.

'What things has he been painting?'

'Some landscapes. Nice ones, actually. I'd buy one if he wanted to sell them. I told him that... that maybe he could make money from selling his work. Perhaps set up a market stall or something. It's good to give them a goal to aim for.'

'So he's just been painting landscapes, then. Nothing else?' Boyd asked.

He heard Shah take a long drag on a vape. 'What are you... a cop or the *Guardian*'s art critic?'

He paused, wondering how much to share. 'You know what he was in for?' he said finally.

'Yes. Of course I do,' Shah replied.

'Right, well, he was fixated on a woman with a certain *look*. His ex-wife, in fact. The woman he abducted looked a lot like her. At the time he was arrested, he'd been painting multiple portraits of youngish, brown-eyed women with hazel-coloured hair.'

'I don't recall seeing any,' Shah told him. 'I can send you a picture of his room if you like.'

'Could you?'

'Uh-huh, we take them as part of the home visit. To show how they've settled in. We send them to the parole board to review.'

'That would be really helpful if you could do that,' Boyd said. 'My phone number is –'

'Email,' she cut in. 'Work email. Just in case you're some tabloid sleaze or offenders list vigilante. I mean, you don't sound like one, but...'

Fair point. He gave her his work email.

'When is he due to contact you next?' Boyd asked.

He heard rustling paper again. 'Oh, actually, he's on my visit list for tomorrow,' Shah replied.

'Okay, well, look... Can I leave you my number? Just in case there's anything you spot tomorrow.'

'You want me to call you?'

'Yes.'

'That's not really how this works.'

'Look. I know, there are proper channels, but this is a case I'd like to keep tabs on... unofficially.'

'Unofficially?' She sounded guarded.

'Please. I've read his case file. I'm no expert, granted, but Ewan Jones's mental condition on arrest and interview was largely played down at his trial. It's a just-in-case thing. Nothing more.'

Shah vaped again. 'Sure, all right. I'll take your number. I'm not saying I'll use it, and I'll want you to reply to my email to your work address first, but let's have it. What was the name again?'

'DCI Boyd.'

He heard her scribble it down, then he gave her his iPhone number rather than his work phone. She assured him she'd send the email as soon as she hung up.

He ended the call and looked up to see the first of CID's night shift had turned up. It was DI Abbott, armed with a coffee and a greasy Cornish pasty – and looking ready for a night dozing in his chair with his feet up on his desk.

42

Boyd had his coat optimistically draped over one arm as he leant into Sutherland's office. 'Is there any news back from Scotland yet?'

Sutherland looked up from his keyboard. 'Oh, yes. Yes, there is. It's a go for tomorrow. Boyd... don't tell me you were hanging around for that?'

He nodded.

'Ah, sorry. Well, yes, we're good to go.'

Boyd gave him a thumbs-up and headed off towards the double doors, muttering to himself about communication. Or lack thereof.

He hurried out of the station into the glow of the amber saturated lighting across the pool cars and parking area. It was icy cold and the rain had turned to sleet. He unlocked his Captur, climbed in and turned the engine on. The windows were fogged up and would need a few moments of the blower to clear. He looked at his phone and saw that there was a text from Charlotte.

. . .

EMMA AND I CHATTED TODAY. You should know she's okay with you. She knows why you did what you did. And I think she's grateful. But mostly she's embarrassed. That's why she's been avoiding you. I get the feeling she no longer wants to date the young man she was seeing.

BOYD TAPPED OUT A QUICK REPLY.

THANKS FOR TALKING WITH HER. I think we were both a bit embarrassed about the whole thing.

HE WONDERED if he should mention his unofficial snooping around Jones to her. So far Charlotte knew nothing about what had happened to Jones after she'd left him. She didn't know either that Boyd had seen her battered and bruised face on the one occasion she'd gone to the police about him. He wondered if he'd ever get that image out of his mind.

What she certainly didn't seem to know *anything* about was the abduction, his arrest and the fact that he'd served fourteen years at Her Majesty's pleasure. Telling her all that would undoubtedly terrify her, and if the man who'd loitered outside her back garden for a couple of nights on the go was just some crackhead, then he'd be unnecessarily waking something up that she'd worked for years to put to bed.

In any case, the talk he'd had with Jones's parole supervisor had sounded encouraging. Yes, Jones was out of the clink, but it sounded as though he might have moved on from obsessing over Charlotte. Maybe it would be better to keep quiet for now.

He tucked the phone into his jacket pocket. The windows had now cleared enough for him to make a move. He reversed out of his parking spot, drove over to the exit and out onto Bohemia Road.

As he passed the paddle pond and the crazy golf course on the seafront, both sporting forlorn Christmas lights and still open for business despite the drizzle, he felt his phone vibrate in his jacket. He resisted the urge to fish it out to see if it was Charlotte again, or Emma reaching out with an olive branch. The number of times he'd beeped at some muppet on his phone while driving and flashed his warrant card for good measure... It would make him the world's biggest hypocrite if he did the same.

He waited until he was parked up outside his house on Ashburnham Road before retrieving his phone to see who'd texted him.

It was an unknown number.

MESSAGING HERE INSTEAD of your work email. I know you're doing this 'off the books' so I'll keep it that way. Just wanted to be sure you weren't a tabloid twat. Pics to follow...

AN IMAGE PINGED up on his screen and he immediately tapped it and zoomed in. The picture showed the interior of a small hostel room. A solitary bay window fogged by a tatty net curtain gave the room a little bland grey daylight. There was a bed, a side table and a small breakfast table with one wooden chair pulled up at it. It would have been a spartan, clinical interior if it hadn't been for the drawings and paintings that crowded the walls. The breakfast table was cluttered with paints and pastels and something that looked like a work-in-progress.

In the photo, he could even see a bit of Ewan Jones himself; his knees with his hand resting on them were visible in one corner. The man was doing his best in a small space to get out of the way and was perched on the end of his bed.

Another photo pinged through. He tapped and zoomed in once again. This one showed the wall to which Jones had stuck most of his pictures – Shah clearly wanted to show the parole board that her client was keeping himself occupied.

And she'd been right: most of the pictures were landscapes – pastel, charcoal and chalk depictions of coastal scenes. He recognised the white cliffs of Dover, a lighthouse, some fishing boats drawn up on a beach, a moody wetland scene with a heavy sky – all of them what Boyd thought of as the kind of art that ends up being ignored on the wall above the fireplace of a grubby pub.

But they weren't all landscapes. His eyes were drawn to one small portrait near the edge of the photo. He zoomed in on it, but enlarged it became blocky and pixelated. He zoomed out again and took in a sharp breath.

It was Charlotte. He was sure. It was a younger version of her, though. Her face was rounder and her hair was pulled back by an Alice band. Her shoulders were narrow... It looked like Charlotte as a child.

Just then he heard a soft tapping that made him jump. He looked up to see Charlotte peering in through the passenger-side window.

'Are you all right?' she asked through the glass.

He put his phone away, opened the door and climbed out. 'Sorry, Charlotte. It's work. Even when you're off, you're not off,' he said quickly, locking the car and rounding the front.

'Mia and I were wondering whether we might be taking advantage of your hospitality...' she began. 'Maybe it's time we stopped being silly and headed back home?'

Boyd shook his head. 'You're not taking advantage, Charlotte. Stay another night.'

'I, well... That's very kind of you, Bill, but... I really need to get back to –'

He placed a hand on her arm to stop her. 'Charlotte... we need to talk.'

43

Her home was a modest one. A two-up two-down terraced house in a part of St Leonards that looked as though it had seen better days. For some reason he'd been expecting more from her, something grander.

In prison, Ewan had often speculated as to whether she'd managed to find another partner or whether she'd decided to go it alone. His instinctive guess had been that she would choose independence for the rest of her life.

He couldn't blame her for that. He'd had time to reflect on what he'd put her through all those years ago.

She'd stepped from her teenage years straight into his arms, and not long after that into a marriage. Of course she'd be single now, and, anyway, her humble little place screamed *spinster living alone*. The only thing missing were cats.

He picked his way through her front room. It was not much bigger than the cell he'd spent the last fourteen years living in. There was an armchair with a side table and lamp beside it. He could see a small stack of novels that she was working her way through concurrently. There was an open fireplace that contained a bed of ashes and charcoal. There was a rocking chair, a grandfather clock – which she must have inherited from her beloved grandparents – and a small after-thought of a TV.

It was all very old-fashioned. But that was so Charlotte. He'd met her when she was young, but she'd always seemed to have such an old soul.

He glanced at the pictures on the walls – there were none of his paintings, of course. He supposed it was hardly surprising. There were a couple of Edward Hopper prints that reflected her own preference for solitude, and a black-and-white photograph of Hastings' promenade from a grander time when gentlemen donned straw hats and women wore bonnets.

He spotted an item on the bookshelf that he recognised from their years together – a flute case. It contained the flute she'd played as a girl with dreams of joining a prestigious orchestra. The case was covered in dust. He wondered if she played it at all now or just kept it as a touchstone to her childhood. She'd rarely played it when they were together.

You never did anything much, did you?

When he'd first met her, she'd seemed like quite a handful. A bubbly girl, prone to fits of laughter and impulsive suggestions. If it hadn't been for her face – that stunning resemblance – her feisty personality might have put him off. But she soon became more manageable. Pliable even. So besotted was she with him that she quickly surrendered her old self and became the muse that he wanted. A life-like mannequin for him to pose and paint. His Pinocchio puppet, who learned very quickly – *clever girl* – that her opinions and spontaneous conversation-starters weren't required.

∾

'Bill? What is it?' asked Charlotte.

He led her into the dining room and they sat down.

'Bill?' she repeated, looking alarmed.

'Charlotte, I did some digging on Ewan Jones,' he said.

She nodded. 'I thought you might. Please don't get into trouble, Bill – it's ancient history. He –'

'You thought it might be him standing outside your garden,' he reminded her. 'So no... it's not ancient history to you, is it?'

She put her head in her hands. 'You're right. I can't lie; I still have nightmares sometimes.' She looked up at him. 'You searched him on your police computers?'

He nodded.

'Please...' Her voice faltered. 'Please tell me you found nothing.'

He was still in two minds about how much she needed to hear.

'Bill?'

He sighed wearily. 'Ewan Jones,' he began, 'went on to violently assault and abduct a woman after you escaped him. He may have been intending to kill her.'

'Oh my God...' Charlotte blanched, and her hand flew to her mouth.

'Look, I'm really sorry to have to tell you this. But we need to take him seriously and we really need to talk about him...'

EWAN JONES SPOTTED a copy of the local paper on her armchair – the *Argus*. He'd seen that paper before in his local café, lying there on a table.

And thank YOU very much. It was in that particular paper he'd glimpsed the photo of Charlotte; her face turned to look back over her shoulder at the press as she knocked on a front door. The news had been all about a train hijacking near Hastings and an off-duty police officer who'd been instrumental in bringing the incident to a close.

That eye-catching story was, of course, nothing compared to the breaking news that Charlotte was apparently alive and well, and living in Hastings.

He recalled having to sit down at the table, trembling as he stared at the grainy depiction of her face. The table was already occupied by another lonely and regular patron. Another ex-con out on licence, no doubt, trying to make his tepid coffee last the whole morning.

He remembered simply staring and staring... the paper rustling in his shaking hands, and hearing the voice for the first time in years. The voice that used to shriek and beg in his head, the voice that had quietened down during his years in prison to little more than a bedtime whisper. The voice that was now back with a vengeance.

My Lottie. My little Lottie.

'SHE *LOOKED LIKE ME*?' whispered Charlotte.

'She looked quite a lot like you, Charlotte. And he was clearly intending to kill her. He had a kit with him to...'

Charlotte felt the air in her lungs escape with a desperate whistling gasp and she struggled to pull another breath in.

'... taking her somewhere to do that, then dispose of her body.'

Some part of her understood that Bill was saying more than she was taking in right now. She was still focused on three words: *looked like you.*

'He's been in prison for the last fourteen years and was released on parole three months ago...' Bill's voice continued.

She was dimly aware that she was feeling light-headed, dizzy. She was glad to be sitting and holding the side of the table, or she might have lost her balance.

Bill was still talking. 'You told me he was obsessed with

painting you over and over? That was his thing, right? His obsession?'

She focused and nodded. 'He called her Lottie. The... girl in his head. The one he kept trying to paint.'

'And you're certain it wasn't you he was referring to?'

She shook her head. 'No. No... I thought it was me, at first. Charlotte... Lottie, right? I thought he was *idealizing* me, *romanticizing* me.'

He wasn't, though. Was he? Maybe at first he was, but then later, when he began to turn frighteningly strange and possessive, he referred to the face in those paintings as if she was someone else entirely.

'He never actually said it in so many words but he was painting someone else. Someone he called Lottie. Someone from his past.' She looked up at Boyd. 'A ghost...'

EWAN SAT down at her small round kitchen table. The room was lit by a sickly vanilla-coloured bulb that hung from the ceiling in a cream lampshade.

Just like me, Charlotte, eh?

He smiled at the thought that with every meal he'd eaten alone in his cell, she'd been doing the exact same at this stark wooden table. He wondered if she ate in silence or whether she put on Radio Three. Perhaps she listened to one of her Erik Satie LPs on the turntable in the living room, to drown out the fact that she was all alone.

He listened to the gentle rumble and tick of her boiler as the central heating came on. Then he reached over to open the fridge. Inside there was a carton of milk and a plate of leftovers. She'd obviously left in a hurry, not worrying about turning the heating down, or emptying the fridge.

He must have spooked her the other night. He'd been a

little too careless, too close to the gate, and that fucking dog of hers had gone ballistic.

Where've you fluttered to, Charlotte? Where've you flown, my little love?

He took the milk out of the fridge to make himself a cup of tea and then checked the cupboards for mugs and teabags. He filled the kettle and then wandered out into the hallway while it started to gurgle.

He tapped his bottom lip with his finger.

Where have you gone, Charlotte?

Not to her parents. She'd been smart about that the last time she'd escaped him. There had been phone calls and letters home, of course, but never an actual visit, because she knew he'd be watching their house. Her beloved grandparents were gone now, and she had no brothers or sisters...

Then a friend. It has to be.

The voice was begging him again. Echoing in the darkness of his mind.

'I WANT you to look at something,' said Boyd. He pulled his iPhone out and set it on the table. 'I had a chat with Ewan's parole supervisor this afternoon. They do home visits just to check that their clients aren't returning to their old ways. Anyway...' He thumbed the exchange he'd had with Shah onto the screen. 'They take pictures for the record... She said Ewan was keeping himself busy with his paintings.' He enlarged the image, and Charlotte craned forward to look more closely.

'They're very different to what he painted when I was with him.'

'How so?'

'Well, before they were mostly Lottie, of course. And they were usually against dark backgrounds.'

'Dark coloured?' Boyd asked.

'Mood. Colour. Composition. All of it was dark. He worked in black, white and red mostly. These...' She gently slid the zoomed-in image across the screen, studying each picture in turn. 'These are natural landscapes. The colours are a bit less stark. Look, there's some green, some yellow there... Good lord, even some flowers.'

Boyd noticed that the frantic tone in her voice was easing a little.

'The pictures he was doing right at the end, just before I got away from him, Bill, they were violent, really disturbing. These look much better.'

'Violent?'

Charlotte looked at him. 'He was painting pictures of Lottie, or me, spattered with blood. Dismembered, with facial disfigurements, with bloody eyes.' She shuddered and turned back to Boyd's phone. 'But these look much healthier. I mean, if this is a representation of what's in his head, then...'

The idyllic image of a couple of fishing boats drawn up on a beach caught her eye. She zoomed in and fumbled the phone, dropping it onto the dining table.

'Charlotte?'

'Oh, God. Oh my God, Bill.'

'What is it?'

He picked his phone up and looked at the painting. There was nothing he could see that was upsetting: just two weathered upturned hulls lying on shingle.

'It's Hastings,' she whispered. She pointed at a row of tall black huts in the background. 'The net huts. They're unique to Hastings.' She glanced at him. 'Oh God, Bill... It is him. He knows I'm here!'

∼

EWAN STOOD IN THE HALLWAY, gazing at the front door, crimson and blue light spilling through the coloured glass from the street lamp outside.

'It's okay... it's okay... I'll find her,' he muttered.

The hallway was empty except for a side table with a small lamp. He turned the lamp on and a warm pool of light illuminated a dark wooden tabletop. There was an old rotary dial phone on it. He smiled. That was Charlotte. Forever stuck in the rose-tinted bubble of her childhood.

Beside the phone was a green leather phone book. He flipped it open, wondering how many names he'd find there. He didn't think that many. This home spoke of someone who was content with her own company.

He was right. There were hardly any entries. Under 'A' in Charlotte's neat handwriting were A. Melford and AAA Taxis. Under 'B'...

Bill Boyd.

Boyd. That was a name he'd heard before. Recently too. She'd drawn a little smiley face beside his number.

Bill. Is that a friend, Charlotte? A 'special' one, perhaps?

Ewan smiled. *Boyd* – he suddenly had it. He'd read it in the same copy of the *Argus* that her picture had been in. In the same article, in fact. Boyd was the off-duty copper who'd been involved in the train incident, wasn't he?

44

The two boys sat on the roof of the tower. The wooden planks up there were thick with dried layers of seagull shit, but it gave a commanding and spectacular view of the wetlands and, further along in the distance, the campsite.

The lanky boy chose a beam of wood to sit down on. 'They built these to destroy Napoleon,' he said. 'If he was gonna invade, like.'

The posh boy sat down next to him and let the shoulder strap of his holdall slide off. 'You hungry?'

'Yeah!'

Posh unzipped the bag, pulled out his lunch box and peeled off the stiff Tupperware lid. 'My name's Ewan, by the way. What's yours?'

'Richard,' replied the lanky boy. 'But everyone calls me Ricky.'

'I've got Marmite sandwiches, an apple and some sweets.' Ewan said. 'And I managed to sneak in a couple of Dairylea triangles when my grandma wasn't looking.'

Ricky peered into the box and grinned. 'Awesome. You got the Batman one,' he said, pointing at the Pez dispenser.

Ewan fished out a sandwich for Ricky. 'So why's this place called Devil's Tower, then?'

Ricky took a hearty bite of his sandwich and talked as he chewed. 'Cos devil worshippers used to sacrifice kids here, didn't they?'

Ewan's eyes rounded. 'Seriously?'

'Oh, yeah.' Ricky nodded. 'Hundreds of 'em, down in the dungeons.'

'There's dungeons?'

'Sure. They go down really far. But it's flooded at the bottom. I reckon you'd find about a gazillion bones if you went down.' Ricky looked at him. 'D'you know, they once raised the actual devil down there?'

Ewan nibbled at his sandwich. All of a sudden he wasn't feeling quite so hungry.

'There's no such thing,' he replied.

Ricky snorted. 'No? They raised him and he ran out to sea. Left big hoof marks in the marsh.'

Ewan shook his head. 'No, I don't believe you. That's ridiculous.'

'Really?' Ricky pointed down at the swirling dips and humps of the marshland below. 'There, look... You can still see the outlines.'

Ewan craned his neck to look over the crenellated brick battlements. There were plenty of round pools below, surrounded by crests of tall grass. 'Are those his footprints?' he asked.

'Yeah.'

'He'd have to have been blimmin' huge!'

Ricky looked at him, dead serious. 'He was. I mean, he was as big as this tower.'

'Pfft,' was Ewan's reply. 'Yeah, right.' The story was sounding far too tall now, and his appetite comfortably returned. If the devil bit was rubbish, so probably was the story about a host of dead children down below them.

Ricky had finished his sandwich. 'You gonna eat that apple?'

Ewan looked down at his lunch box. 'We can share it.'

Ricky reached in and grabbed it. He took a big bite. 'When we're done, I'll show you the dungeon if you like.'

45

Boyd drove to work wondering whether it had been the right thing to do to insist that Charlotte stay at his today. Perhaps it was an overreaction on his part, but since the White Rock Theatre overlooked the beach and Ewan Jones had quite possibly taken a day trip to Hastings to draw his fishing boats, it felt like the appropriate precaution. But it had meant leaving her at his home with nothing to do and plenty to think about.

It's just for today – he'd told her. He was going to call Jones's parole officer later to see if she'd been to do her home visit and for confirmation that he was still in Dover where he should be.

Boyd parked up in the pool-car area and climbed out of his car, making a conscious effort to switch his mind to work.

He'd been copied into an email to Sutherland informing him that Ricky Harris had been arrested early this morning and was in transit down to Gatwick. Boyd decided that he'd give Minter and Warren the job of meeting and taking over custody of him. Warren would be a familiar face for Harris, and Minter's formidable build would be more than enough to convince the wheezy old rocker not to play silly buggers.

He entered the station, grabbed a coffee from the canteen on the top floor, then finally settled down at his desk and logged on to LEDS.

There was an email from a legal firm saying they'd been contacted by Harris and would be sending over a solicitor to sit in on the interview and please could he state when that was scheduled to take place. He tapped back a quick reply. It would most likely be about five, since they were mandated to allow Harris some rest time before they could begin.

Which was good. It gave Boyd time to review the information they'd gathered so far and think through his interview strategy. Harris had been pretty open with them last time, but now he was under caution, and would be accompanied by a solicitor, his responses were likely to be a blanket wall of 'no comment'.

He spotted Minter settling in at his desk.

'Morning, David Ginola.'

Minter looked up, then rolled his eyes. 'Ah, very funny, boss. I'm still not sure I've totally recovered from the *Zoolander* comment.' He frowned. 'Who's Ginola, anyway?'

'An ex-footballer with great hair. Maybe that's what the agency are after, your lovely hair?'

Minter absently raised a hand to run it through his glossy dark locks, then stopped himself. 'Ahh.'

Boyd smirked and gave him the good news that he had the job of collecting and babysitting Harris this morning. 'So you and Warren are off up to Gatwick to collect Harris. His arrival time is eleven thirty.' Boyd looked at his watch. It was 8.47 a.m. 'You'll need to leave here around nine thirty, in case the roads are busy.'

'Righto, boss, nine thirty it is,' Minter replied.

Boyd looked around the floor. 'Do you know where Okeke is?'

Minter shook his head. 'No, I've not seen her this morning.'

'Damn.' He'd wanted to speak to her about yesterday's autopsies. 'Okay. He reached for his coffee. 'Oh, Minter, just a thought. Take vest cams with you. Harris'll have already been cautioned by the Scottish police, but do it again on camera so that anything he babbles on about in the car –'

'– is fair game. Righto, boss, I'm on it.'

Boyd opened up the action log to refresh his memory on the points of the case so far. Warren's research on Dark Harvest, their lyrics, album covers, videos and the various eighties news stories about their on-tour antics were collated tidily for him to review.

He was about an hour into it when his phone rang. It was Sully.

'Morning, Boyd. We've got a surveyor called Arnold here who's waggling around a piece of paper that says he has the right to enter the tower and examine its structural integrity. He says he's been appointed by the UKMTPS to check –'

'Oh, for fuck's sake,' Boyd muttered, cutting Sully off mid-flow.

'Nicely put, Boyd,' Sully said. 'They were almost, but not quite, my first words too. We're nearly at the bottom now. There's only a few feet of water left to pump out and we've installed a whole load of tension beams to brace the walls, as well as more scaffolding on the stairs. So we don't need another Moaning Minnie down here. Personally, I'd tell him to sling his hook, but that piece of paper he has does –'

'Fine,' Boyd said, interrupting him again. 'Just a look. Let him have a quick look and don't let him bloody well touch anything.'

'I know,' Sully replied tartly, and hung up.

Boyd resumed picking his way through Warren's report. The DC had identified a number of lyrics that, in Harris's current situation, didn't look particularly good.

Little angels with their lies, little sirens without eyes.

Boyd made a mental note to present those to Harris this afternoon. Although the murders of Patricia Hemsworth, Chloe Hunter and the other unidentified body were separated by decades, they'd each had their eyes removed. If he was going to delve into cod psychology, then perhaps it said something about guilt or remorse. The dull-eyed accusatory gaze of a dead victim was a thing that killers sometimes struggled with once the red mist cleared. Most often, though, they chose to throw a rag or some clothing over the victim's face.

He reviewed the symbol that had been carved in the brick, which had also been a repeated motif for the band. It was a musical note, inverted, with two crossbars near the bottom, one wider than the other. The obvious symbology being that it was an inverted crucifix as well as a musical quaver. The Devil's Music, of course. It would have been foolhardy of Harris to carve something that was essentially his autograph on a brick near where he'd hidden a body. But then, maybe, he'd presumed it would never surface again. It was quite possibly an act of overconfidence. Or... if he believed in all this woo-woo nonsense, he might have thought it conveyed some preventative power on the body being discovered.

Boyd emerged from his action-log digging at five to one. There was a text from Minter to say that they had Harris in the car and were on their way back down to Hastings. He had also missed a call from Okeke.

He dialled her phone and she answered immediately. 'Hey, guv.'

'Where the hell are you?' he asked her.

'I'm back at Ellessey Forensics. I just wanted to check something out.'

'It would be helpful if you could let me know next time,' he grumbled.

'I know – I'm sorry, guv. It was a spur-of-the-moment thing.'

She paused, clearly goading him to ask. Boyd was keen to get back to work so he bit the bullet. 'And?'

'Since you asked so nicely – all three victims had striation marks on the bone around their orbital sockets, which indicates that their eyes were scraped out by the serrated blade of a Swiss Army penknife. That was the conclusion that Dr Palmer and I reached after we'd compared different tools and blades yesterday.'

'A Swiss Army penknife?'

'Yup. Jay's got one from the seventies, a hand-me-down. So I promised her I'd pop back with it this morning.'

'They don't have one there?'

'Not all the different models, no. Not one that dates back as far as the seventies.'

Boyd winced. 'It's not that long ago, Okeke.'

She laughed. 'Sorry. Anyway, it's a match. For all three bodies. Which at the very least strengthens the case for the same killer with the same knife and the same MO. If Harris turns out to be our man, then he'll have to answer for all of them.'

'Good job,' Boyd said. 'Was there anything else newsworthy from Dr Palmer?'

'If you're hoping for DNA from the bodies, then no. There's nothing back yet. We're still waiting.'

He sighed. A match to Harris on one or other of the bodies would clinch it for certain.

'Right, see you back at the station, then,' he said. 'Good work, Okeke.'

He hung up and rang Charlotte. He wanted to check in on her before he got bogged down in work again. He dialled the house phone and got no answer.

Fine. She's walking the dogs. She'd said she might take them up to the woods around East Hill rather than down to the beach. He tried her mobile and after a dozen rings it went to voicemail.

A queasy flutter of concern shot through him. She normally took her phone everywhere. But it was possible that, with two energetic dogs on leads and pockets full of poo bags, keys and her phone, she'd been unable to answer. He stifled the urge to drive back home and check in on her because... there was an easier way to settle his mind. One that wouldn't make it look as though he was overreacting.

He dialled Ewan Jones's parole supervisor, Sarah Shah. She'd said that he was on her house-call list today. Again, though, there was no answer. He went through to voicemail and this time decided to leave a message. 'It's DCI Boyd. I'm just checking in on your visit to see Jones. Let me know how he is after you've been, if that's okay? I just want to know... you know, he's where he should be.'

He hung up, the feeling of unease deepening. 'Fine,' he muttered to himself. He grabbed his car keys off the desk and got up.

46

Boyd drove back home along the front, frustrated by the maximum speed signs of 20 miles per hour as he approached Pelham Arcade. Really, those signs were pointless at this time of the year; there was hardly a pedestrian to be seen out there in the cold gusting wind. The Christmas lights strung over the road swung dismally on their cables, making the seafront look even more cheerless and abandoned. A half-arsed job was worse than no job at all, as far as he was concerned, when it came to window-dressing a town for Christmas.

He found himself slowing right down to study the one or two hardy fools out this afternoon. With hoods up and woolly hats on, there was little hope of identifying Jones among the passers-by.

Boyd headed inland on the Bourne, then swung a right up the final steep hill of Ashburnham Road and parked his car outside his house.

Usually the unique sound of his Captur's engine would trigger the appearance of a wet brown nose pushed against the window blowing twin circles of steam onto the glass. But not this afternoon. There was no sign of Ozzie.

The sense of foreboding that had been troubling Boyd at work and followed him home now intensified. He got out of the car and walked cautiously up the path to his front door.

It was ajar.

Conventional wisdom would dictate he was *not* to assume the worst. But then conventional folks didn't have a human ear sitting in their safe or suffer from frequent nightmares about their decapitated son and dying wife.

Boyd gently pushed the front door inwards and stepped into the porch, one hand reaching for the walking stick leaning against the rack of wellies. It was a worn and bleached branch that he'd picked up on a walk with Ozzie. It had a pleasing smooth, large pommel of wood at the top that made him feel like Gandalf the Grey. He turned it round so that the weighty knuckle of wood was at the far end.

He stepped forward into the hall and crept past the open door on the left that lead into his study. The bottom of the stairs was ahead, the door to the lounge to his right. The hall leading to the dining room was around the corner. Another two steps forward and he'd have to look in three different directions all at once.

Be ready, Bill, a soft voice cautioned him. He tightened his grip, then quickly stepped forward. He glanced up the stairs – nothing. He peeked quickly into the lounge – it was empty. Then turned the corner, looked down the hall... and let out a long, slow wheeze of air.

He could see Charlotte through the dining-room window. She was out in the back garden hosing down both muddy dogs. She must have thought she'd closed the door properly. Sometimes the latch was lazy and it needed a good slam to engage properly.

He shook his head, almost in a state of collapse as he

returned to the porch and put the stick back. He pushed the front door firmly shut and announced loudly that he was home. A moment later, both dogs nails skittered across the wooden floor as they raced each other up the hallway to greet him.

'Where's your mummy?' he asked Mia.

'I'm her mummy, am I?' Charlotte said, appearing in the dining-room doorway. She smiled. 'What're you doing home so early?'

'I'm just back for lunch,' he replied. 'The canteen's offerings are bloody awful today.'

47

Sully was rather impressed that the surveyor had thought ahead and brought his own waders with him. The depth of the water in the flooded basement was now only about two or three feet, depending on where one stood on the undulating floor. Gavin Marchant had pulled up his hose and departed earlier that day, keen to make a swift exit from this particular job.

Sully had bristled at first when the surveyor – James Arnold – had pushed his way past the tape, waggling his piece of paper around and claiming he had some obscure parochial authority to invade the hallowed space of a crime scene. But, after talking him through the dos and don'ts and then discovering he was a passionate historical re-enactor who specialised in the English Civil War and the Napoleonic era, Sully was beginning to warm to him.

Re-enacting – or, as Boyd and his uncultured merry band would undoubtedly call it, 'playing soldiers' – was an interest that Sully had been courting in recent years. Particularly musket-era history. All that powder smoke and the smell of cordite, the odour of wood smoke and saddle wax from their historically accurate campsites... it was marvellous stuff.

Arnold panned his torch along the walls and then upwards towards the fragmented floorboards above them. 'Yes... you can see some historic bowing of the walls,' he said, 'and that would have happened back when this fort was actually being used. They obviously built this one on ground that they didn't think was going to give.' He looked at Sully. 'They panic-built a lot of these thinking Old Bony was massing his ships to invade, you know?'

'Oh, I do,' said Sully.

Arnold shone his torch along the beams of wood supporting the floor above. 'The presence of water down here all this time has effectively equalised the pressure against the brickwork, otherwise those support beams would have come down long ago. Essentially, being flooded has helped preserve this place.'

'As you can see, we've put up support beams and some scaffolding to –'

Arnold shook his head. 'It's fine as a short-term measure, but, honestly, Stephen Knight is quite correct: this whole void needs filling with concrete as soon as possible.'

The surveyor waded across the uneven floor to get a closer look at the wall on the other side. He stumbled and almost went over into the water. 'Bugger!'

'Ughh... I've got some water down inside my... uhh... It's freezing!' He reached down into the water to see what he'd stepped on. 'I tripped on a bloody basket or something.'

He lifted the something partially out of the water, panned his torch across it and dropped it like a hot stone and recoiled several steps. 'Oh, good God!' he exclaimed. 'Was that a ribcage?!'

48

Boyd hit the record button. 'Interview date: Tuesday, December the fifteenth. The time is 5 p.m. Present in the room are DCI Boyd and DC Warren, the interview subject Ricky Harris and his solicitor...'

'Jason Pinner,' the solicitor supplied.

Boyd settled his notes on the table in front of him, keeping them face down for the moment. 'Hello again, Ricky,' he said. 'Good journey down?'

Ricky Harris stared sullenly back at him. 'Go fuck yourself, Boyd.'

Boyd smiled. 'Well, that's a better start than "no comment", at least.' He picked up the page of question prompts that he'd prepared earlier. 'Right then, let's see if we can take the direct route and save ourselves a lot of time, shall we?' he began. 'Were you, Ricky Harris, involved in the murder of Patricia S. Hemsworth on July the twenty-seventh, 1971?'

Pinner leant in to advise Harris to give a 'no comment' but Harris shook his head. 'I'm not doing no comments, because I've got nothin' to fuckin' hide. The answer is *no*! I wasn't.'

'Were you present at the Martello tower, known as Devil's Tower on that date?'

Pinner leant in again and Harris snapped. 'Just leave it, man! I'm fuckin' fine!' He turned back to Boyd. 'No. I've never even visited the bloody place. I told you that when you were sat drinking tea in my home not so long ago.'

'But you were aware of the tower? Even as a boy?' Boyd continued.

Harris nodded. 'I told you that already too. All the kids in the area knew about the place and the ghost stories that went with it.'

'And what stories were those?' Boyd asked.

'Rituals, child sacrifices, raising devils.' Harris smirked. 'It was all good stuff. Great material.'

'Inspiration for your heavy metal career, eh?'

Harris nodded. 'Of course. Gruesome sacrifices and satanic rituals… It's all bread and gravy for album sales, man.'

'So, in 1989 you bought this tower that you'd never seen before and never visited?' Boyd continued.

'Yes. Like I said.'

'Why did you do that?'

Harris sighed. 'We've done this all before, man.'

'Not under caution,' replied Boyd. 'So…'

'I thought it would be cool as a recording studio. Turned out to be a big fuckin' mistake because a bunch of local arseholes called the Martello Protection Society or whatever and their arsehole-in-chief Stephen Knight said I couldn't do a fucking thing to it. All right?'

'So you had no use for it, then?'

Harris shook his head. 'Nope.'

'Did you try to sell it?'

Harris shrugged. 'Half-heartedly. I mean I wasn't out there going door-to-door, but yeah… If I couldn't do anything with it, I didn't want it any more.'

'But it took you thirty years to find a buyer?'

'Sure.'

Boyd looked down at the notes he'd made this morning. 'Stephen Knight claims he made repeated offers to you over the years to buy it.'

'Yeah. But they were shitty little offers. I was holding out for a decent one.'

'Even though no one else was interested? Even though no one else made any offers? Even though you've admitted you've needed money in recent years?'

'Yeah. So what?'

Boyd was becoming more than a little irritated with his arsey manner. Maybe it was time to give Harris a little shake.

'Ricky, let me put it to you that you bought the tower simply to prevent anyone else from buying it at a later date and either restoring it or developing it.'

'And why the fuck would I do that?' Harris scoffed.

'To keep anyone from finding the body of Patricia Hemsworth and whoever else you'd dumped there.'

'What?! Who the fuck is Patsie Whatever?' His solicitor leant over and whispered into his ear. Harris nodded and said, 'No comment.'

Boyd nodded subtly at Warren to go ahead with his list of questions – which were more of a deep dive into the meanings of his lyrics and the inverted musical-note symbol included on all Bad Harvest's album covers. Harris seemed happy to follow the interview in that direction for a while. He seemed more than a little flattered that someone as young as Warren had taken the time to sift through his old songs to cherry-pick lyrics to cross-examine.

Boyd let them run with it for about ten minutes. Harris's guard seemed to be gradually dropping and he was starting to become more talkative again. Boyd decided to step back in and shake Harris's cage again with the forensic evidence.

'Ricky...' he said. 'We know that you visited the tower; more to the point you visited the tower on the same day that Patricia Hemsworth went missing.' He let that hang in the air for a moment, hoping that Harris might step out of his safe space to ask how they might know that.

He didn't.

'Ricky Harris, your DNA is present on items found alongside her body.'

There was a momentary flicker of a reaction on his face – there one second, smothered the next with an expression of heavy-lidded boredom.

'Can you explain that?' Boyd asked.

'No comment,' he mumbled.

'There was your DNA and there was also someone else's DNA. Come on, Ricky, who were you there with?'

'No comment.'

'See –' Boyd leant forward on his elbows – 'there's an opportunity for you to help us here. To help bring some closure to this. And that's something that could well be taken into consideration on sentencing... Come on. Who was with you that day? Another kid? A school friend maybe?'

'No comment.'

'Was it a game that went too far?'

'I said no comment.'

His solicitor reached for his arm. 'My client refuses to comment.'

Boyd was tempted to bring in the other confirmed body: Chloe Hunter. But until they had DNA evidence from Ellessey to confirm a link to Harris, even though there were MO similarities, he had to keep that powder dry.

'All right,' he said finally. 'I'm suspending the interview for now. The time is 5.26 p.m.'

Warren hit the stop button while Boyd gathered up his notes.

'We'll pick this up tomorrow, then,' said Boyd.

'What time?' asked Pinner.

'I'll let you know.'

Boyd watched as the custody officer walked Harris out of the interview room. Pinner put his notepad into his briefcase, nodded to the detectives and left too.

'And it started out so well,' Boyd said to Warren. 'Hopefully Ellessey will come through with the DNA forensics tomorrow, in which case who knows? He might roll over and give us a name for the other profile.'

Boyd's phone buzzed. He pulled it out and saw that it was Sully calling him. 'How's things over at Faulty Tow–?'

'Boyd,' Sully blurted out. 'I think I've just discovered where that spare humerus came from.'

BOYD CALLED Charlotte as Minter drove the pool car through the rush-hour traffic on London Road: a stop-start stream of brake lights and headlights that caught swirling clouds of exhaust in their glare.

'Hello there,' she answered cheerfully.

'I may be a bit late coming back tonight; we've had a sudden new development on the case,' he said.

'All right,' she replied. 'I thought I'd have a little dig around in your underwhelming kitchen and I've decided to make a casserole. It will keep until you get back. Now, before you go, I have an important question... Are you a dumpling man?'

Boyd, suddenly starving, inwardly cursed this bloody job. 'Dumplings? Love them.' He glared at Minter, who had let out a hastily stifled laugh.

'Good,' Charlotte replied. 'Will you text me when you're on the way back? I'll have dinner ready for you when you get in.'

'Will do. Thanks.' He hung up.

Minter turned to look at him. 'Was that your lady friend from the party asking if you wanted her dumplings, boss?' He laughed. 'Now, what's her name?'

Boyd smiled. 'Charlotte.'

'Yes, that's it.' He overtook a Tesco's home-delivery truck. 'That getting a bit more serious, is it?'

'She's just a friend. Just a friend,' Boyd repeated. He looked out at the darkening sky. It was five o'clock and the last vestige of grey daylight was lingering still. 'Her central heating's packed up. So she's sofa-surfing at mine until she can get it fixed.'

'Bloody nightmare getting a boiler man out these days, eh?'

He couldn't tell if Minter was making conversation or fishing.

'I've heard it can take weeks to get someone out,' Minter said, glancing over at Boyd. 'So how long is she staying, boss?'

Boyd nodded. *Fishing.*

'The way it's going, she'll probably still be here for Christmas.' *Hopefully*, he added silently.

Minter gave him a conspiratorial wink. 'Good on you, boss.'

They arrived at the tower just before six. The pool car's headlights picked out Sully emerging from the tower entrance with a blue body bag, carrying it in his arms like a child.

'So now we have four,' said Minter, as he pulled up beside Sully's van.

'Well, we had four anyway,' said Boyd. 'I think someone would know if they'd lost an arm.' He climbed out of the car. 'Sully.'

'Boyd,' he replied, as he set the body bag down in the back of his van. 'This one was right at the bottom.'

'You can walk on the bottom now?' Boyd asked.

'With waders, yes.'

Boyd noted the other vehicle and the man doubled over beside it. 'That, I presume, is the surveyor?'

Sully nodded. 'Poor chap left most of his lunch down there. Completely compromised the crime scene,' he said, chuckling to himself.

'How much of the body have you got?'

'Most of it,' Sully replied. 'I'll need to bring my team in tomorrow to do a proper fingertip search across the bottom.'

'And after that you'll be happy to hand the tower back to the owner?'

Sully nodded. Then, turning to face Minter: 'Hello there, gorgeous. When's the *Vanity Fair* shoot?'

49

Charlotte looked down at both dogs. They were watching her slice the carrots into batons like a pair of eager sous chefs learning from a Michelin master.

'Oh, I see,' she said. 'I have your full attention now, do I?' She looked down at Ozzie. 'Does Daddy do carrots with you too?'

She held out a freshly cut baton for him and it vanished in a blur without touching the sides. 'Clearly he does.' She held out another one for Mia, who, more demurely, took it lightly from her hand as if it was delicately made sushi.

It felt odd. Nice... but so strange to be making a meal in Bill's kitchen. She felt like an imposter, as though she was indulging in a peculiar role-playing game. A small girl once again playing house, making a meal from Lego bricks on a cardboard-box cooker. She shook her head and smiled at the childhood memory.

You're fifty-five, Charlotte... You should be looking down at your own granddaughter playing little chef by now. Of course, *that* was never going to happen, not from her family line anyway. But perhaps there might be an outside chance of being grandma to somebody else's children one day? If she could let someone else in, that was.

She tutted at her own coded language. *Someone else?*

'Let's be honest,' she explained aloud to the dogs, 'he's years younger and worn a lot better than me, I feel.' She shook her head as she chided herself for previously having told Boyd she was fifty. She really had no clue why she'd done that; perhaps she'd been trying to claim back some of the years she'd lost to Ewan.

Both dogs cocked their heads, as if looking at her knowingly.

'Oh, you disagree?' She added the sliced carrots to the casserole dish. 'Well, that's very generous of you, but I think I might be fooling myself here. I think I might have been – what's the expression the kids use? Friend-zoned?'

Ozzie barked.

'Oooh, need to go out?' She opened the back door and shooed both dogs into the garden before closing it behind them.

More and more in recent months she'd found herself entertaining fantasy vignettes: her and Bill curled up together on a sofa, a book in one hand, a hot chocolate in the other; improbable journeys in a battered old VW camper van, dogs in the back and an empty road ahead of them, on their way down to the south of France... that sort of thing.

'God help me,' she muttered. 'I'm turning into Shirley Valentine.'

The doorbell triggered a little old-fashioned copper bell high up on the kitchen wall – a lingering vestige from the days when Bill's house had been a Victorian girls' school.

She realised it was probably Emma. She'd said she was due back this evening and had probably forgotten her keys.

Charlotte smiled, pleased with herself that Bill's daughter was coming home to the smells and bubbling sounds of dinner on the go. She was well aware that Emma was, to some degree, the gatekeeper to her father's heart. If something akin to a romance ever did blossom between them, she was certain it would require Emma's blessing to work.

She went down the hallway, wondering how to greet Emma this evening... 'I've got a casserole on the go for your dad... Can I tempt you?'

No. It's Emma's home too, don't forget.

'I hope you don't mind my fumbling around in the kitchen... I thought I'd whip something up for dinner.' That sounded better.

She flicked on the light in the porch so that they wouldn't trip over each other in the dark, then pulled the door open.

'Hey there, Emma... I hope –'

For a frozen second she didn't recognise the man. For a heartbeat, it could have been an Amazon delivery driver, a neighbour of Bill's, a colleague.

'Hello, Charlotte,' said Ewan Jones.

Before she could slam the door in his face, his foot was wedged in the gap and the heavy wooden front door juddered uselessly against it. He shoved it inwards and stepped inside, quickly, then calmly shut it behind him.

'It's been a long time,' he said softly. 'I've missed you.'

Charlotte backed down the hallway. 'Get out!' she cried. Then more forcefully: 'GET OUT!'

Ewan shook his head. 'Why would I go when it's taken me all these years to find you again?'

Apart from the fact that he'd aged noticeably, this could have been a badly stitched together continuation of the very last time she'd laid eyes on him.

She knew everything she needed to know about him from their time together: that he was capable of violence, that he was dangerously unwell, and that in the last seventeen years he'd done far worse things than he'd done even to her.

'Ewan... please...' She tried a more reasonable-sounding tone. 'Leave me alone. It's over.'

'It's over when we're dead and gone,' he whispered.

Charlotte turned and ran, assessing her route as she did so. Right was for the lounge – a dead end. On the left was the dining room. Another dead end given that the back door was shut, and there was no way out of the garden anyway.

She reached for the stair rail and scrambled up the first few steps, expecting him to leap on her back at any moment.

'Stupid bitch!' he snarled.

She'd made it halfway up the staircase before she felt his vice-like grip around her ankle and lost her balance. He was on top of her a second later; his full weight was on her back. She felt his hot breath on her cheek and the bristles of his unshaven chin scratching the lobe of her left ear as he whispered hoarsely, 'I've waited far too long for this.'

She desperately attempted to elbow his face, but he pulled his head back.

'Oh, you've grown rebellious,' he said, chuckling darkly. 'Right then... you silly bitch, you're coming with me.'

50

'All right, then,' said Boyd, clapping his hands together. 'There's no point us all standing around out here in the bloody cold. There's nothing more we can do until tomorrow.'

Sully slammed the rear door of his van shut. 'I'll have my team out here first thing in the morning.'

'Hold on,' Boyd replied. 'Shouldn't we get the pumping chap?' He looked at Minter. 'What's his name?'

'It's Gavin... something, boss.'

The rest of the name came back to Boyd. 'Gavin Merchant, that's it. Yes, shouldn't we get him back here first thing tomorrow morning to pump it *completely* dry first?'

Mr Arnold, the surveyor, had recovered his composure and joined them. 'You won't ever get it completely dry,' he said. 'The water will just keep coming in.'

'Well, we can get it down to just a few inches, can't we? Surely you'll need to see the bottom to do a fingertip search, Sully?'

'We can set up a grid pattern and feel our way,' Sully replied. 'It really won't take too long.'

'All the same, I want the water down as low as he can keep it with his pump going. Once we're finished with the searches, Mr Knight can have it back.' Boyd looked at the surveyor. 'Do you want us to remove the scaffolding and tension bars before you —'

'There's no need,' said Arnold quickly. 'Concrete mix can be poured straight in around it all. It'll be fine.'

'Fair enough.' Boyd checked his watch. It was quarter to six. He pulled his phone out and dialled Okeke.

OKEKE DRAINED her coffee and set the mug down on her desk. 'The thing is, Warren... he's a cocky little arse. He'll fit right in with Flack's team, I'm sure. Those cowboys all seem to think they're in an episode of *Breaking Bad*.'

Warren shrugged. 'I bet O'Neal ends up getting DS before me, though.'

Okeke pulled her coat off her desk. 'Rosper is one big resource drain, and it's achieving piss-all as far as I can see. If you're concerned about building up your performance record, then rapid case turnover's the way. But,' she scoffed, 'you've been a DC for, what, all of five minutes...'

Warren was looking down at the penknife that had been hidden under her coat. 'You brought a knife into work?'

'Yeah,' she replied, waggling her head with sass. 'For close encounters with dumbass scrotes.' She picked it up. 'I took it into Ellessey to compare the bone scrape marks around the orbital sockets. It's a Swiss Army knife, model seventy. The first model to have one of these.' She pulled out the short, serrated blade. 'It's a match to the grooves,' she said, miming how the killer would have scraped it around the eye socket like a spoon around a yoghurt pot. 'You need to sever the soft tissue before you can pop out the eyeball.'

'Oh, right.' Warren tried not to grimace. 'An *exact* match?'

She nodded and folded the blade back in. 'Uh-huh.' She held out the knife handle for him to see the whole thing. 'Here's an interesting fact: apparently this was the only Swiss Army model to have a *white* grip texture on the handle. It wasn't a great success. They went back to the normal smooth red handle afterwards.'

She could see Warren's interest waning and set the knife back down on her desk.

Her phone buzzed. 'I'm coming, Jay, I'm coming,' she muttered, then saw it was Boyd. 'Guv?'

'You still at work?' he asked.

'Err...' She was almost tempted to say she was on her way home. 'Yeah, I'm still here.'

'Great. Can you get on to Gavin Merchant, the pump guy? His number will be in the action log. We need him back in tomorrow morning as early as he can make it.'

'Right,' she said with a sigh, wondering why he'd dialled her number and not Warren's. 'I heard something about another body?'

'We've got the rest of the bones that go with our humerus, by the look of it.'

'Always good to have the complete set,' she replied helpfully.

'We're going to do an all-hands fingertip search across the bottom tomorrow. Tell Warren to bring his wellies.'

'Will do.' She hung up and looked at Warren. 'Wellies tomorrow.'

51

Charlotte tried not to look too closely at the glinting blade of the kitchen knife. Half an hour ago it had been slicing carrots; now it was hovering close to her neck.

'Keep your eyes on the road, Charlotte,' said Ewan.

'I haven't driven in years,' she said shakily.

'And you weren't that good back in the day, were you?' He shook his head. 'Pathetic really...'

She nodded. *Keep him calm.*

'Where are...'

'Where are we going?' he finished, in a mock whiny voice.

She nodded again.

'Don't worry your pretty little head about that,' he replied. 'I'll do the thinking.'

They were heading north out of Hastings; the traffic was moving more easily than she'd have liked. 'Ewan...' she began, uncertain which line to take. Plead with him? Reason with him? Argue?

'You don't need to talk, Charlotte. Just drive. There's a good girl.'

You have to get him to talk. You have to!

'Ewan...' she began again. 'I know you were going through something back then. I know I could have been more –'

'Shut up,' he snapped.

She glanced at him. 'But you were starting to frighten me.'

'Oh dear,' he said, chuckling. 'You were a bit of a mouse in those days, weren't you? Everything frightened you.'

'No,' she replied. 'Not everything. It was just *you*.'

'Ooh, defiance?' He grinned. 'That's new. I like it!'

'I've grown up, Ewan. I'm not your child bride any more.'

He laughed. 'Oh, but you were, weren't you? So young and naive. A little starstruck too, if I recall.'

She had been, of course she had. His face had been in several newspapers, his artwork hung in galleries in London and New York. And, yes, he'd been dashing, glamorous, worldly: the 'rock star of oil on canvas' a Sunday paper had once dubbed him.

'I left you because... because you were *scaring me*. There was no one else –'

'I don't fucking care if there was anyone else or not!' he snarled. He pushed the tip of the blade into the soft skin at the corner of her jaw. 'You're nothing to me, you stupid bitch! You weren't then and you're even less so now!'

They were on the outskirts of town, out of the regular amber street lights and into periodic beats of darkness and light.

'Turn right at that junction,' he said.

She did as she was told. A signpost pointed towards the A28. They were heading east.

'You know, Charlotte, you were just a meat mannequin for me to pose and paint; that's all you were. Nothing more.'

She knew she had to keep him talking. 'So why did you pick me? Why did you marry me then?'

He made a long sucking sound with his teeth. She heard

something wet rattle in his mouth. Dentures perhaps. He'd never been great with his teeth.

'I liked your look,' he replied after a while. He turned to her. 'I liked your eyes.'

52

B oyd let Minter drive back to Hastings. The Welshman grumbled all the way along the road from Rye as they crawled home at the rear of a long train of vehicles that had built up behind a truck carrying a holiday trailer.

Boyd thought it best to let Charlotte know he was going to be delayed by a slow-going wide load. He called the house line and let it ring only a few times before trying her mobile. It rang until it switched to voicemail, once again.

'Hi there, Bill here. Just to let you know my ETA is looking like it's going to be seven thirty, maybe quarter to eight. Hope those dumplings are juicy and plump.'

He hung up and tucked the phone back into his jacket pocket.

'Oh, dear, dear, dear,' said Minter with a grin on his face.

'Please,' Boyd replied, rolling his eyes. 'You're better than that, right?'

'It's not just the dumplings, boss...'

'Then what?'

'It's *Bill* now, is it?'

Boyd shook his head as Minter laughed. He was saved from

explaining himself further by the phone buzzing in his pocket. He pulled it out, expecting to see Charlotte's name, but it was the parole officer Sarah Shah.

'DCI Boyd,' he answered.

'You asked me to call you if Ewan Jones broke his parole conditions? Well, he just has,' she said flatly.

'What's he done?' Boyd asked.

'I went around for a home visit earlier today. There was no answer. I tried again just now and, the long and short of it is, it looks like he's done a runner,' she replied.

'Today?'

'None of the hostel residents have seen him for nearly a week.'

'But you said...'

'That he's required to call in. Which he has been doing. But obviously he's not been calling in from home.'

'Shit,' muttered Boyd.

'There's something else... One of his neighbours reported their vehicle as stolen a few days ago. Unless I'm adding two and two and getting five, that could well be him.'

'Have you gained entry to his room?' Boyd asked urgently.

'I'm just waiting to... I have to have a police officer with me before I can go barging in.'

'Call me back if he's there,' he said, and hung up.

'Problems, boss?' asked Minter.

Boyd redialled Charlotte's mobile number, but it went straight to voicemail again. 'Charlotte, it's Bill. Call me as soon as you get this message. It's urgent!' He hung up.

'What's going on?' Minter asked.

Shit. Shit.

He explained the basics to Minter and picked up his phone again.

'We should probably get a patrol car around to your place, boss.'

'What do you think I'm doing?' Boyd snapped.

~

CHARLOTTE HAD HOPED for a chance to escape the car as they drove through the village of Camber. Ahead of them had been a pedestrian crossing outside a Premier off-licence and as they'd approached she'd prayed there'd be someone waiting to cross, forcing the traffic lights to red and thus giving her a chance to brake and scramble out. But the lights remained green and a few moments later they were back in dark countryside once again, heading along country roads flanked on either side by skeletal trees and leaf-choked ditches.

They drove in silence. Charlotte had noticed a sign for Dungeness. If they kept going in this direction, they'd be in Kent soon.

She finally mustered enough courage to try again. 'Ewan,' she said. She'd already squandered too much of the drive in silence. 'Whatever you're thinking of doing...'

Keep your voice even. Calm. Firm... and keep talking, dammit.

'... we can change whatever that plan is.'

'What makes you think I have a plan?' Ewan replied. 'I'm just doing what she tells me.'

'She?' Charlotte was almost too afraid to mention the name. 'Lottie?'

He looked at her. 'You never really did understand, did you?'

'Could you explain it to me?'

He huffed out a breath. 'There were three of us in that marriage.'

She thought about that. He'd been fixated on a girl that he'd kept painting. A girl who looked very similar to her. He'd given a name that she'd initially thought was a pet name for her. Charlotte had believed that she'd posed and modelled for an artist who'd started out creating an idealised version of her... which had somehow become quite real in Ewan's troubled mind. A doppelganger. A twin. So, yes, in a sense... there had been three of them.

'Lottie's just an idea, Ewan,' she whispered. 'She's just a figment.'

He shook his head. 'She's real. She's real. And she's so fucking angry.' His voice rose in pitch to a child-like whine. 'I'm sorry! I'm sorry! I'm so sorry!' he cried.

Charlotte was almost certain he wasn't directing that at her.

'Ewan,' she said softly. 'We can work this out. We can get you help.'

He turned to look at her. 'No one's helped so far!' he snapped. 'Nobody fucking can! Don't you get it, you stupid bitch? I'm alone with this. It's my fault. My fault. My guilt! I've been trying to make it right again, all my fucking life!'

53

M inter growled at the slow-moving traffic. 'Want me to put on the blues-and-twos, boss?'

Boyd shook his head. 'And go where?' he replied grimly. 'If everything's okay, then it's fine, but if Jones has done anything, then the patrol car will be there in a minute.' His stomach dropped. Voicing the options out loud felt like... making them real. 'We need to know if he's in his room first. Alive or dead.'

He tried to calm his mind. If Jones *had* grabbed Charlotte, then the first useful thing to know would be the registration of the stolen car so that he could put an all-points out on it. If Jones had taken her, presumably he'd take her to familiar ground.

Which was where? Not where he'd recently been put up. To Jones that would be a random room in a random town. It would have to be a place he'd lived, spent time. A fairly isolated place where he felt confident. Boyd ground his teeth with frustration. He wished the bloody patrol-car plods would hurry up and confirm that Charlotte was safe at home... or not. He kept checking his phone, waiting on Jones's parole officer to let him know whether Jones was in his room. The lack of response was killing him.

He picked up his phone to call Okeke. She was still at work, with LEDS at her fingertips. She could dig out Jones's file and give him a list of possible locales where Jones might head. He was about to tap her name in his recents list when his phone buzzed.

'Shah?' he answered.

'Yes, we're in.'

'And?'

'He's not here. Which means he's in breach of his parole conditions.'

The bastard's arrestable. 'Right. Can I talk to the police officer with you?'

'Sure.' Boyd could hear the rustle of the phone being handed over and the clipped chatter of radio traffic in the background.

'Who's this?' asked a male voice.

'DCI Boyd, Sussex CID. Who am I speaking to?'

'PC Ben Lloyd.'

'Listen, Ben, I need a reg number for the car that was reported stolen outside Jones's hostel. The parole officer said there was a report of a TWOC in the last few days.'

'Right, sir. Let me just call it in and –'

Boyd's phone beeped. There was another call coming in. *Shit.*

'Ben? Call me back on this number when you've got it, all right?'

'Yes, sir.'

He ended the call and found himself speaking to another uniformed officer: 'Sir, this is PS Chaffey. I'm inside your house. The front door was open. No sign of a forced entry but your dogs are shut outside in the back garden...'

Boyd could hear them both barking and yipping desperately.

'There's no one in the property, sir, but there are clear signs of a struggle...'

Keep your cool, whispered Julia. *If he's taken her, she needs you thinking clever.*

Boyd fought to stay calm. 'Chaffey, there's been an abduction. The victim is called Charlotte Bellefois; she's female, white and fifty-five years old. The suspect is her ex-husband, Ewan Jones, white, sixty-two years old. The suspect has previous for violent assault, abduction and attempted murder. They'll almost certainly be in a stolen vehicle; I'm waiting on the details of that now...'

'Right, sir.'

'I want you to search the house again. Just make sure she's gone... and...'

Think clever, Bill.

'... look for any indication of *where* he's taken her. Get a patrol car to her home too.' He gave the officer her address. 'I'm somewhere out near Rye, but my colleague DC Okeke is at the station. She's your point of contact for any news. Have you got that?'

'Yes, sir.'

Boyd ended the call and dialled Okeke.

'Guv?'

'Charlotte's been abducted. Her bastard of an ex-husband got into my house and grabbed her!'

'What? Ohmygod, what the actual –' she rasped. 'Guv? Abducted? Are you sure?'

'His name's Ewan Jones. Pull him up on LEDS; he's a fucking nutter.' He immediately heard the clatter of her nails on a keyboard. 'He's got previous for abduction, violence, attempted murder and he's been trying to find Charlotte for years.'

"It's up,' said Okeke. 'Ewan Lester Jones, sixty-two. Paroled a few months ago.'

'That's him. There are boots on the ground at mine and boots heading over to her place. Call Control and get this fucking elevated. Please. She's almost certainly with him in a stolen car –'

'You got a reg?' Okeke asked.

'I'm waiting on it. Look, you're my point of contact. Minter and I are stuck in the middle of the bloody countryside with no idea which way to head. You're –'

'I'm on this, guv. Just –'

'Don't tell me to stay calm. I *am* fucking calm!'

'I was going to say just sit tight,' she said. 'We'll find her. Who's getting the registration number?'

'It was a TWOC reported in Dover a few days ago.' Boyd fumbled in his mind for the address. Dammit. The street name was all he bloody needed. Something like Mullerton, Fullington...

'Bullenden Avenue?' said Okeke.

'Yes! That's the one.'

'Silver Peugeot 206. Registration FP79 FDV. I'll call that into Control. All-points warning'

'Thanks.' He hung up and looked at Minter. 'She only told me about all this a couple days ago. She's...' He shook his head. 'She was married to a bloke who –' His phone buzzed again. 'Sorry, got another call.'

It was Shah.

'Yes?'

'This is PC Ben Lloyd, sir. I've got the vehicle details –'

'So have I. I need you to put out an APW across your force. Tell Control the contact point is Sussex Police, Hastings CID, DC Okeke.'

'O-Car...? How's that spelled?'

Fuck's sake.

'O-K-E-K-E. There are two adults in the car: one male, white, sixty-two. One female, white, fifty-five. The woman has been abducted and is at extreme risk of violence or murder.'

54

The twin headlights of the Peugeot picked out the low humps of a grass verge either side of a single-lane road that was riddled with potholes. Beyond the verges she could see nothing but black. It was as if all that existed was this one winding road taking them into an endless dark void.

Charlotte's mind rattled through branches of possibilities – if she slammed on the brakes, would she be able to get out of the car before he rammed that knife into her neck? If she got out, did she stand a chance of outrunning him? If she screamed for help... was anyone going to hear her? Was compliance her only survival option? Should she let him do what he wanted to do and hope that being cooperative would buy her more time and the chance to escape? Was he going to kill her? Would he kill himself? Was that what he'd meant by 'making things right'?

'Ewan, p-please... talk to me,' she pleaded. 'Who is she? Who is Lottie?'

Ewan began to rock in his seat. 'Let me tell her,' he whispered. 'Let me. At least let me do that. Come on. She deserves... What? No. Please...'

Oh God help me. He's actually hearing her?!

She felt what little reserve of strength she had left sliding away. Madness like that, madness with voices, wasn't something that could be workshopped away, was it? It was hardwired. A broken brain misfiring. Ewan's lifelong achievement had been managing to contain it, to hide it. Venting it through his art.

'Shhh, it's okay,' tried Charlotte. 'It's okay. Forget her. Forget her, love. Listen to me instead... ignore –'

Ewan stamped one foot in the footwell and thumped his knee with his fist. 'I can't! I can't!' He spun his head towards her. 'You have NO FUCKING IDEA! I can't just... ignore...' Then he was shaking his head frantically. 'No, no, no, NO!!!'

Charlotte leant away from him, as far as she could. The hand holding the kitchen knife was flailing around danger-ously close to her neck.

I could crash. She could try that, spinning the wheel and hoping for the best. But she couldn't see what was beyond those grass humps. It was just a featureless black out there. Was it sea water? Marsh? Mud?

Oh God help me.

Ewan's rocking and whimpering gradually subsided and then he began nodding, as if he was listening to a phone call, some sort of pep talk down the line. 'Okay,' he said. 'Okay. We're coming,' he muttered. 'Soon... soon... soon.'

55

The skeleton crew of night-shifters were beginning to clock on and settle in for the evening. They shot curious glances at Okeke and Warren, who were sitting at Okeke's desk.

'Haven't you two got homes to go to?' said DI Abbott, as he eased himself into his seat, setting his coffee and box of Krispy Cremes down on his desk.

The phones on the CID floor rang and Warren picked up the one at Okeke's desk. 'Hastings CID?'

'This is Control Room, Sussex Police. I'm PCRO Tammie Nelson. Are you the ones who put out the APW on the silver Peugeot 206?'

Okeke, who'd been leaning in to listen, snatched the phone from Warren. 'Yes. This is DC Okeke speaking. What have you got for me?'

'We had an ANPR hit on the vehicle from a static cam outside the Premier off-licence in Camber about twenty minutes ago. It was heading eastwards out of Camber.'

'Camber?' Okeke looked at Warren and waggled a finger at her screen. He jumped onto her keyboard and pulled up the

FCN – the ANPR fixed-camera network. He typed in the location and on Okeke's monitor a local map appeared with a marker peg flashing red.

'Thank you.' She hung up and studied the map alongside Warren. 'Zoom out,' she ordered.

He clicked on the scale slider and dragged it downwards. The map revealed more of the East Sussex coastline.

'Boyd's just come back that way, hasn't he?' said Warren.

Okeke traced the road into Camber from the east – Lydd Road. It ran right up against the beach along Camber Sands and towards Jury's Gap.

'They might have even passed each other,' added Warren.

She scrolled the map left. 'Christ.' She pointed at the screen. 'The Martello tower isn't a million miles away.'

'Do you think this is linked to the case?' asked Warren.

BOYD HAD Minter stop in a layby while they waited for more news.

His sergeant pulled out a packet of Polos and offered him one. 'It'll help take your mind off things, boss.'

Boyd looked at him with barely veiled incredulity, but he took one all the same. 'Jesus,' he said. 'We really try to put a wall up, don't we? Between what we do for a living, and who we are.'

'It's us and them, boss...'

Boyd nodded. 'Because we think of crime as what happens to *them*. Not us.' He shook his head. 'Shit. And then something like this happens and suddenly it's not just a job any more.'

His phone buzzed in his hand. He hit answer and rattled out, 'Okeke? What's the news?'

'We've had an ANPR sighting of the silver Peugeot 206,

registration FP79 FDV, on Lydd Road at Camber. It's heading out to Jury's Gap.'

Minter immediately swung the car round out of the layby and back the way they'd come. This time he didn't ask: the lights and siren went on.

'How long ago was this?' asked Boyd.

'About half an hour. Guv?'

'Yes?'

'Jones was caught before, attempting to abduct and kill someone. He had a kill-and-dump kit, right? Well, the tower's that way,' she said. 'He's heading towards the Martello tower.'

Pieces that he hadn't considered might conceivably be linked suddenly clattered into place like ball bearings descending a marble run. Jones was roughly the same age as Ricky Harris, wasn't he? And hadn't Jones's LEDS record mentioned that he was born and raised in Kent?

And Jones's paintings – not the pictures of the girl but the endless painted landscapes of bleak marshes and moors? He remembered thinking they bore an uncanny resemblance to the forlorn wilderness around the tower.

'Just a second.' Boyd lowered his phone and called up his brief thread of messages with Sarah Shah. He tapped on the photo of Jones's room that showed the wall plastered with his charcoal and pastel drawings. He scaled it up and slowly scrolled along. The landscapes shared a similar theme – wetlands, marshlands, beaches with grass-crested dunes. The muted colours gave them a melancholic, vaguely foreboding tone.

He stopped scrolling when he came across the one small portrait. Again he was struck by the aged-down picture of Charlotte. He hadn't scrolled beyond it previously but this time continued looking. The image at the very edge of the photo was another marsh, painted in muddy colours. But the faint smudged outline on the horizon was unmistakable. A tower.

Boyd put the phone back to his ear. 'Jones knows the tower,' he said. 'Fuck it. It's him! He's the one who's been dumping bodies there!'

'That was my thought,' replied Okeke. 'He could be our other DNA profile from Hemsworth's –'

'Okeke! Every unit that's close by –'

'I'm on it.' She hung up.

56

The headlights had been picking out the sheen of tidal pools and mud flats for a while as the car snaked along a rutted gravel road. Finally out of the solid darkness, Charlotte caught sight of something reflecting light back at them. It looked like the chevron-patterned tape that police strung up around a crash site or a crime scene.

For a moment her hopes lifted. Where that tape was found, police were usually close by. Right?

Then, amid the gloom, twenty yards beyond the tape, the headlights picked out a round brick tower. The gravel road ended there.

'Stop the car,' said Ewan.

Charlotte did as he asked. He reached over, unlocked and pushed open the driver-side door. 'Get out.'

She climbed out of the car and he joined her swiftly, grabbing her wrist, not that there was any way to escape. They were in the middle of nowhere.

'Ewan? Please... whatever –'

'Shut up!' he snapped, pulling the police tape aside and dragging her after him.

The Peugeot's headlights cast thick beams through skeins of swirling mist onto the tired old brickwork of the building.

'W-what's in there?' she whimpered.

He ignored her and led her towards an arched doorway. The tower looked like some old fortification that might once have housed early-warning plane-spotters during the war. She was dimly aware that her branches of opportunity were disappearing fast.

She took a deep breath and tugged her arm hard to escape his grasp, almost pulling him off his feet in the process. Ewan responded by punching her in the face with the handle of the kitchen knife. 'Fucking bitch!' he snarled as she dropped to her knees, stunned by the impact.

He released his grip on her wrist and instead wound his fingers into her hair and grabbed a fistful. He began to yank her forward again, through the arched door and inside the building. She yelped with the pain. Nothing hurt more, nor commanded compliance more than the agony she was feeling from his grip right now. Still she tried, squirming and dragging her feet, both her hands clasping his tightly, trying to ease the sharp tugging agony and peel his fingers clear of her hair.

At last he let her go and shoved her roughly to the floor.

'Down!' he said.

Initially she thought he was telling her to stay lying, but then, by the light of the car's headlights spilling inside, she saw that she was beside an open trapdoor with a ladder leading down into complete darkness below.

'Ewan, no...' she pleaded, aware through her broken voice that she had lost any hope of reasoning or negotiating her way out of whatever he had in store for her now.

'Get DOWN THERE!' he screamed, once again holding the tip of the knife to her throat. 'MOVE!'

She complied slowly, swinging one leg and then the other over the lip of the trapdoor and onto the steps of the ladder.

Feeling her way down, she descended until one foot tapped down onto a sheet of plywood. She looked around to see that the whole floor was a patchwork of plywood boards.

Ewan came down quickly behind her, dropping the last few steps and thudding onto the floor. From far below, Charlotte could hear a soft splash of water as grit and flakes of rotten debris cascaded into a pool or a well.

'Why...' she began.

'Enough talking now,' his voice growled in the darkness. 'Not one more fucking word!'

She heard him fumble for something, then heard a soft click. A small key-fob torch suddenly wiped away the pitch-black, giving her a monochrome, almost dungeon-like context of dancing shadows and glistening wet stone.

He pointed with his knife. 'Go.'

She turned to look where he was gesturing and saw a weathered wooden post beside the curved wall and steps leading down through the floor and out of sight.

He shoved her. 'GO!'

BOYD HAD What3words open on his phone. He'd placed a peg to remember the tower's location the first time he'd gone out to it, and now his focus was on watching their location jitter painfully slowly across an almost featureless map towards it. A grim fairy tale for the smartphone generation – knight, monster and maiden reduced to one blue dot and one red one.

Minter had turned the sirens off. His headlights were on full beam and he was driving foolishly fast along a winding narrow gravel strip that offered little room for error – a corner too fast and they'd be thrown into a tidal pool.

Boyd tried to keep his attention on the dots – the distance between them narrowing slowly. That gap was all that mattered until they got there, then he'd widen his field of thoughts to *What the fuck next?*

Their eyes – a snippet of Okeke's voice – *scraped out by the serrated blade of a Swiss –*

He shook his head as if he could shake that thought out of it. *Not Charlotte. God. Please. Not that for Charlotte.*

He'd had a moment when he'd queried whether he – or his job – might somehow bring the horror of real life to her front door; make her a lightning rod for disaster or danger.

But her story had gatecrashed his. She'd come with her very own monster. A very patient one who'd been biding his time, hiding his fucked-up pathology for years behind a smokescreen of compliant parole hearings and harmless landscape drawings.

∾

'EWAN... PLEASE... TALK TO ME.'

He'd dragged her down here, at knifepoint, to this sodden dungeon for what reason? She kept trying to reassure herself that the knife was his means of coercing her to this place and no more. He'd smacked her with the handle – her head was still ringing from the blow – but he hadn't stabbed her. Maybe there was a little hope left in that?

He seemed to have run out of intent and purpose, and was now squatting on a pile of glistening algae-covered bricks beside her, staring at the rippling water around them.

She noticed scaffolding poles glinting in the darkness. They provided a glimmer of hope – this place wasn't some long-forgotten ruin but a place that was actively being restored. Outside, there could conceivably be a cabin somewhere in the gloom, containing – she could only hope – a surly security guard resigned to spending a Scrooge-like Christmas alone. Weren't security guards meant to patrol every few hours? To make a cursory inspection?

'Ewan?' she tried again. 'W-why are we down here?'

He stirred from his thoughts to look at her. This time the knife wasn't thrust in her face but instead hung limply in his fist.

'She's stopped,' he said softly. 'She's not crying any more.'

Charlotte knew better than to ask who 'she' was again. 'Is this what Lottie wants? You d-down here?'

He shook his head. 'Not me. It's you,' he replied. 'She wants you.'

She was afraid to ask, but...

He's talking again. I've got him talking.

'Why does she want me, Ewan?'

His bottom lip suddenly curled and his face crumpled. 'We killed her,' he cried. 'We left her to die down here all alone. I'm sorry. I'm so sorry.'

'We? What happened, Ewan? Tell me...' she whispered.

'We were just kids...' he said, sobbing.

'Did you hurt someone?' asked Charlotte. 'Was there a... an accident down here?'

'There was another boy...' he replied. 'I didn't even really know him....' His voice had changed in timbre to the whine of someone younger, a child. 'We'd just met on the beach. We were both bored. He said he knew a cool place...'

'Was it this place?' she prompted.

'Yes.' Ewan sniffed. 'He said we should go and explore it. I didn't want to... but...'

Charlotte began to suspect where this tale that he was tiptoeing slowly towards was heading. 'Was Lottie here? Was she another child who was playing here?'

He nodded absently, one hand incessantly tugging at the bristles on his chin. 'It was... only meant to be a game...'

'There!' Minter pointed ahead.

Boyd looked up from his phone and out through the mud-spattered windscreen. Ahead of them – although it was hard to tell if the track was going to lead them straight there or meander some more – he could see the headlights of a stationary vehicle and the base of the tower caught in the glare of their headlights.

Mercifully, the last leg of the track ran straight to the tower and a few moments later Minter pulled up a dozen yards short of the Peugeot. Boyd reached for the torch in the driver's well and they both jumped out.

'Careful,' whispered Boyd. 'He could be armed.'

'Gun-armed, or knife-armed?' queried Minter. He was holding up a pair of stab vests pulled from the rear seat.

It could be either. Boyd shrugged and held his hand out for one of the jackets. 'Call Control and let them know we're here,' he said as he approached the Peugeot.

'Boss? It might be best to hold back –' Minter began. 'No,' he continued, shaking his head, 'because when have we ever done that?'

Boyd snapped on the torch. The silver Peugeot was empty.

They were inside the tower, then.

He stepped past the tape and approached the arched doorway, grimacing at the noise behind him: the growl of the pool car's engine and the crackle and squawk of radio chatter.

I need to bloody hear.

There was no way Ewan Jones wouldn't have heard them arrive and no way he wouldn't have registered the blue flickering lights coming from their car. So there was no point making a slow and stealthy approach. Charlotte's life could quite possibly be measured in seconds left.

Boyd cupped his mouth as he stood in the doorway. 'EWAN JONES! THIS IS THE POLICE!'

He leant in and panned his torch around. There was no one on the main floor. He crossed the floor, lay down and panned his torch through the trapdoor. There was nothing to be seen on the floor below either.

'EWAN JONES!' he called, this time his voice boomed as it reverberated off the curved brick wall. 'THIS IS THE POLICE!' There was no bloody chance that he could have missed that – but still there was no response.

He'd left Minter outside, waiting for back-up. There was only room for one foolish arse in here. But Charlotte had to be somewhere below and doing nothing was not an option. He quickly clambered down the ladder and dropped heavily onto the floor. It creaked and groaned alarmingly beneath his weight. There was an unnerving give to the plywood sheets that covered the old planks beneath. In the centre of the floor was the large gap where the floor had caved in. Cautiously, he made his way towards the outer curved brick wall and grabbed hold of the post that marked the top of the stairs. Even that wobbled uncertainly as he held on to it.

He heard the sound of creaking wood and the soft clanking of the scaffolding poles that shored up the floor and the stairs.

'EWAN JONES!' he tried again. He pulled out his phone and held it in both hands as if it was a gun – an old trick from his uniform days. 'OFFICER WITH A TASER!'

Nothing.

'CHARLOTTE? ARE YOU DOWN THERE?'

He thought he heard water sloshing gently, as if it had been disturbed by someone moving around. He took several steps down, placing his feet close to the wall to mitigate his weight on the old steps. He still wasn't entirely confident that the scaffolding was secure enough to be taken for granted.

'Hello?'

He couldn't see a thing, even now that his eyes had adapted to the full darkness. It was disconcerting. Above him he heard Minter's heavy footsteps clonking across the plywood-lined floor.

'You okay down there, boss?'

'Put the mini gen on!' Boyd called back.

'The what?'

'The generator! We need lights on down here!'

He heard Minter's heavy steps as he crossed the floor again, then the click of a switch. The generator whirred to life and the floodlights on the floor above and down in the basement below winked on.

Boyd winced in the intense glare. Sully had quite clearly emptied his department's stock cupboard of 500-watt tripod lamps in an attempt to recreate the mothership scene in *Close Encounters.*

It took him a few moments for him to take in what he was looking at.

57

The last time Boyd had been down here, the water had been lapping halfway up the stairs; now it was well and truly down to the bottom, revealing an undulating mountainscape of fallen bricks, timber and the remnants of Second World War crates, surrounded by a black sea of silt-thickened water.

In the middle of this was Charlotte, cowering and covered in blood on the left side of her head and neck. It had soaked into her cream jumper and even down into the sodden corduroy skirt she was wearing.

Beside her was Ewan Jones, squatting like a stone gargoyle, staring down into the gently sloshing water. He was holding a large kitchen knife. Boyd realised from the blue plastic handle that it was *his* kitchen knife.

'Ewan!' he called out. 'Drop the knife, mate.'

Jones slowly looked up at Boyd as if he were nothing more than an annoying distraction.

'The knife!' snapped Boyd. 'Drop it!'

'Where's she gone?' he replied plaintively. 'Where's Lottie gone?'

Lottie – Boyd could only suppose Jones was referring to one of the bodies. 'We found her, mate,' he said. 'And the others. It's over.'

'She has to be here!' Jones cried. 'She was crying! She...' He staggered off his perch and across into the brackish water. 'She must be here somewhere!'

He waded into the water, dropping down to his neck as he fumbled the bottom with his hands. He was wandering further and further away from Charlotte. A little more and maybe – if Boyd shouted at her to run – she'd be on the steps before Jones could wade back to her.

'Where are you, Lottie?' Jones whimpered as he continued his frantic ducking and wading. 'I did what you wanted,' he cried. 'I brought her here!'

Minter had crept down the stairs. 'Boss, we've got an ARU on its way,' he said softly from behind Boyd.

Boyd nodded. 'Good. I'm not sure if we're going to be able to talk him down.' He looked at his sergeant. 'We should taser the bastard first, though. You didn't happen to...?'

Minter shook his head. The Armed Response Unit would undoubtedly have one, so it was just a case of keeping the crazy bastard occupied until they turned up.

'Ewan... she's not down there any more. We took her away.' He paused. 'So she can finally have a proper burial.'

Jones had waded across to the far side of the basement. Panting with the effort and the cold, he rested against one of the construction-support props that had been recently installed.

It was bracketed to a pair of horizontal tension bars that reached out on either side to the bowing basement walls. A large metal square brace sat at the end of each arm, firmly pressed against the bricks, almost like a pair of broad splayed hands: a scaffolding rendition of Superman holding two crushing forces apart.

'Ewan,' said Boyd again. 'It's over. There are police with firearms on their way. Let me come down and help you both get out of here.' He took another couple of steps towards the bottom.

'We can get you some proper help, Ewan,' he added. 'Not prison time, mate, I mean help. Real help.'

Jones was clinging on to the support prop, panting out clouds of breath, reminding Boyd that the water had to be close to freezing. Charlotte so far had remained silent, clinging to the bricks she was sprawled upon.

'Ewan,' she uttered softly. He looked up from the swirls of dark water. 'Ewan, it's okay, my love... it's okay.' She managed to conjure a warm and caring smile across her bloodied face. 'I can hear her now... I can hear Lottie.'

Jones's expression changed. 'You... you can hear her?'

Charlotte nodded. 'She's happy now. She's not crying.'

Boyd took advantage of the distraction to take the last few creaking steps down to the bottom and stood still, ankle-deep in the water.

'What's she saying, Charlotte? What's she saying?' Jones asked.

Careful, thought Boyd, *you can't possibly know what she sounds like in his head.*

'She...' Charlotte turned to look at Boyd, who was now wading across the treacherously uneven ground beneath the rippling surface. The look on her face said it all. *What do I say now?!*

'WHAT'S SHE SAYING!' shouted Jones impatiently.

'She's saying... it's all over n-now. She says thank you, Ewan. Thank you for bringing –'

'DON'T FUCKING LIE!' Jones snapped, banging the pole with his fist. The kitchen blade clanged noisily off the metal and the sound echoed ominously around the basement.

'She says it's okay... She... she knows you... didn't mean to drown her –'

'LYING BITCH! DO YOU THINK I'M STUPID?' He slammed his fist into the pole again, but this time its base made a grating sound as it slid along something beneath the water. 'SHE DIDN'T FUCKING DROWN, YOU SILLY BITCH!'

Boyd saw it happen in slow motion: an almost predictable sequence of events that started with the bottom of the construction-support pole sliding further off-centre, and then lurching away into deeper water as if it had been kicked out.

The support beams, which had until now been perfectly horizontal like the arms of a crucifix, sagged downwards and the wide square braces, lacking the tension that was holding them firmly in place, crashed down into the water.

There was a held-breath moment when it seemed as though nothing further was going to happen, then, to the right, a brick clattered out of the wall into the water, followed by another, and another.

Boyd waded across to Charlotte, grabbed her hand and pulled her to her feet, just as the rest of that particular section of wall sagged inwards like melted wax and crashed into the water.

A viscous bulge of sodden peat the size of a boulder spewed through the ragged hole like toothpaste out of a tube, then behind it gallons of muddy water cascaded in.

Boyd and Charlotte scrambled through the chaos back to the stairs and up onto them as the muddy avalanche consumed Jones where he stood.

'UP! UP! UP!' yelled Boyd as he felt the stairs vibrate from the sudden impact of thick muddy water smashing against the supporting scaffolding. Minter reached down, grabbed Charlotte's arm and pulled her up behind him. Boyd followed in hot pursuit as he felt the scaffolding give way, then a moment later the steps themselves.

He had just set foot on the top one when the entire structure collapsed beneath him and he hurled himself up onto the plywood-covered floor. Even that felt unsafe, though.

'Keep going!' He flapped his hands at Minter. 'Get the fuck out!'

Minter shoved Charlotte up the ladder first, then followed her up, hefting her up and out with his shoulder. Boyd flew up the ladder behind them. As he pulled himself up through the trapdoor, the entire floor below collapsed into the swirling mire in the basement.

As the floodlights and generator descended along with the plywood boards and the ancient timber into the depths, Boyd looked down and caught one last snapshot image of a vortex of glistening liquid piling in to fill the void.

The three of them emerged from the arched doorway to see the twinkling headlights and flickering blues of a convoy of patrol cars weaving their way along the marshland's winding lane towards the tower.

'They're like bloody London buses,' Boyd panted.

58

Boyd watched over Charlotte as she woke up in stages over a period of ten minutes. The stitches on the side of her temple ran back into her hairline, which had been shaved down to the skin to allow the doctor to close the wound. There was a kind of Frankenstein's monster look to it. A cool look if there'd been a Halloween party for them to head off to.

'Hello there, sleepy-chops,' he said.

Her left eye was completely bloodshot, not pink but a solid red moat that surrounded her pupil. The doctor had said it wasn't permanent. It would clear in due course, but for the moment it looked unsettling.

'Hello, Bill,' she whispered. 'Ooh, my head stings.' She reached up towards the stitches, but Boyd intercepted her hand.

'Be careful. You have a bit of an ouchie up there.'

She smiled. 'I'm presuming that's not one of your forensic terms?'

He laughed and took her hand. She glanced at a glass vase of flowers on the table beside her and frowned, puzzled.

'They're from Emma,' he explained. 'She dropped them in earlier. You had one hell of smack to the side of your head,' he continued. 'Hence the stitches. Other than that, though, apart from some scrapes and bruising, you're fine.' He smiled. 'You're a tough old bird.'

'Charming,' she replied. She closed her eyes for a moment, then opened them. 'What happened to...?'

Boyd shook his head. 'He didn't make it.'

'Right,' she said, and nodded. 'Right. Okay.'

'They pulled his body out a couple of hours ago,' Boyd added. 'He drowned.' He tried to interpret the look on her face. 'Do you need something for the pain?' he asked.

She nodded and squeezed his hand. A tear rolled down her cheek. 'It really hurts.'

'SHE'S AWAKE. The guv'nor's talking to her,' said Okeke, peering through the gap in the curtain that had been drawn around Charlotte's bed. Minter and Warren got up from the hospital's bucket chairs and joined her.

'Just good friends, my arse,' said Minter.

'For fuck's sake,' Okeke whispered. 'Time and place!'

'It looks like he's told her Jones is dead,' said Warren. He frowned. 'Why's she crying?'

Okeke looked at him. She shook her head with exasperation. Men, she mused, could be so moronically binary.

The three of them watched in silence as Boyd gently held Charlotte in his arms. Okeke suddenly felt uneasy. They were watching something that Boyd was assuming was a private moment.

'Enough,' she said, grabbing Minter's and Warren's arms and herding them back to their seats. Then: 'I heard from the D-Sup that Boyd's off the case.'

Minter looked at her. 'He told *you* that? Not *me*?'

'No, well, he didn't exactly tell me. I sort of overheard it,' she confessed. 'He was letting Boyd know that because of the personal connection he needed to step away from the case.'

'Did you happen to hear who's going to be replacement SIO, then?'

She shook her head. 'It'll probably be you, Minter, as his second. But don't let it go to your head. Don't be an arse about it. You're not getting a "guv" out of me,' she said, grinning.

'I suppose we'll find that out soon enough,' said Minter. 'As long as it's not that idiot Abbott,' he added.

'I shouldn't think it'd be him,' Okeke replied. 'I think Sutherland's hoping he'll get bored sleeping through his night shifts and take early retirement.' She looked at Minter. 'Which of course would leave a slot open for a new DI. Race you?'

Minter laughed. 'I've got a good head start, Okeke, so why not? Game on.' He looked at his watch. 'Well, I think I'm going to head off home now. You need a lift?' he asked Warren.

Warren nodded.

The two men pulled on their coats. 'See you tomorrow, then, Okeke,' said Minter.

She waved them off. Then a moment later: 'Minter?'

He paused. 'What?'

'You might want to bone up on the action log,' she said, 'if you want Sutherland to hand over SIO to you. Best be prepared.'

He tapped his head. 'Right.'

'That's one conversation *not* to screw up, mate,' she added.

59

Emma handed her dad a mug of tea. She sat down beside him on the sofa and they both stared out of the bay window.

'How's Charlotte doing?' she asked eventually.

'She's okay. She's got stitches along her temple and up into her scalp. They had to shave a bit away so she's kind of sporting the Bride of Frankenstein look right now,' he said, smiling.

'Nice, Dad. Really nice. You know... really sympathetic.'

'She makes it look good,' he said, adding, 'The flowers were a nice idea. Thank you.'

Her dad had told her the gist of things. That Charlotte had been staying over, not because of her central heating going on the futz but because of Jones. She still couldn't get her head around the fact that an actual real-life serial killer had broken into their home and snatched Charlotte. It made the place feel vaguely contaminated, as if he'd left the sulphurous smell of evil behind him.

The other thing that she was struggling to make sense of was how Charlotte could have been married to a man who'd done what he'd done to those girls. How could a person be married to another and *not* know they were capable of something so vile and horrific? It was, she thought, like watching crime docs on the telly. You always asked yourself... *How could the wife have not known? But maybe she did? Maybe she knew all along and chose not to acknowledge it?*

But Charlotte wasn't *that kind of woman...* Emma found herself starting to think that maybe Charlotte and – although she didn't think she'd ever admit this – her dad had had a point about Patrick.

'Do you think this is going to change her, Dad?'

'What do you mean?'

'Well, from what you told me... she must have been pretty sure she was going to die, right? I mean, that kind of thing messes with your head. Makes you re-order your priorities. Doesn't it?'

He sighed. 'Didn't really change me that much, did it?'

'Again...' She sighed. 'That's so sympathetic of you.'

She shook her head as he took another run at it. 'What she experienced was terrifying. But... I hope there'll be something good that comes out of it for her.'

'Jesus. Really, Dad?' Emma looked him incredulously.

'Ems... she spent God knows how many years looking over her shoulder for him, you know? She had no idea he was inside and she'd been hiding all that time.'

She watched her dad as he ran a hand up Ozzie's back, ruffling his fur the wrong way. Oz grumbled for a moment and then rolled onto his back, legs splayed.

'I hope...' he continued, 'I hope this'll be a release for her.' He shook his head. 'You know, that's what didn't make sense to me about her...'

'What didn't?'

'I think, I may be wrong... but I think she's actually a very outgoing person. An extrovert. But...'

'You think hiding changed her?'

He nodded. 'Exactly. Before that, the sheer bloody terror of being married to someone that bloody cra–'

'You can't say crazy, Dad. That's not actually a term these days.'

'Batshit crazy, then,' he said defiantly. 'I've heard you say that more than once.'

She laughed – he could have that one.

'That's going to knock corners off you, right?' he continued. 'Gnaw at your confidence.' He took a sip of his tea. 'She was still a kid, really, when she first met him. And...'

'Is this you clumsily segueing your way into discussing Patrick?' She'd been expecting this for a while and was surprised to find she didn't mind as much as she'd thought she would.

He raised a hand. 'What? No, I wasn't...'

'Okay,' she said. 'Well, we might as well get this convo sorted out now. It's done, all right? We are no longer a thing. I don't even work the same shifts as him any more. I asked to be flipped to mornings.'

'I wasn't –'

She raised her hand. 'I'm not done yet. I understand that I might have been a bit, I dunno, naive or whatever. But it's all good. Nothing really bad happened.' She gave him a thankful nod. 'Now, let us not speak of it again. Ever. *Comprendez*?'

'*Comprendez*.'

Ozzie rolled lazily off the couch and went to join Mia, who was sitting beside the fire and gazing wistfully at the flickering tongues of flame.

'So when's Charlotte coming out?' Emma asked.

'Tomorrow morning. As soon as the consultant signs off on her.'

'Is she going to stay here for a bit longer?'

He looked at her. 'Is that going to be a problem?'

Emma shook her head. 'Totally not a problem. She's all right. I like her.' *And I think someone else does too.*

'Good. No... She... I don't know.... The offer's there if she needs a few more days with some company. I imagine the thought of going back to her place right now, being alone... that might be a bit...'

'Unsettling?'

'Yup.' He looked at her. 'But you're sure you're okay ...?'

Emma smiled. 'She can stay as long as she wants. You need a Charlotte in your life.'

He frowned. 'What the hell does *that* mean?'

'Work it out, numbnuts.'

60

'Ah! It's Cardiff's answer to David Beckham!' crowed DSI Sutherland. 'Come on in and grab a seat.'

Minter closed the door behind him and sat down. 'Hardly,' he replied, beaming. 'I just got given a business card is all, sir. I'm not sure if I'll even call the number.'

Sutherland grinned. 'Well, don't forget your friends when you're rich and famous, eh?' He cleared his throat and assumed a more serious expression. 'Now then, you know why you're here, sergeant?'

'Because DCI Boyd's off the case.'

Sutherland nodded. 'For obvious reasons. It's nothing he's done wrong, you understand, just... you know...'

Minter nodded. 'There are personal connections.'

'Indeed. You're Boyd's second. I presume, despite gallivanting up and down hills and dales for your Lion Man competition... and launching a modelling career... you're up to speed on his case.'

Minter suppressed a smile. 'Ironman, sir, but, yes – we got lucky with Ewan Jones.'

'You got very lucky. Fortunately the press aren't sniffing

around yet. I'm not sure what they'd make of the SIO's *girlfriend* suddenly becoming the latest victim of the very serial killer he's investigating.'

'The woman's just a friend of his, sir.'

'Hmmm.' Sutherland snorted. 'Nevertheless, there's a personal connection, which is why I need you to stand in as acting SIO going forward.'

'Yes, sir.' Minter sat up a little straighter.

Sutherland scratched his head. 'Anyway, I just want to make sure I'm up to speed myself: this tower relates to two different suspects, so we effectively have two lines of enquiry that may actually be linked?'

'Sort of, sir. We have three female victims, all dumped there who we believe were all Jones's victims, starting with Chloe Hunter in 1999; Laura Kahn – potentially - who went missing in 2003, being the most recent. We're still trying to ID the third body, but... she's almost certainly one of Jones's.'

'And there's this little girl, Hemsworth...'

'Yes, she went missing in 1971, and it's likely that's when she died. We're almost certain Jones had something to do with her, despite being a minor at the time. And probably Harris too.'

'Harris's DNA was in her... lunch box, wasn't it?'

'In *a* lunch box, sir. Harris's DNA is confirmed as being on items found in it, which was in the same bag as Hemsworth's body. If we can identify Jones's DNA, we'll have a forensic link putting them both in the same place at the same time as Hemsworth. And,' he added, 'there's also the suspicious activity regarding Harris's ownership of the tower itself.'

'In what way?'

'Well, buying it in the first place, when he must have known there was nothing he could actually have done with it. Then aggressively holding on to it for thirty years. Maybe young Jones and young Harris were childhood friends. They encountered Hemsworth at the tower and she somehow ended up murdered, mutilated and dumped in that bag.'

Sutherland had the action log on the screen and pulled up both men's details. 'Christ, they'd have been just boys when...'

'Right, sir... Harris thirteen, Jones eleven.' Minter shook his head slowly. 'It beggars belief, so it does.'

Sutherland scrolled through the notes on Ewan until he came across the photos of the art in his hostel room in Dover. 'Good god, those drawings of his...'

'They're quite bleak, aren't they, sir?'

Sutherland curled his lips. 'If there was an award for gloomiest landscape exhibition...'

'The same themes go all the way back to the eighties, when he was on the brink of becoming successful. They're all of marshes, towers, deep wells, dark colours, dark moods... And then there's the girl he kept drawing.' Minter got up and leant over the desk. 'Do you mind if I show you something, sir?'

'Be my guest.'

Minter walked around to Sutherland's side of the desk and clicked through the action log until a photo of a young girl appeared on the screen. 'Patricia S. Hemsworth. This was the image from the misper file.' He then clicked on one of Ewan's paintings from the eighties and lined it up alongside the portrait from his hostel room.

'Good grief,' said Sutherland. 'He's been painting Hemsworth all along?'

Minter nodded. 'That's what we think. The other victims – Chloe Hunter, Laura Kahn... if we can confirm her, and the woman who escaped him back in 2008 – also bear a passing resemblance to Hemsworth.' Minter pulled their pictures up.

Sutherland nodded slowly as he took them in one at a time. 'Yes, I see... There's definitely a certain look to all of them.'

'We think that whatever happened back in seventy-one with Jones and Harris imprinted on Jones's psyche. He was only a boy, then. Perhaps he was trying to relive or atone for that moment in his youth over and over?'

'And what about Harris? Do you think Harris had anything to do with the later victims?'

Minter shrugged. 'It's possible. But we have no corroborating evidence.' He sucked in a deep breath and let it out slowly. 'The best we can pin on him at this stage is a possible involvement in Hemsworth's death.' He pulled a face.

'What?'

'Well, that hangs on the lunch box DNA, doesn't it? He could argue that he met Jones earlier that day. Shared a bit of his lunch with him, then went off on his merry way.'

'And you're interviewing him when?'

'This afternoon. We're just waiting on Ellessey to give us the full results on the third body and DNA swabs. We've retained him on joint enterprise for Hemsworth's murder, but... who knows? We might have him for the others too.'

61

Okeke watched Minter emerge from the pier's café with a plastic tray. She dropped her cigarette butt and toed out the ember, kicking it through a gap in the planking and down into the frothing sea below.

Minter set the tray down on the table. 'No fish-finger sandwiches today. I got you a chicken wrap instead.'

'Crap.' She sighed. 'I wanted something hot.'

Minter sat down. 'The coffee's hot.'

She peeled the lid off and blew on it. 'So what's the strategy with Harris this afternoon, then?'

He raised a brow. 'So what's the strategy with Harris this afternoon, then...?' He repeated her question and looked at her expectantly.

She shook her head. 'Nu-uh, I'm not saying it.'

Minter relented. 'Well, while we're waiting on the DNA swabs from the later victims, I think we double down on his involvement with Patricia Hemsworth's death. We'll tell him we can get him on joint enterprise, unless he can give us a credible account that excuses him.'

'Which we can't,' she replied. 'It's just he-said-she-said. Plus, it was fifty-something years ago.'

'Well, we'll let him think we can,' replied Minter. 'Maybe he'll open up and tell us what happened in 1971.'

'Or a version of.' She sipped her coffee. 'You know we can't mention anything about the later victims until we hear from Ellessey, right? Or the eye-gouging thing?'

Minter looked up. 'Yes, I know all that, thanks, detective *constable*.'

'I'm just checking.' She picked up her wrap and looked at it with little enthusiasm. 'Truth is, though, I reckon it was Jones who led whatever happened that day – I mean, the same MO years later? When Harris was already stuck on that island? And I was picking through the evidence taken from Jones's room. He was seriously fucked up.' She set the wrap back down. 'Have you read his notebooks?'

'Not yet. Jesus, Okeke, where do you find the spare hours in a day to do this stuff?'

She smiled sweetly and carried on: 'He was convinced that Hemsworth was commanding him to bring her a body so that she could – I don't know how – possess it and live again. He was completely convinced that if he dragged someone down into the tower, Patricia would rise from the depths and all would finally be forgiven.'

'Well, that's artists for you, isn't it?'

'How do you even get that batshit crazy, though?'

Minter shrugged. 'Let's also make sure we keep all that from Harris too. If he gets wind about any of the crazy stuff, he'll use that to blame everything on Jones.'

'You think, *boss*?' she said, rolling her eyes.

He smiled. 'See? That didn't hurt so much, did it?'

'Oh, piss off,' she huffed, and took a swig of her coffee. 'So, is Sully done with the tower now?'

'I should think so. Or what's left of it anyway. I'm not setting foot anywhere near it now. It's a bloody death trap, I'm telling you.' Minter took a bite of his pasty. 'We're going to hand the tower back to Knight and Arnold to finish the renovation. The sooner it's officially out of our possession, the better. I think the whole thing's going to tumble down at any moment.'

Okeke nodded. 'What time's the interview room booked for?'

Minter checked his watch. 'Three.'

She got up and grabbed her coffee.

'You going?' he asked, mouth full.

'I might check in on Boyd. See how Charlotte's doing,' she said.

'Not to his house, you're not. It's nearly two now. We need to war-game the interview!'

'You're spitting crumbs,' she replied. 'Relax. I'm just gonna call him.' She headed down the pier, then stopped and turned round. 'You should probably get Warren out with those release forms?'

'Huh?'

'Before the tower collapses?'

She was right. He nodded. 'My desk, no later than two thirty. I want to –'

'War-game... I know.'

He watched her go and shook his head. Okeke was a bleeding nightmare to line-manage. And so infuriatingly right all the time. He honestly had no idea how Boyd coped with her.

'PRESENT IN THE room are DS Steven Minter, DC Samantha Okeke, interviewee Richard Harris and his solicitor...?'

'Jason Pinner.'

'So where are the other two?' asked Harris. 'Batman and Boy Wonder?'

'They're on other duties,' Minter replied.

'That makes you two the B team or something, then?' He turned to Pinner. 'I'm not sure I'm happy about that.'

Minter ignored him, shuffled his notes, then set them down. 'Ricky Harris, we have you at the scene of Patricia Hemsworth's murder, July the twenty-seventh, 1971, at the Martello tower known as Devil's Tower. We have DNA evidence that puts you there on that particular day. We also have your purchase of that same Martello tower, then holding on to it for thirty-plus years. In addition, we have conflicting statements that Stephen Knight made several decent offers to buy the tower over the past thirty years, but you claim that they were, in your own words, "shitty little offers". Would you like to take this opportunity to explain any of that to us today?'

Harris leant forward. 'No comment.'

'Okay.' Minter pulled a printed chart from his notes. 'So, a lunch box was found with Patricia Hemsworth's body; a lunch box that contained a preserved apple core. What we have found on it are traces of DNA that match your profile, along with another DNA profile. So... it's evident that you and one other person were present in the tower with Patricia Hemsworth. Do you know who that other person was?'

Pinner leant in towards Harris and whispered something. Harris nodded.

The solicitor raised a hand. 'Can we suspend this interview? I need a private moment with my client.'

'Already?'

'Please. If you don't mind?'

Minter shrugged. 'Interview suspended at 3.05 p.m.' He paused the recording machine and got up. 'You've got fifteen minutes.'

Outside the interview room, with the door clicked shut, Okeke finally spoke. 'That sounds hopeful.'

'Maybe he's thought about it and realised he's got someone else to blame it on?' Minter said.

'Which means we'll probably get a load of complete bollocks out of him,' she replied.

'Anything's better than "no comment".'

She tutted, but nodded. 'Maybe.'

They waited in silence for a while, then suddenly Minter shucked out a laugh.

'What?'

'Batman and the Boy Wonder,' he said, smiling. 'That's a classic.'

She nodded. 'Boy Wonder... ooh, Warren's going to love that. Not.'

There was knock on the door from inside and Jason Pinner's face appeared. 'We're ready to continue.'

'ALL RIGHT, THEN,' began Minter. He un-paused the machine. 'Interview resumed at 3.12 p.m. Mr Harris, your solicitor has just informed us that you now intend to explain how your DNA was found at the scene of Patricia Hemsworth's murder –'

'Lottie,' Harris said.

'Sorry?'

'She said her name was Lottie...'

Minter frowned at Okeke.

She looked up from her notes. 'Scarlotte,' she said. 'Her middle name was Scarlotte.'

62

'**B**loody hell, this is... incredible,' muttered Ewan. His voice echoed around the cavernous interior of the tower.

Ricky nodded. 'It's like dungeons and dragons down here, mate. There's like vaults and caves right at the bottom,' he said, pointing down the ragged hole in the floor, 'and don't forget the human sacrifices. Little girls were –'

'Who's there?'

The two boys jumped out of their skins, then looked at each other, eyes bulging with a rush of adrenaline. The voice was female. A girl. It had a sing-song quality to it as its reverberation bounced around the brick walls from somewhere above.

'Is someone else down there?'

A wooden board creaked above them; dust and grit fell through the gaps and clattered a moment later into the water far below. A torch shone down the ladder and lit up the damp brick wall.

'Who's that?' called up Ewan.

'I'm Lottie,' she replied. 'Who are you?'

'My name's Ewan.' The torch beam fell onto him. He pointed at his tall new friend. 'This is Ricky. We're exploring Devil's Tower.'

Lottie came down the creaking ladder carefully, holding the

wooden rungs as she descended. 'Me too,' she said as she finally approached them. 'I'm from Peckham,' she said. 'That's in London by the way.'

'I'm on holiday,' said Ewan. 'Are you staying at the campsite?'

Lottie nodded and smiled, suddenly recognising him. 'Oh, hold on. I've seen you on them climbing frames. You're that posh boy, aren't you?' She gave him a furtive smile, then aimed her torch at Ricky. 'Who's this ugly mug?'

'Bog off,' Ricky replied.

She laughed at him. 'Bog off? Are you simple or somethin'?'

HARRIS BLINKED and forced himself to return to the version of events that he'd been telling the coppers.

'So this girl and Ewan, you're saying they took an instant dislike to each other?' Minter asked.

Harris nodded. 'She took the piss out of him and I could tell he wanted to smack her one.'

'So what happened next?' asked Minter.

'I told everyone to chill... then we played for a bit. You know, dare games, arsing about, that kind of thing and then finally...' Harris shook his head. 'Man, it was so long ago...'

'Try your best,' said Minter. 'Whatever you can remember.'

'Well,' continued Harris, 'if I remember... we got separated somehow. We were playing hide-and-seek, I think. The other boy, Ewan, was with the girl, and I was on my own.'

'WHERE'S EWAN, DO YOU THINK?' asked Lottie. 'He's never gonna find us.'

Ricky grinned. 'He got bored, I guess. It's just you and me now.'

They were hiding beneath the wooden steps that curved around the wall above them. With the torch off, it was almost completely dark, with just the faintest glimmer of daylight leaking down.

Ricky realised he really wanted to touch her. He noticed that Lottie had started growing titties, despite being so small. He just wanted a little touch, that's all. The darkness and the fact that they seemed to be alone emboldened him. He reached across and grabbed her chest, curious to see what a girl's breast felt like.

'Hey!' she yelped, and slapped his hand away.

'Ah, come on,' he said. 'Just a little feel.'

'Piss off,' she said, standing up and emerging from beneath the steps. 'Perv.'

Ricky emerged too. 'Come on, Lottie. I was just having a laugh.'

'No, you weren't. You're like a dirty perv.'

'It was just a little titty squeeze. What's your problem? Are you a lez or something?'

She bent down, scooped up a handful of mud and flung it at him. It splattered across his shirt. 'Hahaha... now you're a proper dirty perv.' She bent down again to scoop up some more, but Ricky stepped forward and grabbed her wrist

'Right, just for that...' He wrestled her into an armlock, hands bent behind her back, and held both her wrists in one of his big hands.

'Get off me! You pissing weirdo!'

With his free hand, he had free reign.

And that's when she started screaming.

'So, you heard her screaming?' Okeke asked him. 'And you did what?'

'I came running down from the top of the tower, didn't I?' Harris lied. 'She was screaming something about Ewan feeling her up and he was chasing after her. I mean, I had no choice, man; I came running down to save her.'

'And what did you find?'

'They were on these wooden steps that go right down to the very bottom. The other lad, Ewan, had her pants in one of his hands and was holding on to her ankle. The girl was crying, I mean, really crying and screaming and...'

'What're you doing?!' *shouted Ewan.*

Ricky looked up. He'd thought the boy had got bored and buggered off. The little bitch had managed to get free, but he'd caught up with her halfway up the stairs. He'd just grabbed hold of her again and now mummy's boy was back.

'We were just snogging,' said Ricky. 'Then suddenly she started screaming –'

'Help me!' Lottie screamed again. 'He's hurting me! Please!'

Ewan took several steps down. 'Let her go! For God's sake!'

Ricky lay on top of her, pushing her against the steps to prevent her squirming, then he pinched her nose. She opened her mouth to scream again, so he shoved her pants in to shut her up.

'Quiet!' he snarled, holding his palm over her stuffed mouth. He looked up at Ewan. 'Come on, mate. Gimme a hand.'

'No!' Ewan looked horrified. 'No. Jesus. Ricky, let her go!'

He shook his head. 'She'll tell, right? She'll go to the police or something and we'll both get it.'

Ewan shook his head. 'You let her go right now or –'

'Or what?'

'I'll...'

Ricky chuckled. 'Come on... You can have a little feel too while I'm holding her if you like. Then it's my turn again.'

Ewan looked like a rabbit in the headlights. Ricky could tell he wanted to help her, but he was just too chicken.

'You just gonna sit there and watch, are you?' said Ricky, grin-

ning wildly now. This was fun in a way he hadn't ever realised was possible.

Catch, Wrestle and Sex. A new game. Kiss and Chase, but just taken to the next level.

Lottie's screaming was still fairly loud, even though it was muted by her underwear and his palm. 'What's it going to be, Ewan? You playing or not?'

'This is wrong, Ricky. Let her go,' Ewan mumbled.

'What? You a bender or something?'

'Let her go!' he repeated, more confidently this time. 'You're bloody hurting her!'

But a part of Ricky's mind was already telling him that Lottie couldn't be allowed to go anywhere. That there'd be no telling tales or going to the police. That Lottie from London was going to have to vanish.

'If you don't give me a hand, I'll just tell the police it was you who did it!'

~

Harris's account of events had finally ground to a halt. He was sobbing, or pretending to, into his cupped hands.

Okeke leant forward, impatient with his tears. 'So, Ewan Jones what?... You're saying he actually assaulted her?'

Harris wiped his face and shook his head. 'It's so long ago, you know? It's all jumbled.'

'Just tell it how you remember it,' said Minter calmly.

'He... Look, I was scared... I should've stepped in sooner,' whispered Harris. 'It's... I could have saved her. I know I could but...'

'But what?'

Harris slid down in his chair and buried his face in his hands once again.

Pinner interceded. 'Can't you see my client's distressed?'

'Come on, Ricky,' said Minter. 'This is your chance to get things off your chest. To tell us what really happened.'

'She fought him off,' said Harris. 'That brave little girl managed to get him off...' He began to cry again.

'My client needs a break.'

Ockе held a hand up to shush him. 'Harris? What happened?'

'Ewan pushed her,' he whispered. 'She fell off the steps, down to the bottom.'

63

Warren checked the satnav on the dashboard, then looked out through the windscreen at the home in front of him. 'Bloody hell,' he muttered.

It was a large Alpine-chalet-styled building with green storm shutters (for effect, obviously) flanking each window and a darkly stained wooden facade along the front, giving the impression that it had been built from freshly cut and treated pine lumber. It sat in the middle of a large square lawn at the end of a vanilla-coloured paved driveway.

There were Christmas lights strung across the front, and all the place needed was several tons of fake snow dumped on it to transport it from the drab, grey overcast Sussex countryside to some exclusive ski resort.

He grabbed the folder off the passenger seat and climbed out of the pool car. He patted his hair down, straightened his tie and cleared his throat so that his voice sounded a little deeper, then he stepped up to the porch and rang the doorbell.

He was about to ring it again when he heard a chain slide on the inside and the door opened.

'Mr Knight?' said Warren.

Stephen Knight took a moment to place him. 'Ah, it's PC Plod,' he said.

'No, I'm DC Warren,' he corrected. 'Do you mind if I have a quick word, sir?'

Knight shrugged and backed up to let him in. Warren stepped into the large foyer as Knight closed the door behind him. 'What can I help you with there, son?' he asked.

Warren brandished the folder. 'I have a form for you to sign. It's a release form – for the tower. We're done with it now and you can get your workmen back in.'

Knight smiled. 'It's about bloody time. Let me get my glasses.' He gestured for Warren to take a seat in the lounge. 'Go and sit down, young man; I'll be with you in a moment.'

Warren watched Knight disappear up a grand set of stairs.

'Bloody hell,' he muttered again as he stepped into the lounge. Thick, roughly cut pine beams ran across the ceiling, a white shaggy carpet covered the floor and, on the wall at the end, a large TV mounted above a fireplace was showing *The Chase*, the volume muted. Along the walls were items of historical weaponry: muskets, sabres and an armoured breastplate, each with a spotlight artfully uplighting them.

He could hear music playing somewhere else in the house. It sounded like a military marching band, all pomp and oompah-oompah brass and kettle drums. He wandered over towards the fireplace, which was crackling away with several logs piled high. To be honest, if Bradley Walsh's face hadn't been glowing down at him from the giant TV, he'd have thought it a classy place.

'I FOUND her down in the water at the bottom,' said Harris.

'Dead?' asked Minter.

He shook his head, lips pressed firmly together.

'Dying?'

Harris nodded. Minter was struggling to tell whether Harris was putting on the tears and snot. From his experience as a copper, it was only possible with the benefit of hindsight. All those retired detectives who gave it the old 'I knew those were crocodile tears' were talking shite.

Harris wiped his nose again and let out another long I'm-pulling-myself-together breath. 'I could have run for help... but I panicked. I just ran.'

'You left Patricia Hemsworth dying?' asked Okeke. She wasn't doing such a good job of keeping her voice level and neutral. Minter cut back in before she decided to lean across the desk and break his nose.

'You left her to die, alone, in the dark?' he said.

Harris nodded. 'Jesus. I was scared. I panicked. I... I'm... that day has haunted me...'

Minter clenched his teeth. *If he starts crying again... I swear...*

Harris's chin started to wobble. 'But... there was n-nothing I could d-do.'

'You and Ewan both vacated the tower at that point?'

Harris nodded. 'Ewan was long gone. I never saw him again.'

'So what happened then?'

Harris sipped his cup of water. 'I went back home.'

'And you didn't bloody well tell anyone?' snapped Okeke.

Minter was tempted to step on her toe under the table, but from the look on her face she'd probably kick him right back.

'Look, I'm going to have to insist that my client has a recovery break,' said Pinner. 'He's clearly distressed. This is totally unacceptable.'

Minter sat back. 'Fine. All right. Interview suspended for half an hour at –' he checked his watch – '4.47 p.m.'

They watched as Harris was escorted out of the small interview room and waited until his solicitor pulled the door shut.

'What do you make of that?' asked Minter.

'That Jones tried to molest her, Harris tried to defend her, then she was pushed and fell.' Okeke pulled a dismissive face. 'It could just as easily have been the other way round, you know? With Jones dead, we only have Harris's version. The question we need to ask Harris when he's finished crying like a baby is... which one of those little bastards came back later, fucking mutilated the poor little girl and stuffed her in a bag?'

'No prizes for guessing what his answer will be,' Minter muttered.

64

'The consultant won't be much longer,' said Boyd. 'Then I'll get you home.'

Charlotte was already dressed and sitting on her bed. 'Ugh, I hate hospitals. Honestly, I feel good enough to just get up and go.'

He smiled. She was sounding more like her usual self this afternoon. It had quite possibly been the lunch offering of watery curry on a bed of rice and greyish broccoli that had spurred her enthusiasm to get out.

He checked his phone to see whether there were any messages from Minter or Okeke. They'd said that they were interviewing Harris again this afternoon. They were probably well and truly stuck into it by now.

The consultant finally turned up. After a quick inspection of the stitchwork under the dressing, he declared Charlotte fit enough to leave, and she gladly led the way out of the ward, exiting Conquest Hospital at pace and climbing thankfully into Boyd's Captur.

'Right, Parker,' she said in a surprisingly good Lady Penelope voice, 'take me home.'

Boyd smiled. 'Right you are.'

'Wait.' She looked at him. 'Can we take a walk along the beach first?'

'You sure you're up to it?' He nodded at the window. It was dark already. 'It's getting late.'

She nodded. 'I really could do with some fresh air, Bill... and just a little normality.'

'All right.' He put the car into gear, pulled out of the hospital car park and onto Little Ridge Avenue to head down to the front.

65

Oh, he'd heard everything – those two boys and the girl were standing right above him, their raised voices booming and filling the entire cavernous interior of Devil's Tower.

He'd heard the scuffle and the girl's shrill scream as she'd plummeted from the stairs, then the splash as she'd landed in the water, only a few yards away from him.

The two boys had scrambled in different directions: one ran away, the other had raced down the creaking stairs to find this Lottie, gasping and wheezing as she lay impaled on a jagged shard of wood.

He had lingered for a few minutes, whimpering tearfully, 'I'm sorry. I'm sorry. I'm sorry.' Then he'd backed away, scrambled up the stairs and a moment later was gone from the tower.

There was only the dying girl with him now, whimpering in the dark. Distressed. Another chance to play with his new penknife.

'INTERVIEW RESUMED; the time is 5.37 p.m.,' began Okeke. 'Present are DS Minter, DC Okeke, interviewee Ricky Harris and his solicitor Jason Pinner.'

She looked at Harris. 'Better now?' she asked sarcastically.

He nodded. 'Yeah, thanks.'

'Right, well, before the interview was suspended, you told us that both of you had found Patricia Hemsworth at the bottom. You said she was still alive.'

'I said *dying*,' he replied. 'There was no doubt about it.'

'And that's when you left her there?'

Steady there, Sam, Okeke reminded herself. Oh, she so wanted to grab that skanky beard of Harris's and slam his face down onto the table. She repeated her earlier question: 'You left her to die, alone, in the dark?'

He nodded. 'Jesus. I've told you already.' His chin started to wobble again. 'Why do you keep making me go over it?'

She glanced at Minter and he nodded subtly. *Let's go for it.*

'So which one of you two went back to the tower? All the way down to the bottom so that you could mutilate her body and then stuff it into the holdall?'

Ricky Harris's face froze.

CURIOSITY DREW *him away from his souvenir-hunting expedition. He often came down to the lowest level, where the marsh water was seeping in, gradually edging its way upwards and covering the fallen debris of decades and centuries past.*

Curiosity drew him out of the storage bunker he'd been sloshing around in, looking for coins, brass percussion caps or uniform badges.

Curiosity compelled him to cross the uneven floor of the base-ment, to the dying girl. He snapped his torch on as he stood over her. In its stark glare her skin looked almost ghostly white, the blood bubbling out of her mouth an incredibly vibrant crimson. One of her arms twitched and spasmed as she struggled for breath on the wooden shard, like the gull on the beach earlier this morning... Well, she was going to die anyway.

The boy pulled out his penknife...

∽

WARREN WAS ADMIRING one of the muskets on the wall when Knight returned to the lounge with his reading glasses and two glasses of whisky.

He joined Warren, both of them standing there studying the long-barrelled gun resting on its display plinth.

'Ah, yes, the Brown Bess musket, model 1810. Used by the British army. This one was fired at the Battle of Waterloo, you know? Incredible little bit of history right there. A seasonal warmer, young man?' Knight asked, handing Warren a whisky.

Warren could smell from his breath that Knight had already had one or two.

'Umm... I really can't, Mr Knight. I'm still on duty.' Warren took the glass, though, not sure where exactly he could set it down.

Knight gently placed his tumbler on the display plinth and lifted the musket. 'The men in the line regiments were expected to load and fire three rounds a minute in battle. During the struggle for Quatre Bras, some of the soldiers there recounted firing over a hundred and twenty times, you know?'

'Oh. Right,' Warren said, not entirely sure how to respond.

Knight held the gun out to Warren. 'Want to have a hold, lad?'

Warren did. He set his tumbler down beside Knight's and took the weapon from him.

'Whoa, it's heavy!'

Knight chuckled. 'And the recoil was horrendous. There

were riflemen whose shoulders were dislocated or whose collarbones were actually fractured by it.'

Warren squinted and aimed down the long iron barrel with the bayonet fixed at the end. He was already struggling to keep the heavy thing level.

'The problem with muskets in general, though,' continued Knight, 'was the build-up of discharge powder around the flint-lock mechanism. Bloody thing could get clogged.' He reached out and took the weapon from Warren. 'In the middle of the fight the soldiers would often have to clean it out with the tip of their bayonet or a stick or...' Knight patted his pockets, reached in and pulled out a jangling set of house keys. Dangling from it was a penknife. He grabbed the knife and unfolded a short, serrated blade.

Warren felt something jolt inside him, almost as if he'd rested his hand on an electrified cattle fence.

'You all right there, lad?' asked Knight.

'Is that... a Swiss Army knife?' he asked, trying to keep his voice steady.

Knight looked down at it. 'Yes. Well spotted, son. It's a model seventy.'

'They changed the handle from red to white... for that one only,' said Warren slowly.

Knight was positively beaming, rather impressed with the young man's knowledge. 'That's right! They didn't sell very well and decided to switch back to the red...'

'It was the first ever model to have the serrated blade,' Warren said, absently backing away a step.

Knight grinned. 'Well, well... you know your stuff, son!'

Warren was vaguely aware that he should probably shut up now. He was mentally racing through his internal action log and all the fragments of information he'd consciously and unconsciously dumped there. Knight was the right age to have been a teenager in 1971. He'd grown up in the area: a boy with local knowledge. He'd been trying, according to Harris and indeed Knight himself, to get his hands on that tower for nearly thirty years.

Shit. Shit. And shit again.

The smile that had been plastered across Knight's rosy-cheeked face was slowly fading. His watery grey eyes locked firmly onto Warren's.

'Mr Knight, may I ask you… how long have you have had that penknife?' Warren said as neutrally and as calmly as he could manage.

Knight's left cheek ticked ever so slightly. He smiled again. But this one was tight and strayed no further than the white bristles of his goatee.

'I think it's time you headed back off to Hastings, lad, don't *you*?' Knight's fists were tightening around the musket as he lowered the wooden butt and raised the business end. 'Rush-hour traffic's a bit of a bugger and you don't want to –'

Warren cleared his throat and said formally, 'Stephen Knight. You do not have to say anything. But it may harm your defence –'

With a flick of his wrist, Knight twisted the bayonet off the end of the musket and let the antique firearm clump heavily onto the thick white carpet. He lunged suddenly with unexpected agility, the eighteen-inch blade flickering across the space between them in a blur.

Warren staggered backwards, losing his footing in the ridiculously dense carpet and landing on his back. The old man advanced and loomed over him, the bayonet raised above his head, ready for a downward plunge that was almost certainly going to prove fatal.

Warren raised both hands to try to catch Knight's fist – rather than the blade – and managed to catch hold of it with the tip of the blade just probing the knot of his tie. The old man's face was crimson with rage and exertion as he put his body weight behind the task of pushing the bayonet down and into Warren's trembling Adam's apple.

Warren was dimly aware that he was losing this fight. The tip of the bayonet was embedded in the knot of his tie and was highly unlikely to slide off target. The only thing stopping it riding all the way through his gristle and bone and into the carpet beneath was the waning strength he had in his forearms.

Knight was hissing spittle out from between his stretched lips with the effort of finishing the job, jerking the weight of his whole body in an attempt to add that extra needed momentum to push the blade home.

And all Warren could think was to plead, *No-no-no-no-no!*

He could feel Knight's hot breath, the saliva dribbling onto his knuckles. The man's hissing face was so close.

I'm dead. I'm dead. I'm dead in seconds if I do fuck all...

He let go of Knight's fist with his left hand, extended his index finger and jabbed it hard into the man's bulging right eye.

The effect was instant. Knight screamed and lost his hard-fought momentum, giving Warren the time to ball his left hand into a fist and swing a blow to the man's right temple.

Knight, knocked senseless, lost his grip on the bayonet and rolled off Warren like a dislodged beanbag.

66

Minter uploaded the interview recording into the directory allocated to the action log. He'd get one of the civilian LIOs on the floor below to transcribe it tomorrow, if there were any available that was. For now, though, he had to start thinking about how to proceed with Ricky Harris. At best they had a historical manslaughter charge; the CPS would probably wimp out on and downgrade it to gross negligence manslaughter. Harris would undoubtedly walk free.

They'd had two extension periods granted already in a bid to keep Harris in custody, but, given the content of this interview and that Harris had provided an explanation for the presence of his DNA, he doubted they'd be able to keep him locked up.

Minter's phone buzzed on his desk.

It was Warren calling. The idiot was probably lost somewhere in the Romney Marshes, following a satnav arrow along some middle-of-nowhere dirt track. He let out a sigh and picked up the call. At least he'd get a chance to try out Warren's new nickname.

'What's the story, Boy Wonder?'

'It's Warren...' he gasped.

'What's the matter, boyo? You broken down somewhere?'

'It's DC Warren,' he gasped again. 'I've just made an arrest... I think'

'You think you've made an arrest or you've actually made an arrest?' Minter asked, grinning to himself.

'I'm not sure if... if I, uh, worded the caution right, but –'

'Warren,' Minter cut in. 'Who the hell have you just arrested?'

'Stephen Knight,' he wheezed.

'What the –' Minter spluttered. 'You were only supposed to get him to sign the bloody release –'

'He's our man!' Warren rasped. 'He's the killer! I've got him down on the ground. I've cautioned him; he's fucking struggling...' Minter heard Warren shouting to *hold the fuck still*, then he came back on the phone. 'Minter... I need some uniforms over here right now!' For a moment Warren sounded like a regular Hollywood alpha. An Arnold-bloody-Schwarzenegger...

'Please, sir,' he whimpered to Minter, completely ruining the illusion. 'I need some help,'

67

Boyd pulled the beanie out of his donkey jacket pocket and gently pulled it onto Charlotte's head. He eased it gently over the shaved part of her scalp, covering the dressing.

'There,' he said, stepping back to admire his handiwork. 'You look less like a patchwork plushie. We don't want to frighten the kids, eh?'

She smiled as she adjusted the woolly hat on her head. 'Thank you, Bill.'

Combined with her duffle coat, it made her look thirty years younger. At a glance, she could have passed for a student on her way down to the Old Town to meet her hipster friends in one of the ironically trendy bars along George Street.

They walked from George Street, through Market Passage and, a few moments later, emerged from Cutter Lane to look out across the seafront.

It had just gone six in the evening. Usually at this time during the winter months it would have been quiet here – but it was well into December; lights had been strung across the road and it seemed as though a significant portion of Hasting's denizens had suddenly woken up to the fact that there weren't that many shopping days left until Christmas.

They crossed the road and walked along the promenade past Pelham Arcade. The crazy golf was still busy with hardy fools playing pitch and putt in the freezing cold. They ambled past the paddle-boat pond and finally onto the shingle beach.

It was pitch-black out there. Boyd could hear the waves tumbling onto the beach and hissing as they withdrew.

'You know, I still can't recall what happened,' said Charlotte. 'The last bit I can remember was Ewan coming at me.' She took in a deep breath and let it out slowly. 'Anyway, it's over now, isn't it?' she said.

'The hiding?' Boyd asked.

She nodded. 'And the waiting. I always thought... No, I always *knew* he'd find me again.' She sighed. 'The strange thing is, I don't know how I feel about him now.'

'You don't have to feel anything for him,' Boyd said. 'He was dangerous, violent, disturb–'

'*Tormented*,' she said. 'I think he was tormented. I think he did something terrible to Lottie when he was young. Something to do with the case you've been working on.'

'Possibly,' Boyd agreed. 'It's ongoing, though, so I can't, you know...'

She nodded. 'Guilt...' she began, then stopped.

'What?'

'Guilt can drive you mad. It can push you over the edge. Can't it?'

He adjusted his scarf and cinched it more tightly beneath his chin. 'It sounds as though you feel sorry for him?'

She nodded. 'I suppose I do. Now that I'm not utterly terrified of him.'

'Well... as you said, it's over. You can get on with your life again.' He winced at how glib that sounded coming from him.

'Bill?'

He looked down at her. 'Yup?'

'I need to go home.'

He nodded. 'Yeah, it's pretty bloody nippy out. Do you fancy grabbing some chips and heading back to –'

'No, I mean *my* home,' she said. 'I need to do that.' She rested a hand on his shoulder. 'I've worked so hard to rebuild myself... I know it's no Victorian mansion, but it's my space. It's me. Does that make sense?'

'Sure,' he said, feeling his good mood deflate. 'Actually, that makes total sense.'

'But thank you for having me. For looking after me. I can never tell you how much it means.'

'That's what friends are for, right?' he said flatly.

The first large drops of rain began to fall from the dark sky. It never snowed at Christmas time in the UK, he reflected. It just pissed down with freezing cold rain.

'Better head back,' he said.

They turned and walked up the promenade. As they cut back through onto George Street, to the sounds of music spilling from the trendy vodka bar opposite the Pump House, Boyd's phone buzzed in his coat pocket.

He pulled it out and looked at the screen. It was Minter.

Boyd sighed. 'Bloody work. Even when I'm off... I'm on. You don't mind if I...'

'You take it,' she said, and squeezed his hand.

He tapped the screen. 'Boyd!' he said, sighing into his phone. 'What's new, Minter?'

68

The rain was heavy that night. It poured down onto the south coast of England like a tropical monsoon, albeit a freezing cold one. The news the next day would be full of stories of flooded riverbanks, ruined homes that had been carelessly built on floodplains, drivers caught out in deeper-than-they-thought road puddles, and trains that had had to be cancelled due to waterlogged tracks.

The collapse of an old brick tower that dated back to Napoleonic times would headline only the local news. The gusting winds and the surging level of rainwater had finished it off at last.

If you'd been there in the early hours of the morning, you might have heard it go: the walls beneath the earth finally giving way under the pressure from outside, the tower above toppling sideways into the marshland, the crack of ancient oak timbers snapping, the clatter and splash of bricks as they cascaded into the mud and silt.

And, amid all that noise, you might have heard something that sounded not unlike a scream of anguish, not unlike a girl's voice crying with righteous rage at a life cut brutally, unfairly short.

THE END

[ACKNOWLEDGEMENTS, etc]

DCI BOYD RETURNS IN

GONE TO GROUND available to pre-order

Gone To Ground

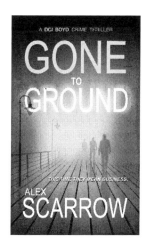

ALSO BY ALEX SCARROW

DCI Boyd

SILENT TIDE

OLD BONES NEW BONES

BURNING TRUTH

THE LAST TRAIN

Thrillers

LAST LIGHT

AFTERLIGHT

OCTOBER SKIES

THE CANDLEMAN

A THOUSAND SUNS

The TimeRiders series (in reading order)

TIMERIDERS

TIMERIDERS: DAY OF THE PREDATOR

TIMERIDERS: THE DOOMSDAY CODE

TIMERIDERS: THE ETERNAL WAR

TIMERIDERS: THE CITY OF SHADOWS

TIMERIDERS: THE PIRATE KINGS

TIMERIDERS: THE MAYAN PROPHECY

TIMERIDERS: THE INFINITY CAGE

The Plague Land series

PLAGUE LAND

PLAGUE NATION

PLAGUE WORLD

The Ellie Quin series

THE LEGEND OF ELLIE QUIN

THE WORLD ACCORDING TO ELLIE QUIN

ELLIE QUIN BENEATH A NEON SKY

ELLIE QUIN THROUGH THE GATEWAY

ELLIE QUIN: A GIRL REBORN

ABOUT THE AUTHOR

Over the last sixteen years, award-winning author Alex Scarrow has published seventeen novels with Penguin Random House, Orion and Pan Macmillan. A number of these have been optioned for film/TV development, including his best-selling *Last Light*.

When he is not busy writing and painting, Alex spends most of his time trying to keep Ozzie away from the food bin. He lives in the wilds of East Anglia with his wife Deborah and four, permanently muddy, dogs.

Ozzie came to live with him in January 2017. He was adopted from Spaniel Aid UK and was believed to be seven at the time. Ozzie loves food, his mum, food, his ball, food, walks and more food...

He dreams of unrestricted access to the food bin.

For up-to-date information on the DCI BOYD series, visit: www.alexscarrow.com

ACKNOWLEDGMENTS

I'd like to thank Debbie Scarrow for her ruthless, sometimes, brutal editing. You flourish that red pen, Debbie, like a bloody sabre. But, after, the slaughter of innocent words... I have to admit the manuscript is always better for it. A thank you also to Wendy Shakespeare who copyedits the words that survive and ensures they make sense. Wendy, you spare my blushes many times over with every book.

I'd like to thank my regular Beta-readers for their early feedback - early enough that there's time to make changes if necessary! With this book the beta team were: Lesley Lloyd, Maureen Webb, Sallie Greenhalgh, Lynda Checkley, Marcie Whitecotton -Carroll and Andrew White.

A huge thank you to the lovely folks of UKCBC, the most supportive group on Facebook and one of my favourites :)

As always, my heartfelt thanks go to Spaniel Aid UK for allowing us to adopt our adorable boy Ozzie in 2017. He's loving being the most impawtant member of Team Boyd. If you would like to know more about Spaniel Aid UK and the work they do, please visit their website: www.spanielaid.co.uk

We share another of our dogs with Team Boyd. We adopted Charlotte's Mia from Brittany's Needing Homes in 2019. They work tirelessly to save dogs at risk in Spain and find them their forever homes in the UK. If you would like to know more, please look them up on Facebook.

Printed in Great Britain
by Amazon

76451620R00189